THIS BOOK WAS GRACIOUSLY GIVEN TO ME BY DR ATKIN DR ATKINS through A RAFFLE DRAW.

Thank you Dr. Atkins, Jané

# Haffling

CALEB JAMES

Published by
Harmony Ink Press
5032 Capital Circle SW
Ste 2, PMB# 279
Tallahassee, FL 32305-7886
USA
publisher@harmonyinkpress.com
http://harmonyinkpress.com




Cover design by Paul Richmond



ISBN: 978-1-62380-894-5
Library ISBN: 978-1-62380-930-0
Digital ISBN: 978-1-62380-895-2

Printed in the United States of America
First Edition
July 2013

Library Edition
October 2013

“Come away, O, human child!
To the woods and waters wild,
With a fairy hand in hand,
For the world’s more full of weeping than you can understand.”

W. B. Yeats “The Stolen Child”

# One

I DIDN'T want to get up. The dream was a good one, and it was disappearing. I could still see his eyes, soft and brown. He was going to kiss me… my first kiss. That's when my phone started to strum. I'd set it on the harp; the other rings were too jarring. I hated waking up. I especially didn't like waking to fire alarms or old-time telephones or any of the other choices on my iPhone. I wanted that kiss, and it wasn't going to happen.

I lay there in my tiny curtained-off bed, my feet hanging off the end. When I went for my school physical I was six foot one and one hundred and fifty pounds. It was seven months later, and I'd added at least an inch, but I was way too skinny. Not like the boy in my dream. He was… perfect.

I heard my sister, Alice, on the other side of our room. To be precise, on the other side of the curtain in our eight-by-ten excuse of a bedroom. Smaller than a lot of people's closets. If I reached to the right and pushed my hand through the shiny fabric we'd pulled from a dumpster, I could touch her mattress. I lay still and let sounds creep in. It was the quietest time of the day, not yet light out.

I heard the click of dog nails in the apartment above, my gaze fixed to the rough spot on the ceiling where years of overflowing dog food and water bowls had caused a steady leak that melted the plaster. A chunk of it fell down a couple years back, along with half a dozen dried mouse carcasses. They were really small rats, but I called them mice to keep Alice from freaking. Mom was too scared to call the landlord or let the Section 8 people know just how bad a place this was. So I nailed up a drywall patch, bought a two-gallon tub of contractor's compound, and following a book on home repair from the library, did my best. It wasn't pretty, but this was an old building, and when the Section 8 inspectors came through last year they didn't even notice.

The day the ceiling caved in, I'd stormed upstairs. I'd been furious: "What if my little sister had been in bed? She could have been hurt. She could have…." The adults upstairs didn't speak English, and if possible, their apartment—which was the exact same as ours—was worse. In the room like the one where Alice and I slept, I'd glimpsed two sets of bunk beds. In front of one of them was an array of dog food bowls. I counted four kids in their kitchen, a small pack of Chihuahua mixes making a mess of their chow, and a woman in a torn housedress smoking a cigarette while washing dishes. All my angry words had choked in my throat. What was I supposed to say? At least now the dogs have bigger bowls and a broad strip of lime-green linoleum to put them on, courtesy of me… and Macy's dumpster.

From the dogs' clickity clack I listened for Alice—not yet awake. Her breath was soft, but if I concentrated and pictured her blonde head and clear-blue eyes on the other side of our Little India curtain, I heard her. I wouldn't move until I did. If she was breathing and she was in bed, she was okay. My day could start.

As to the other sounds, even at the quietest time, there was a lot going on—the East Village Symphony. Maybe that was pushing things, I didn't know what kind of composer would call this music—a siren downtown, the hum of building exhausts, pigeons in the alley, and Nimby flitting in my ear, telling me it was time to get up. Maybe it was just noise.

And Nimby…. "Alex, get up. Alex, get up."

Her tiny voice was an unwanted constant in my life and in my ear. I was good at shutting her out; I'd had sixteen years of practice.

But not when I first woke up and not as I was dropping off to sleep. It's like she was always waiting on either end of the Wonderful World of Nod. I spotted her out of the corner of my vision, six inches tall, orange-and-black wings with specks of blue and red on the tips—like a swallowtail butterfly. Her tiny black feet perched on my shoulder. She wanted me to look at her, to acknowledge her existence. I didn't. I don't, and I wished—every single day—she'd disappear. I used to yell at her to try and get her to shut up and leave me alone. And that made me look like a loon, and we had enough of that in this family.

"Get up, Alex," Nimby sang. "You have school."

She wanted me to respond. I didn't. I pictured a brick wall inside my head, and I pushed her to the other side. I imagined her tiny red eyes welling with tears as her fragile wings beat against my mental prison. We went through this every frigging morning. And then she was gone, and it was time to start the day.

I skooched to the edge of the bed and my feet connected with the floor. I kept quiet, wanting Alice to get the extra half hour sleep while I got our world on track for the day.

The morning air was chilly through my green scrubs—courtesy of the Cabrini Hospital dumpster. Give me a cool spring day over the miserable heat and humidity of our East Village hovel in July and August. Then it wasn't the symphony of sound that greeted me in the morning, but the smell of slow-cooked garbage steaming through the open windows. It wasn't bad today, or maybe like everything else in my messed-up life, I was used to it, and I shut it out.

I pushed through the curtain between our bedroom and the apartment's kitchen/living area/demilitarized zone that separated Alice and me from our crazy mother, Marilyn. I glanced at the door to her room—no curtain there, but solid oak, with a lock facing into the kitchen. That was my doing. Because sometimes… I locked that door with my mother inside. I was sure that made me a bad person, but it was low on the list of things that would land me in hell… unless of course I was already there.

Our kitchen was basic tenement. A tiny sink—the only one in the apartment—then our combo bathtub/kitchen counter, and to the right of that a gas stove and an ancient refrigerator that Mom painted in a dense forest motif. Lots of woodland creatures with staring eyes and birds swallowing insects. There was a double window over the tub/counter, and across from that a table with three mismatched chairs. Next to that was the front door with a police lock that had a steel rod that ran from the lock plate to its hole in the floor. There were two other locks, both with deadbolts.

I started a pot of coffee—for me. I drank it black, and while it dripped, I pulled together our book bags. I laid them out on the kitchen counter, which was a piece of plywood I cut to fit over the bathtub. To be fair, it was a big tub. But who wanted to get naked in a place where there was no privacy?

I checked Alice's homework. I scanned the sheets of her fifth-grade math and English to make sure she'd get full credit. I made a couple quick corrections, making my handwriting match hers. Then I made us each a couple snacks—peanut butter between crackers and a bag of carrot sticks for each of us. We got the free lunches, which weren't bad. There was one juice box left in the cabinet, and I popped it into Alice's knapsack.

I liked this time of day. Just me, Nimby locked away behind my mental brick wall. Alice safe in bed and Mom well sedated until sometime around noon. Through the bars of the kitchen window, I watched a pair of pigeons, and beyond them the building across the alley. Every window with a story, most of them darkened, all of them barred with security gates like ours. Every so often someone new moved in, and they forgot to put up gates, or they didn't know. They got robbed, and it happened fast. The day after all their stuff was stolen and what couldn't be carried got trashed, they got the gates.

As the coffee dripped, traces of my dream floated in my head—who was that boy? He was going to kiss me. What would that be like? Something about him was so familiar, but try as I might to remember the details, all I saw were those brown eyes, little flecks of gold and thick lashes. I couldn't see his face, just those beautiful eyes and the feeling something important was about to happen—my first kiss. I was sixteen years old, and I'd never been kissed. I was also gay, which on the list of things that kept me up at night, barely registered.

# Haffling

I poured coffee into a mug advertising one of the antidepressants my mom'd been on—"Have a Zoloft morning." I took it from her shrink's office—Dr. Norman Katz. He said I could have it. Thought it was cute, me wanting it.

Taking a first swig of black coffee, I padded on bare feet to Mom's door. It wasn't locked. I tried to remember when I saw her last. She hadn't been home for dinner or when we came home from school. Must have been this time yesterday; she'd been passed out in bed. Like instructions on the shampoo "wash, rinse, and repeat." I turned the knob and pushed.

Mom's room was the biggest of our three, and that's because Alice was supposed to sleep in here—it was the only way Section 8 and the Office of Children and Families Services (OCFS) would approve this too-small apartment for the three of us. Boy children and girl children after age six weren't supposed to sleep in the same room. It was a rule, and I was real good at keeping track of those.

Mom's room was dark, the windows blacked out with drapes. One wall was covered with closets I'd knocked together out of two-by-fours and plywood I'd scrounged from some guy as he was taking down the window displays at an electronics store on Canal Street. In the middle of the room was her platform bed, which had a pullout trundle where Alice was supposed to sleep. It took my eyes a few seconds to adjust. My brain pulled shapes into images. The unmade bed, blankets, and pillows, my ears straining for her snores. "Mom." Looking at the mounds of bedding. *Is she there?* "Mom? Mom? Marilyn?"

I clicked the switch and the overhead light flooded the room. Dozens of faces stared at me from the walls and from on top of my do-it-yourself closets. But from the bed, nothing. No sleeping Marilyn Nevus. With coffee in hand, I thought this through. She hadn't come home last night. I last saw her… *did you really see her?* I swigged coffee and heard Alice head into the small closet that contained our toilet. "Did you really see her?" Liking the sound of my voice, something real to hang onto in the craziness of Mom's room.

Her artwork was everywhere. Framed, unframed, hanging one on top of the next. Our apartment was tiny, but the ceilings are ten feet, and every inch of her room was covered with her insanity—her schizophrenia. Paintings and collages of mythical creatures—ogres with names scrawled on the frames—Gork, Gehrmond. Winged fairies, self-portraits of Marilyn, weird mosaics pieced together from psych pills she refused to take. Along the far wall was her worktable, an old door laid across some salvaged metal filing cabinets. The table was pretty cool, all covered in layers of paint and glue, like the pictures on the wall had melted onto it. Which I suppose was kind of true.

"So where are you, Mom?" Wondering how much it mattered this time.

I didn't hear Alice come up behind me.

"There's a note," she said.

I turned and faked a smile. Alice looked up at me, her blue eyes wide, her corn-silk-blonde hair mussed from bed. She held a piece of paper ripped from one of Mom's journals. "What's it say?" I asked.

She read, "'*Had to go. You'll figure things out.... M.*'"

"Okay then." I searched Alice's face, wondering how she was taking this. "You all right?" My own emotions were too knotted up to name—anger, resignation, sadness, numbness... or "E," all the above.

She shrugged. "Where do you think she is this time?"

"No clue. But she'll come home. She always does, right?"

"Sure." And she pushed past me into Mom's room. She walked to the worktable and looked at the most recent creation in her series of pill art. A half-completed composition of an ogre. The detail was amazing, all the pills coming together like brush strokes. Alice gently brushed her hand across the surface. "I bet we could get money for some of these."

"The pills or the art?"

"Both, I guess."

"Yeah, don't think selling pills—art or otherwise—is smart."

"She used to sell things," Alice said. "Didn't she?"

"Long time ago. Do you even remember that?"

"I think so. I remember rooms with white walls and paintings... and big windows looking out on the street."

I touched the back of Alice's hair and smoothed it down. "That's right. You would have been tiny. She had shows, and the prices on her paintings—serious money, thousands. Some of those on the top are what she used to do.... That one." I pointed to a long canvas of a busy sidewalk. It showed people in a hurry, only the closer you looked at it, you realized things were weird. The ears were too pointy on a baby in a stroller, a lady with shopping bags had eyes the color of fresh blood—like Nimby's—a dog chased a rat down a sewer grate, but the rat had eight toes per paw, and the dog had three.

"I like it," Alice said. "It's like those puzzles where you have to find the hidden things. But that's my favorite." She pointed to a painting of the two of us. In it, I was eight, and she was three. Light and dark: her, blonde, fair, and blue-eyed, and me with hair the color of a crow's wing, olive skin, and green eyes. The day I learned the basics of genetics was the day I realized Alice and I had different fathers. No clue who they were.

"Come on," I said. "We need to get going."

"Are you going to look for her?"

"Not now." I pulled down a box of house-brand Frosted Flakes and got the milk from the fridge. I sniffed—still good, but not for long. I made a mental note to hit Gristede's after school. I checked my wallet to see how many food stamps we had left for the month. Less than twenty bucks, and ten days before we'd get more. Not critical. "It's Tuesday. We'll hit the food bank after school."

Alice poured milk into her cereal. "Why don't we put one of her non-pill paintings on eBay? She'd never notice."

"Probably not... it's not a bad idea. Maybe one of the old ones...."

"You're not the only one with a brain." Alice smiled; it looked forced.

"I know." I could see she was worried. "We're doing okay?"

"We are," she said.

"Good."

But we weren't, and we knew it.

# Two

ON THE walk to school, Alice in her regulation plaid skirt and white shirt, and me in skinny jeans, killer clown T-shirt, and red Chucks, I tried to understand why so many people wanted to live in Manhattan. Like it's some great destination. Why we stayed, I didn't know. Why I fought so hard to get our crummy HUD apartment in the East Village—again, something of a mystery. Mom, in her semi lucid moments would go on about what a great place this was. How if you wanted to be an artist—which she was—New York was the one and only. I didn't see it as we passed a homeless guy with his shopping-cart possessions and his cardboard-box bed. Yeah, maybe if you had a bazillion-dollar apartment with views of the park and cab rides to wherever, and ate every meal at one of the twenty million restaurants. Yeah, maybe New York was swell for some.

"That could be us," Alice said, checking out the homeless guy.

"I know." I was struck by the image of my beautiful sister in her school uniform and the defeated man passed out on the ground, probably mentally ill like Mom, with a drug problem on top. "And isn't it sick that it makes me feel better that there's someone worse off than us?"

"There's a lot of people worse off." She cracked a smile. "What's wrong, Alex?" she asked as we headed down Avenue A toward Houston.

I recognized the opening of a game we played. We had our own. The rules to this one were easy. Keep listing the crap in your life and whoever can't come up with something loses. The other rule is you can't break the rhythm. "What's wrong is we live in a shit hole. What's wrong, Alice?"

Without breaking stride, she answered. "What's wrong is we live in a shit hole, and my clothes come from thrift stores. What's wrong, Alex?"

"What's wrong is we live in a shit hole, your clothes come from thrift stores, and our mother has schizophrenia. What's wrong, Alice?"

"What's wrong is we live in a shit hole, my clothes come from thrift stores, our mother has schizophrenia, and you don't have a boyfriend. What's wrong, Alex?"

We turned the corner onto Houston. "What's wrong is… oh shit!" I grabbed her hand and stopped.

At first she thought I'd lost the game—not likely, considering the laundry list of what was wrong in our lives. And then she saw them, like a band of trolls from one of Marilyn's paintings. Gregor Slotnik—six foot four and two hundred fifty pounds, and his gang of shaved-head, steroid-pumped, high school cretins. They were twenty feet away, hanging out in front of the Korean grocers.

"What's wrong," I said, abruptly turning ninety degrees and heading to cross Houston and get away from them. Maybe they hadn't spotted us. "Is we live in a shit hole, your clothes come from thrift stores, our mother has schizophrenia, I don't have a boyfriend, and Gregor Slotnik wants to beat the crap out of me."

"Hey, Nevus, what's the hurry?" Slotnik was right behind us.

"Run?" Alice asked.

I looked for escape routes. "Too late." Across the busy four-lane street, I spotted Biff Knapp's shaved head, and coming up on either side, two more of Slotnik's thugs. "They were waiting for us."

"No," she said, "they were waiting for someone. It's just *our* lucky day."

"Leave us alone, Slotnik," I shouted back.

"Not a problem, fuck face. Give me twenty bucks, and you'll be on your way."

We were on the corner where First becomes Allen. It's a busy intersection, and as people hurried past on foot and in cars, a few glanced our way. Did anyone understand that a sixteen-year-old kid and his eleven-year-old sister were about to get mugged? If they did, would anyone stop or try to help? Sometimes I hated this city. If I had twenty bucks, I might give it to Slotnik. If I were alone, no way. But Alice was here, and she didn't need this kind of shit. "I don't have any money, Slotnik."

"Too bad." And he and Knapp and three others were closing in, pushing us back toward a chain-link fence that separated a discount lighting store from a used restaurant supply house. It was clear they knew their flanking technique. Alice was probably right, and this wasn't personal. I felt her hand in mine as she glared at Slotnik.

"Your sister's getting pretty." He smirked and was so close I felt the spittle fly from his lips. "I know people who pay good money for little blonde girls." And then he did the unforgiveable. He reached his meaty paw out and grabbed her by the arm.

Suddenly, it was personal. In moments like this, my brain did funny things. I should have been scared or pissed off. But for me that came later. Right now all I could think of was how to get us out of this. Alice was on the same wavelength.

She screamed like a banshee. And while New Yorkers were good at staying in their own iPod bubbles, the eardrum-shattering noise that came from Alice could not be ignored.

I watched Slotnik hesitate, and the thought that ran through my head—*take out the leader, and the others won't stop you.* I let go of Alice's hand, and before Slotnik knew what I intended, I dropped to the ground, and with a practiced sweep, knocked his legs out from under him. Then a knee to the groin.

He gagged and doubled over. His eyes bugged.

I could have stopped there. Maybe I should have. But in war it was a mistake to leave your enemy mobile. I rolled to my feet, glared at

Knapp and the other miscreants, and aimed my heel at Slotnik's right kneecap. It was fast and surgical. A move I'd practiced thousands of times in Sifu William's Dojo. I didn't want to think about the crack of bone as my foot connected or the sick twist beneath my heel that let me know I'd hurt him bad. As in have-to-go-to-the-emergency-room bad. As in if this wasn't self-defense, I-could-land-in-juvie-for-assault bad. As in I'm sixteen, and they'd probably try me as an adult bad.

Alice had stopped screaming, and a circle of onlookers had formed. Several had their cell phones out, and I think a couple were filming.

Gregor rolled, screaming on the sidewalk. His broad face was beet red, tears streamed, and snot ran.

I heard a siren and saw a police cruiser turn off Houston. It was heading toward us.

I grabbed Alice. "Run!"

I wondered if Slotnik's hoods would follow, but a glance back and I saw them running off in the other direction, leaving their leader bawling in pain.

We ran. All I could think was how Alice's starched white shirt practically glowed. We zigged and zagged toward Chinatown and had to slow when we hit the crush of Mulberry Street, which even at seven in the morning was jammed with foot traffic, cars, cabs, and double-parked delivery trucks.

Alice whispered, "I think we're okay."

My height was both an advantage in that I could look over most everybody's head, and also a liability—tall white boy in killer clown shirt in Chinatown. If anyone were following, I wasn't hard to spot. I didn't see any cops in pursuit, and I was pretty sure Slotnik's gang was several blocks north. And then it hit me. "Damn."

"Don't think about it," Alice said.

I didn't even have to tell her what I was thinking.

"You had to hurt him, Alex. And you had to hurt him a lot or he'd just come after us. You had no choice."

Tears welled. I did not want to cry. But why did this stuff have to keep happening to us?

"Let's go in here," she said, looking in the window of a Chinese bakery.

"I don't have any cash."

But she'd already gone in. I trailed after her, breathing the wonderful smells of fresh-baked pork buns and cream-filled pastries. A Chinese woman behind the counter was bringing out a tray of steaming almond cookies. She smiled at Alice. "Such a pretty girl."

Alice flashed her the sweetest smile. Her blue eyes practically glowed in the fluorescent light. There was something in her expression, and I'd seen her do this many times. The word that came to mind was "irresistible."

The baker woman put down her tray. "Would you like a cookie?"

Alice beamed. She was looking directly at the woman, their gazes connected. "I don't have any money."

The longer the woman looked at my sister, the brighter her own smile became. Without looking, she pulled a paper bag from the counter and filled it with half a dozen cookies. "Here," she said. "When you have money, you'll come back." She handed Alice the pastries. As her fingers brushed my sister's, I saw a spark in the woman's eyes. Like just having that little contact with Alice had brought her joy.

"Thank you," Alice said. And clutching her bag of cookies, we left.

Once outside, she passed me one of the still-warm treats.

"How the hell do you do that?" I asked.

"I don't know," she admitted. "It's kind of a feeling. Like it made her happy to give me those cookies."

"Great, you make people happy, and I make people want to beat me up. Awesome." As I said that, I realized that before we went into the bakery I'd been on the verge of tears over how bad I felt for hurting Gregor Slotnik. And now…. "These are dammed good cookies." They really were, crunchy on the outside, chewy inside with a rich almond flavor, and still warm.

And for the three remaining blocks to get us to the School of the Transformation on Mott Street, where Alice was in the fifth grade, we ate the delicious cookies and nothing bad happened.

# Three

I HELD the empty bag from the bakery and watched Alice line up with the other uniformed kids in her class. I was mesmerized by the neat patterns of children—a little army in blue-and-green plaid with bulging backpacks. "Off to war," I muttered, and my thoughts were pulled uneasily back to Gregor Slotnik—*you hurt him bad, Alex.* I could still hear and feel the bone shatter beneath my heel. I reminded myself he was going to hurt us, that it was justified. But was it? Was it okay to hurt someone like that? Who was I to make that decision? Maybe he'd have left us alone once he realized I had no money to give him.

"I know you." A boy's deep voice came from behind my back.

I startled. "You talking to me?" I turned and met the most amazing pair of brown eyes, surrounded by incredibly long lashes. I swallowed as I took in the full effect of his shaggy hair that wasn't brown or red, but somewhere in between. My mouth was dry. Say something, Alex. "We go to school together."

"Duh," he said. "You're Alex Nevus. I'm Jerod Haynes. We're in like three classes together."

*Of course you are*, I thought, wondering what the hell I was supposed to say while making several rapid connections. Jerod sat two seats behind and off to my right in AP English. He was at the next table in Organic Chemistry lab with his partner Joanie something. In AP Calc he was also behind and to my right. He was dressed like me, only his jeans looked expensive, and his untucked polo shirt probably didn't come from the dollar bin at the Goodwill. I snorted as I made the awful connection.

"What?" he asked. "What's so funny?"

"You don't want to know." More importantly, I'd have to be held at gunpoint to tell this totally straight boy I'd just realized—he was the boy in my dreams. *Okay, Alex, fine, you're not going to say that. But for God's sake say something.* "So what are you doing here?"

"My little brother's in third." He broke gaze and looked across the lines of kids as they got sucked into the doors. "And… he's in."

"I've never seen you here before," I said.

"Yeah, our au pair's sick… but I've been here before. I've seen you."

In three years of going to the same high school, this was probably the most I'd ever spoken to Jerod Haynes. What did you say to the most beautiful boy in class, who had an au pair and jeans that cost more than Alice and my entire wardrobes combined?

"Oh," I stammered, wondering how I could possibly have missed him and trying to think if it meant anything that he'd noticed me.

"Yeah, you usually seem pretty focused on your sister. That's her, right?"

"Yup." And while I normally had no trouble finding words, it seemed like I'd have to make do with single syllables and small sentences.

"So you heading to Stuy, or what?"

"Yeah." Although with Mom AWOL, I'd contemplated cutting school to try and track her down. He was giving me a funny look, like I was slow or something.

"We should get going," he said. "I've got too many tardies as it is."

Walking helped. I didn't have to look him dead-on and think about how in the sunlight his eyes were flecked with gold.

"You kind of keep to yourself, don't you?" he said.

"I guess." I knew he was being polite, doing what people do to fill the airspace. But it felt nice, and I don't know what possessed me. "I don't fit in."

"Because you skipped a grade?"

"Yeah," I said, taking the easy out.

"I think it's cool. If I could have cut a year or two off my time I would have jumped at it. Sadly, I'm not a genius."

"Give me a break. You're in all AP classes, and you're on two varsity sports? Then you had the lead in the senior class play and…."

"Huh?" he responded.

Suddenly, I felt like a stalker. *That was way too much information, Alex.*

"But you don't really try, do you?" he said. "I mean, we've been in the same classes for years, and this is the first we've spoken."

I didn't want to contradict, but I could think of at least three occasions where words had passed. In chemistry he'd asked to borrow a reagent. In English, I'd commented on his essay about the roles of women in the medieval romances of Christian de Troyes—although maybe that didn't really count, because it was more talking about than talking to. And finally, a couple weeks back in the cafeteria, he'd asked me about the specialty coffee I'd splurged on between classes. I'd tried to respond to him, but had just burned my tongue and had shrugged like a moron. "High school is just something to get through."

"You're pretty intense, Alex Nevus. I wish I had your focus."

*Is he making fun of me?* I could only imagine what I must look like to him… tall dork who could barely string a sentence together. "Trust me, you don't." To make the awkwardness even worse, my mental brick wall constructed in the morning had crumbled. And while I'd mostly shut her out since the melee with Slotnik, Nimby had been batting at my shoulder for the last half hour. I would not look at her or listen as she sang, "Alex and Jerod kissing in a tree…." I couldn't begin to explain to Jerod how spot-on he'd been about my focus. So while trying to appear like a normal person, I was simultaneously mortaring down imaginary bricks to block out my pointy-eared fairy. I've been doing this for so long it was automatic. But as we waited at a crosswalk for the light, I caught Jerod's gaze.

"Do you have *any* friends?" he asked. His tone seemed sincere.

"Not really," I admitted. "Just me and Alice… and I guess my Sifu."

"Like martial arts, Sifu?"

"Yeah."

"That's cool. What kind?"

And I told him about Wing Chung, thinking like most people he wouldn't know what it was, or think it had something to do with a weird band from the eighties, but no.

"That was Bruce Lee's form," he said.

"Yeah."

"It's like all close fighting stuff, right?"

"Totally, which when I was little was great," I said, finding my tongue had finally loosened. "It gave me confidence, so that even if I was fighting someone a lot bigger—" *I am not going to think of Gregor Slotnik.* But of course I did, and Nimby made a crunching sound in my ear. No, I wasn't going to listen. I caught a glance of Jerod. He was smiling over perfect teeth. Was anything about this guy not right? *What were we talking about?* "Yeah," I said. "So even when I was little I knew how to leverage my strength. Wing Chung pulls from your center, and your arms and legs are kind of like a praying mantis's claws. Everything in tight." Thinking about Sifu, I chuckled.

"You laughed?" Jerod said, as if shocked.

"You mocking me?"

"I don't think I've ever seen you laugh."

Something in my chest fluttered. I clamped down the words that wanted to blurt out: *"You've been watching me? You noticed my existence?"* Instead, I shared what had flashed to mind. "Sifu William is a funny guy—funny good. He's incredibly old, at least in his seventies, maybe eighties, smokes like a chimney… little guy. He says stuff like 'little movement, much strength'. He's not kidding. These big guys come into the studio and they're all buffed up and have been doing martial arts forever. They take one look at Sifu and think the guy's a pushover. So they challenge."

"Like in the movies?"

*What the hell?* Just the sound of Jerod's voice made my organs go squish. "Are you talking kung fu movies?"

"Oh yeah. Love 'em. Not the new ones, but the old ones from Hong Kong. And all the Bruce Lee ones, those are amazing. So what happens when these guys challenge Sifu William?"

"He teaches them an important lesson. Sometimes he doesn't even put out his cigarette, but brings them down with one hand."

"No shit?"

"No. After that, one of two things happens. The guy gets pissed off and leaves, or he realizes he's been wasting a lot of time, asks Sifu if he can stay, and becomes a student."

"Do you think maybe sometime you could take me?" he asked. "It sounds awesome."

"It is." But I wondered if I'd built up Sifu's basement studio into more than it was. Would Jerod be disappointed and not see what I saw? And probably he was just saying he wanted to go to be polite. Although his voice sounded sincere, and I had a freakish ability to know when someone was lying. We rounded the block and came to Battery Park. The Tribeca Bridge was off to our right and Stuyvesant High School loomed in the distance. Ten stories high, with its central entryway and tan brick walls. To many, it was considered the top academic high school in the city. To get in, you needed one of the highest scores on the admissions test they give in eighth grade. I was lucky to be going here. Kids would spend tens of thousands of dollars taking review courses for that stupid exam. I had just studied my ass off, knowing I needed to get in, as it had a lot to do with my bigger plans.

Jerod and I headed toward the stairs outside the enclosed walkway that was the school's official entry. My moment with Jerod was just about over. To drive that point home, a tall, model-pretty blonde girl with long curls tied back in a ponytail, flawless skin, and blue eyes waved to him. She was with an Asian girl and a tall Asian boy—Joseph Kwan. The blonde's smile was bright, and from the way she was hanging by the bicycle racks I got the impression she was waiting for… Jerod. Yup, and Nimby was right in my ear. "Oh no." Her tone was high-pitched and mocking. "He's got a girlfriend." *Of course he does*, I thought. I knew that.

"I want you to meet some people," Jerod said.

*Crap!* "Sure," I answered, feeling dull and awkward in my too-tall body.

"Hey, Ash!" he called to the girl.

"Hey, cutie." Her tone was flirtatious. She skipped toward him, her skirt flaring out over her long, tanned legs.

I felt him pull away, our walk and talk over. I watched pretty Ashley thread an arm through his. She tilted her face up, he leaned in, and they kissed.

It felt like something had just landed on my chest. I looked away. *Alex*, I thought, *this is pathetic. He's straight, and of course he's going to kiss the prettiest girl in the class.*

"Ashley, this is Alex," he said, pulling back from the kiss.

She wrinkled her nose, and dimples formed in her cheeks. Her smile seemed forced. "Hi."

I nodded, unable to rip my focus from her arm twined through his.

The two other kids had joined us. I said hi to Joseph, who'd been my lab partner in Physics last year. And was introduced to Anna Sui, another junior.

Ashley pulled Jerod toward the lines of kids going up the stairs. Anna was on the other side of him. I hung back with Joseph, who asked me if I'd started in on college applications. It was the kind of stuff we'd talk about, both of us wanting to get into good premed programs. His options wide open, mine much more limited.

"Yeah."

"And?"

"NYU," I said, keeping my voice low, feeling if I said it too loud something bad might happen.

"Awesome! You going to shoot for early decision?"

I nodded.

"That's really great, Alex."

"And you?"

"Yale, Stanford, MIT. Not necessarily in that order. Actually, I think flip it, and that's the way I'd want it."

"Eggheads rule," I said, easily picturing him getting into MIT.

"I hope so." He glanced toward Jerrod, Anna, and Ashley. The trio's conversation—or rather Ashley and Anna's portion of it—was easily overheard.

"My dress is gorgeous," Ashley gushed. "Sexy but not slutty." Her words were directed to Anna, but her gaze was glued to Jerod. Even from behind, I saw the flush in Jerod's cheek.

He turned back and looked at me. "You going to the prom?" he asked.

"No." And I hoped the conversation would drop. It didn't.

Ashley's head pivoted, "Why not? OMG, you're talking a once-in-a-lifetime thing… okay, not for me. I've been going every year since I was a freshman. But OMG, Alex, don't you have a girlfriend?"

"No," I said, and hoped she'd drop it.

"Why? I mean, sure, you're a year younger than everyone else. You're really good-looking. I mean, not that I'm shopping around, but TDH is classic."

This was far too much scrutiny for me. Couldn't somebody just jab a stick in my eye, or maybe the ground would open up and swallow me.

"Huh?" Jerod asked.

Anna offered, "TDH—tall, dark, and handsome."

Jerod caught my eye. I felt my breath catch. I couldn't read his expression. And while my intuition is good, I'd not expected him to say, "He is that."

"Gross," Ashley commented. "You're not supposed to notice… you going gay on me? God, I hope not. At least not till after the prom."

Jerod didn't answer as we headed toward the security guards at the school's entrance.

I let myself get pulled back in the morning crush. I didn't want Ashley fixing me up with someone for the prom. I didn't want a make-believe girlfriend, and I didn't get the prom. Or maybe I did and just knew it was so far out of my world that it wasn't worth thinking about. Kids spent a ton of money on clothes, limos, even hotel rooms. What must it be like to have that? And not just the money.

I drifted through the morning. The rhythm of the day was nice and mindless. Homeroom, followed by physics lab, and then AP English. Figuring this morning was an anomaly, I headed to my seat, and pulled out our reading assignment—*The Duchess of Malfi*—a gory play about a woman being driven insane by relatives who wanted to steal her property. I felt a tingle down my back, and thought it was Nimby. Then I heard Jerod's voice.

"Sorry about Ashley," he whispered. "She likes to stir the pot."

"It's okay." I felt his breath on my neck. It sent shivers.

"But if you want her to fix you up, just let me know. I'll make sure she finds you someone cute."

"Thanks." I couldn't breathe, and I stared straight ahead, willing Mr. Jurzak to start the class, which he did. I wasn't out at school. I didn't see the point. There were a fair number of openly gay and lesbian students at Stuy, and for the most part it was no big deal. I knew in a lot of other places that wasn't true. But I wasn't busting my butt to get through high school to get a date. That kind of stuff didn't matter.... I just had to get through this. I had to get into college. I had to do well, and I had to get older, old enough to where... and I felt the vibration before the muffled sounds of the harp strummed through the outer pocket of my book bag.

Mr. Jurzak, who'd been reading from the play, shot me an annoyed glance. "Alex, don't make me have to take your phone. Turn it off."

"Sorry, sir." And I reached down, pulled it out, and glanced at the caller ID. "Shit!" In glowing backlit letters: *State of New York OMH.* I turned off the ringer and glanced at the clock. This was bad. My mind spun through the possibilities as to why I'd be getting a call from the Office of Mental Health. Obviously it had to do with Mom. Best-case scenario was someone—probably her caseworker, Lorraine

Needleman—had located Mom and gotten her an inpatient bed. Worst-case scenario… so many to choose from, and why things like the prom and dates, and maybe having a boyfriend, didn't matter.

The bell rang, and I bolted for a quiet corner outside the sixth-floor library. Figuring it had to be Lorraine calling, I dialed her direct number.

She picked up on the second ring. "Alex, where's Marilyn?"

"At home, I guess," I lied.

"She's not, Alex, and don't bullshit me. I need her here, like an hour ago."

Lorraine, who'd been one of the few staples in our lives over the past four years, did not pull punches. She was worried. "What's the problem?" I asked, praying that it was something small.

"I'm at DSS," she said. "It's Marilyn's annual redetermination review. Where is she?"

"Why didn't you tell me?" I shot back before I could stop myself.

"Excuse me?"

"I'm sorry," I said, realizing that pissing off Lorraine was about the worst thing I could do. Alice and I lived in a house of cards, and this was the kind of shit storm that could blow it down. "It's just if I'd known…."

"Right, you would have made sure she was here. Right?"

"Yeah." And this was why, four years ago, I put a lock on my mother's bedroom door. Sometimes she needed to be locked up.

"Alex, I need the truth. Do you have any idea where she is?"

"No."

"Shit! But you can find her, right?"

"Yes," I lied.

"Okay, here's what I'm going to do. I'll tell the hearing officer… crap, I don't know what. This is bad, Alex. On so many levels. Do you have any idea how far I've put myself out for you and your sister?"

"I do." And I did. I felt Lorraine's anxiety pulse through the phone.

"How quickly can you find her?"

"I could get her there tomorrow."

There was silence. "Alex, I don't have to tell you how serious this is. I know you get it. I should have told you about this. I'll see what I can do to get them to rebook for tomorrow. I'll let you know. Just be prepared." She hung up.

My mind raced. This was a catastrophe. If Lorraine couldn't talk the DSS hearing board into squeezing Marilyn in, things could unravel in a number of horrible ways. The $864 we got each month from her social security disability was our major source of income. Her status as disabled also qualified us for our incredibly cheap—by Manhattan standards—apartment. That was just scratching the surface. The DSS board was comprised of social worker types, who for the past four years raised the issue of Marilyn Nevus's suitability to care for her two minor children. Each year Lorraine presented clear and compelling documentation of how well we were doing. And each year I made certain that Mom was well medicated and that she nodded and smiled through the hearing and didn't say or do anything too bizarre or disturbing. Yes, Lorraine should have told me about the hearing. Then again, why get mad at her? She had a caseload of over thirty adults with serious mental illness. My mother was a single case, and I didn't want to think how much time Lorraine spent with her—too much, probably. Basic math told me that if she spent the time with each of her clients that she spent on us… not enough hours in the day. This was my fault. Every year Mom had to go for a DSS hearing. I should have tracked down the date. I should have locked her in her room.

"What's wrong?"

I startled and looked across into Jerod's brown eyes. "Everything. I got to get out of here."

"You're skipping?"

"Family stuff." I couldn't look at him.

"Anything I can do?"

I stopped and realized how he and I lived in different worlds. He had no clue of the nightmare I faced. Yes, Lorraine's call was like a tornado set to touch down, but it wasn't the only one. This was my life, and handsome Jerod, with his *America's Next Top Model* girlfriend, lived on a different planet. "No, but thanks." And I bolted for the stairs.

# Four

MY BREAKOUT from Stuyvesant at ten thirty was easy. I presented myself to the nurse's office. My eyes were hooded, a pained expression on my face. The nurse—who'd danced this dance with me before—examined me. "How bad is it?"

"I just need to get into a dark room and take my pill."

"Do you have one with you?"

"I don't."

"Alex, you know you're supposed to keep one with you at all times, and take it when the migraine first starts."

"I know. I thought I had one. I just need to get into a dark room."

She nodded, her expression was sympathetic. "They're awful things," she commented while scribbling the pass that would let me out through security.

Ten minutes later, and I was outside. I only pulled the migraine ploy when absolutely necessary. Truth was, I loved school, everything about it. The routine, the normalcy, the work-hard-and-improve reality of it. Loved it. But now… it was time to dive down the rabbit hole and track down Mom.

Like faking migraines, I'd been here before. Years from now, when I was finally an adult and Alice was safe, I'd find myself a therapist and I'd excavate the layers of my rage. I'd whirr like a band saw through all the bad stuff we'd been through and scream at how fucked up my childhood was. I didn't know if any of that helped, but I was so sick of having to hold it together. Why did Marilyn have to do shit like this? Why couldn't she be normal? Why did I have to clean up her messes?

As often happened when I slipped into self-pity, Nimby broke through my mental prison.

"Oh, waa, waa, waa. It is what it is, Alex. Time to hunt down mother Marilyn." She started to sing, "Oh where, oh where has Marilyn gone? Oh where, oh where can she be?"

"Shut up!" I needed to focus and not be reminded of the sure sign of my own madness, a bare-breasted black fairy with butterfly wings on my shoulder.

My first step in tracking Mom, and why I'd splurged with our pathetic funds—albeit augmented by a grant from the Department of Mental Health—for cell phones, was GPS. I clicked on the app for Marilyn's phone finder and prayed she had it on her. The good news was, she did. The bad news was, she wasn't close. "What the hell?" I stared at the screen, and with two fingers, enlarged the map surrounding the blinking "X" that indicated her location. She was at the very tip of Manhattan—past Harlem somewhere, in Fort Tyron Park.

I checked my cell's battery; it was fully charged. Hopefully she'd stay put, and I jogged toward the Chambers Street Subway station. "You can do this," I told myself. "There's nothing you can't do, Alex." I fed myself uplifting messages while Nimby ran through an annoying stream of show tunes. As she launched into "The Sun Will Come Out Tomorrow," I resurrected my brick wall and shut her up and out.

Sitting on the A train, I fidgeted with my phone. Reception underground was iffy, but I still checked. I didn't want to think about how many things could go wrong as I stared at the blank screen. But I did. My gut clenched—what would happen if Lorraine couldn't talk the board into postponing Mom's hearing? It had taken years to get Marilyn's disability approved. She'd been turned down three times before Lorraine found an attorney willing to take her case… for a cut, of course. That had been a desperate year, not the worst, but close. The worst—hands down—had been the one before, when I was eleven and Alice was six. The year we'd been pulled from Marilyn's custody and put into foster care.

It was the year Alice was molested.

It was the year I killed the man who did it.

The knot in my stomach tightened as I pictured Sean McGuire's surprised expression. His red-rimmed eyes, the whites bugging like a cartoon, his arms flailing as he fell backward down the cellar stairs. I heard the crack of his skull on the cement floor, and I could still feel my palms against his chest as I'd pushed him hard. That had been the worst year, and no way in hell would I let that happen again.

It took nearly an hour to get to the 190th Street station. I bolted from the train and ran up the escalator, praying Marilyn hadn't wandered to some new location. I checked the GPS. She was close, or at least her phone was. "Just stay put." My eyes fixed on the screen as I headed north up Fort Washington Ave. I felt the tension in my jaw as Fort Tyron Park came into a view, a wall of green behind a spiky iron fence, lots of gray boulders, and meandering paths. I glimpsed The Cloisters on the hilltop, a medieval castle keeping watch at the north end of Manhattan.

The "X" for Mom was close, but weak. I checked the battery—still had eighty-eight percent. The map on the screen showed her less than a hundred yards away. I jogged across the street and entered the park. Dappled light spilled through the canopy of budding trees. With each step, the city sounds grew fewer, like stepping from one world into another. The path was steep, and the higher I climbed, the closer I got to the "X." But as I came to what should have been "X" marks the spot and Marilyn—like I was right on top of it—the "X" blinked and went out.

I stood still. Birdsong in the trees above and one of the best views in the city. Far below was the Hudson River, with Jersey on the far shore. All around me lush woods and beautifully tended walking paths. I glared at my phone; my rage was near the boiling point. The "X" was gone. I powered down the phone and rebooted. For a moment or two there was a faint "X" right where I stood, and then it went out again. "Shit!" I bit back the scream—it did no good. My teeth clenched. "Where the fuck are you?"

I turned in place, biting back my fury. Sifu's words were like oil on rolling waters. *"Dive into your pain, Alex, find the stillness below."* Scanning with my eyes, listening, smelling. I caught the whiff of patchouli, and in the midst of this artfully manicured woods noticed an unintended path in a yew hedge. Tiny branches had been snapped, and the ground was smooth. If we were out of the city—like at the McGuires' little house of horrors—I'd say it was a deer run. I looked at my phone—"Useless." I squeezed through the hedge, wondering how bloodhounds did this. Was the patchouli stronger? Was it even hers?

There were scuffed footprints in the dirt, some old and some that looked fresh. This seemed a well-trod path.

Nimby emerged. "Go home, Alex." She sounded scared.

Alone in the woods, I acknowledged this sign of my own insanity. 'Cause I'd long ago faced the fact—my mom had schizophrenia, and I heard and saw a little pointy-eared black fairy. "Why?" I asked, breaking my own rule about not talking to my imaginary hitchhiker; it only made her more real. "I need to find her, or everything goes to shit."

"Go home, Alex," she repeated. Her voice was tinny—she was frightened. Which, considering she was a hallucination, was merely an echo of my own fear.

I definitely smelled patchouli, more than before.... My gaze fixed on a tiny glass bottle on the ground. Like the ones drug dealers use to sell crack and meth. I know, because we were forever finding them in the hallway of our building. Mom liked to use them in her art and for the perfumes and potions she made whenever she got manic. I picked it up. There was a small amount of amber fluid in the bottom. I sniffed—okay, so she was here somewhere. I didn't want to think how it had been over twenty-four hours since I last saw her. I checked the phone again, no "X" at all.

"Go home, please!" Nimby squeaked and pleaded.

Holding the vial, I did something else I never do—I looked directly at her. "Why do you want me to go home?"

My hallucinated fairy hovered in front of me. Her tiny red eyes stared, her mouth twitched, revealing pointy white teeth. When I was little, those had frightened me—not human, and not the kind of teeth used for munching salad or a sandwich. They were like something from a horror movie. They were made for ripping meat, probably from something that wasn't dead.

"Go home, Alex. This is bad."

I held her in my gaze, noting the swirling gold tattoos on her cheeks, eyebrows, neck, and naked torso. They glowed against her black skin, catching the filtered light through the trees. Her only garment was a ragged skirt the same orange as the dominant color of her fluttering butterfly wings. As hallucinations went, she was crisp as a new penny and exactly how I remembered her as a little boy. "I have to find her and bring her home."

She moaned and shook her head. "Noooooo."

She seemed in pain. But the health and well-being of my hallucinated fairy wasn't really important. "Are you of any use?" I asked. "Or are you just here to remind me I'm going to wind up in the nut house?"

She shuddered. "Please! Go home." Her gaze darted nervously.

"Where's my mother?"

She shrieked, and her hand flew to her ears. "Don't ask questions! Go home, Alex."

As I watched her face, I observed how, more than once, she'd glanced down and to the right. I moved in that direction.

She grew more agitated. Her wings beat so fast they blurred orange, black, and blue.

I realized that she was another type of GPS. The farther I headed down the path, the greater Nimby's pleas. She was screaming by the time I arrived at a towering and untended weeping mulberry. It was the size of a three-story building, its ancient limbs arched high and then dripped down to the ground, creating a dense curtain of interlaced living and dead branches. There were tiny bits of broken stem on the dirt. Someone had been here recently.

"Go home, Alex!" Nimby shrieked.

I reached a hand into the thickly meshed branches, some budding with tiny heart-shaped leaves, others old and dead.

Nimby dove back and forth from my shoulder to in front of my face. The patchouli smell was stronger than ever.

"Go home!" Nimby wailed.

If I'd had the patience, I would have blocked her out. I pushed my hands further into the thick mesh. The deadwood snapped and scratched my hands and wrists. Little twigs fell to the ground. Yup, someone had been here before, and not that long ago. *Let it be Mom.* "Please let her be here." The fingers of my right hand broke through to the other side. I moved my left to meet it. "Mom," I called out. "Mom, it's Alex. If you're in there, please say something."

There was no reply, the only sound the snapping of branches and Nimby's screams.

"Leave here. Please, please, please, Alex, go home!"

I inched my hands together, the fingers touching inside the wall of branches. Then slowly, like one of my Wing Chung moves where the hands move strong from the body's center, I pushed them apart, creating a window.

I peered into the dark. "Mom?" My voice echoed.

Like the whoosh of a soda bottle, I caught a strong pulse of patchouli. Other smells rushed through the opening. Weird! Cookies out of the oven, ripe strawberries, and chocolate. Saliva rushed into my mouth. "What the…."

I breathed deep. The patchouli was now an undertone in a symphony of smells. I thought briefly of the Chinatown bakery and pictured Alice conning that woman into giving us cookies. Although she hadn't done anything dishonest. Just being Alice with her irresistible smile and luminous eyes.

"Go home!" Nimby screamed. "This place is bad! You mustn't be here. Bad, bad, bad."

I shook my head. Confused. *What am I doing here?* My hands plunged deep inside a tree, like a veterinarian about to pull a calf from its mother. “I need to find Mom.”

I angled my right shoulder into the hole between my hands. Then I twisted my body to follow. I backed into the branches, protecting my face from the scratch and the scrape.

I expected resistance as I sunk my weight into the dense tangle. But suddenly, like I’d hit some tipping point, the mesh of branches gave way. I wasn’t expecting it. I lost my balance. I fell back.

Nimby screamed, “Nooooooooo!” Her words blurred. “Ask no questions. Neither a borrower nor a lender be. Stay away from May!” The branches shut her out. *Why didn’t she follow me? She always follows me.*

I grabbed at thin air, and before I hit my head, had the thought, *Who bakes cookies in the middle of the park?*

# Five

THE back of my head throbbed from where it'd hit the ground. My fingers played over a tender lump where Alex met… what, a rock? I tried to move, but couldn't. *Give yourself a second, you're winded.* My eyes were shut. And that smell…. I salivated as I cracked my lids. I expected to be in the dark center of the weeping mulberry tree.

"Wha…?" Bright lights forced my eyes shut. *Okay, clearly this is a dream. That's why I'm having trouble moving.* I reminded myself of facts from physiology. That when we dream, the brainstem is shut off. So we're essentially paralyzed while asleep. In response to that, I again felt the lump on the back of my head with my very mobile fingers. So much for that hypothesis.

Regardless, this had to be a dream. I eased my eyes open, letting them adjust to the glare. Blinking back tears, I stared up at a domed ceiling dotted with rows of theatrical lights. The one directly overhead warmed my body; it felt nice, like that first step into a hot tub. Goose flesh traveled down my arms and across my face.

I heard a woman's musical voice and deeper grunted responses from somewhere in the distance. My other hand played at what should have been the forest floor. Only it was hard and smooth… and clean. I tried to move again, and this time my feet responded. My hands pushed against the floor—the tile floor. My fingers played across the surface, not perfectly smooth, but tiny pieces of…. I rolled onto my side. So pretty, squares of colored glass, none bigger than an inch, inset between a spiderweb of dark grout. My eyes played across the mosaic surface. It was like a stained glass window, only on the floor, and lit from below. It was an intricate woodland scene, and I'd never seen anything like it. I couldn't imagine the cost, but more than that, it was a masterpiece, like the Tiffany windows at the Metropolitan Museum… only more intricate.

Again, I heard the woman's voice, and pulled my eyes from the glowing floor. "Okay," I said aloud. "This is a dream." There could be no other explanation for the scene before me. I was in a TV studio—of sorts. Some kind of cooking show in a kitchen that would have made Martha Stewart weep with envy. From the magnificent floor that merged seamlessly to cabinets made of colored glass. Not just a single color, but hundreds—maybe thousands—of shades. The last color of the floor was continued in the cabinets, and from there it was picked up by the stone countertop. To say the effect was beautiful is like saying *Starry Night* is a pretty picture. My analytic mind searched for the wires and bulbs that would make it all possible—I couldn't see them.

It was lovely and seamless. Ignoring the throb in the back of my head, I turned toward the woman's voice. Every moment or two I reminded myself, *It's a dream. Has to be a dream.* That helped as I stared at the source of the voice.

She was perfect, with skin the color of cream and a wave of blonde hair held off her face with a white silk ribbon. She reminded me of a housewife from a 1950s TV show. Her red-and-white dress flared out like a bell at her tiny waist and came in tight around her full breasts. She was posed with one hand on the glowing countertop and the other holding a cupcake covered with cherries. Her red-lipped smile was dazzling as she looked into….

What the hell was that? About two feet away from the perfectly coiffed and made-up hostess stood an eight-foot, mottled green-and-brown… ogre, dressed in khakis and a striped polo shirt. *It's a dream, Alex. You've hit your head, and you're unconscious in the middle of Fort Tyron Park dreaming about… Gork, the ogre in one of Mom's pill pictures.* I gaped at the green-faced, red-eyed ogre holding what wasn't a camera but a sort of mirror in front of the hostess. Because this was a dream, I figured the mosaic floor was my unconscious reinterpreting Mom's paintings. Yup, things were pulling together. All I had to do was wake up. But I couldn't.

What I could do was stare at Gork. The mirror he held reflected the beautiful blonde and her delicious-looking cupcake. The mirror's surface shimmered. Not glass, but water. Which, how does water stay upright like that without falling off?

The woman studied her reflection, and as she did I noticed subtle changes. The ends of her hair curled up, and then down, finally growing a few inches to where they lay neatly on her bare shoulders. She held the cupcake in front of her glistening lips, as though searching for the best angle. First she held the treat out, then near the corner of her mouth. Her lip color changed, matched first to a dark, almost purple bing cherry, and then to a maraschino red. Her smile vanished. She glared at the ogre. "It's no good. It's dull. It's boring. It's been done to death. This is the best I get!"

The ogre shrugged, and I heard gasps behind him. Someone in the shadows murmured, "Oh no." I glimpsed a darkened area with several creatures on wood and canvas director's chairs.

Keeping with my—this is a dream theme—I put names to the barely visible audience. A couple of the little squat guys were probably trolls, although based on their muscular arms and chests—trolls who spent time in the gym. There were two slender, fairly human-looking women with curved, pointy ears like Nimby's. Only they were full-sized, and I couldn't see if they had wings. One's face was green and the other a powder blue. Their skin reminded me of those chalky pastel mints they have in bowls next to the cash register in diners.

The latter, who had a pencil wedged behind her ear, offered, "Cupcakes have been done to death. They're not sexy anymore."

The hostess's smile returned. The corners of her lips pulled back over sparkling teeth. In a flash, the cupcake flew from her hand and splattered in the pointy-eared woman's face. The impact dislodged the pencil. "Useless!" the hostess shrieked.

She snapped her fingers and pointed over the heads of her shadowed crew. Lights popped on, and with the bell of her skirt swirling, she advanced on them. Her head twisted to the side with a crack, as she gracefully dipped at the knees and picked up the fallen pencil. She examined it briefly before stabbing it into the forehead of the pointy-eared woman.

A dark green fluid swelled around the entry wound. The creature gasped and fell back. Her fall was cushioned by two pairs of spasming wings.

"I don't mean to be a bitch," the hostess said in a sweet voice. "But clearly the importance of what we're doing has not been fully communicated. Cupcakes are garbage! And not even today's garbage. Last week's. Last year's! I need tomorrow, next week, and next year. I need the hot new thing for ten years from now. Nothing less. Little cherries on sweet cupcakes are not going to bring the fey back. Now…." She made slow eye contact with each of the trolls, a badger with a human face, and a thin man with snow-white hair that fell to his waist. "Give me the new, the next. And give it to me now!"

Her glares were met with silence.

From my spot on the floor, I saw the blue woman's twitching wings. The movement was getting less, so either she was passing out or was dying… over a cupcake. Which—all I could think was how delicious that cupcake had looked. I would have eaten it.

But this was absurd. *Alex, wake up.* I remembered my cell phone and reached into my pocket. I pulled it out and clicked it on. The app for the GPS flashed onto the screen, and sure enough, the "X" for Mom's phone lined up with the "X" for my phone. *So where is she?*

Slowly, I pushed up from the floor. I didn't want to think how, if this were a dream, things should be shifting. But the gorgeous floor was even better viewed from above. Dream or no, I wasn't ready to face the murderous hostess; I just wanted to find Mom and get back home.

Gork, the mirror-holding ogre, broke the silence with two grunted words. "Guest spot."

"Yes." And the hostess's smile returned. Her eyes swept the room and landed on me.

*Hell no*, I thought, wondering what guest spot entailed. Scared, but fascinated, I caught the color of her eyes—a vivid green-gold, like a cat.

She winked at me. "I see you," she sang. She glanced at the ogre and his mirror made of water. "So pleased," she said. She stared into the mirror, and the color of her hair shifted, now more honey blonde than ash.

I felt drugged. Like I knew I should be doing something, but all I could think about was how nice it might be to change your face, your hair. Today I'll be blond, tomorrow a redhead. I flashed on a pair of brown eyes, but that was another dream, and a walk to school… or maybe that was the dream and this was reality. And for all the activity in this crazy kitchen/TV studio, it was quiet save for the hostess. I looked at my cell and pressed the app for my contacts. Mom's number was right under Alice's. I touched the number to send a call. "Find Mom," I said aloud. "Go home, wake up. Just do it."

Time passed, and I listened to the hostess. "So excited, so pleased, our next guest is an innovator and an excavator. She is the conduit and the keeper, and most importantly, the woman who will make the world mine. So pleased, so excited, as I know you will be too…. I give you the one, the only, the fabulously fertile… Marilyn Nevus."

My jaw dropped. I stared across the studio, and I heard Mom's phone ring.

# Six

THE jury was still out on whether this was a dream or maybe I'd fallen, hit my head, and was in a coma. Kind of a *Wizard of Oz* scenario. But waltzing—literally—across the glowing kitchen floor came my mother, Marilyn Nevus, in the arms of a tall blond man who could have been the younger brother of the guy with the silvery hair watching from the shadows. This dude in his pirate shirt and skintight britches was gorgeous—like off the cover of a romance novel. He smiled at Mom, holding her gaze. He whispered as they swooped in graceful circles toward the hostess. Mom was in a red silk gown, her arms and shoulders bare. Her hair, raven black like mine, was pinned up with tiny red roses. Her lips were parted; she was laughing. It was weird.

My mom didn't laugh, at least not the way regular people do. Her laugh was wooden and short and came at the wrong times. It was the laugh of a person who thinks something is funny but isn't sure, so they fake laugh to try and pass for normal. Only it did the opposite.

I'd never seen her like this, graceful and lovely. And who the hell was that man?

A soft green spotlight shone on a raised platform next to a wall of ovens. On top of it a group of frogs and brightly plumed birds—with instruments—played a waltz. A pair of birds, one a muted blue, the other a brilliant scarlet with a marigold beak, twittered harmonies back and forth. Behind their plaintive song—I assumed something about love—the frogs kept a croaking beat.

In Intro to Psych, which I took last year, I read about dreams… and schizophrenia, and why teenage boys shouldn't be hearing and seeing fairies. Especially boys with mothers who had schizophrenia. Anyway, why I figured this had to be a dream was that all the pieces made a weird sense. There were rules here—and I was the king of those. Something about fragments of the day or week you'd just gone through show up in twisted ways in your dreams. Ashley had been talking about the prom—and here was my mom in a prom dress. I found my voice. "Wake up, Alex."

Against the pulse of the music and the twirling pair on the illuminated floor, I strained to hear Mom's phone. I held my cell, and like another duet, hers answered from off to my right. It was behind the counter.

"And here she is!" the hostess exclaimed as the frogs and birds came to a sudden stop. The hostess reached out her arm.

Marilyn eased from her partner's embrace, her movements fluid as a ballerina's. She took the hostess's hand. "Your highness."

"Marilyn, my pet, it is so nice of you to join us." The lights grew bright along their stretch of counter. "I beg you… show us something new."

I stared as Mom, graceful and assured, let go of the hostess's hand. She turned toward the ogre with the mirror and smiled. Her expression faltered as she caught me in the periphery. "What are you doing here?"

As she said that, there was a croaking of frogs and a giant numeral one flashed on a screen over a bank of glass cabinets.

"What the hell was that?" I asked.

As the words left my mouth, another round of croaks and a second numeral one appeared. I looked at Mom and then at the giant illuminated numbers. Over the first was a picture of her, and over the second, there I was. And then I heard her phone. "Just wake up," I told myself.

The hostess's expression was radiant, her eyes a glittery gold. "Sweetheart." She was talking to me. "You are awake. Wide awake." She stared at my mother. There was hardness beneath her smile. "It's time for you to give us something new. It is what you do."

"Of course," Mom said. She glanced in my direction and shook her head. "Ask no questions, Alex. The cost is too high." She seemed at home in this unreal reality show. Her movements were unhurried as she glanced at the ogre with the mirror and directed his focus to a stretch of counter bathed in white light. "Today," she began, "we're going to take medication." She laughed. It sent my thoughts skittering back, back before the McGuires' house of horrors, back before I'd ever heard the word schizophrenia. "Yes," she repeated, "we're going to take medication, and find a real use for it."

She waved her hands like a game show hostess over the countertop where dozens of pill bottles and a pile of capsules and tablets awaited.

"All it takes," she continued, "is some brightly colored pills, a glue gun, and your imagination."

As she continued with her demonstration, her cell phone clicked over to voice mail. I couldn't figure out where it was, and for some reason that seemed important. Leary of leaving the periphery, I sidled toward the edge of the cabinets. As I inched across the mosaic floor, lights from underneath shot colors up my legs. I held out my hand, and I could see the patterns and pictures from the floor like tattoos on my skin.

I glanced at Mom. She was brightly lit, talking to the mirror while her fingers pressed pills onto a Masonite artist's board. If this were a dream, the images would shift, and one scene would flow to the next. That wasn't happening. And if this wasn't a dream… then the number one bet was I was mad as a hatter. Number two… and that was a distant second… this was real. That thought scared me, like that first day in the McGuires', not knowing what to do, knowing we were in danger and having no clue how to get out of it.

I glanced at my right shoulder… no Nimby. The one time in my life I could actually use her, and she'd abandoned me. *Why?* I'd have thought she'd be right at home. I remembered how frightened she'd been. She'd told me not to ask questions. Neither a borrower nor a lender be, and stay away from May, which I was guessing had to be the blonde running this tea party. *Okay, there are rules here. You're good with those. Yeah, and you've already broken two of them.* I remembered one of Sifu's sayings. *"All of your senses are open, this is how you learn."* I focused on the scene before me, letting the information rush in. Mom, more normal than I'd ever seen her—that was important. And her dance partner, now standing off to one side, his gaze fixed on her, and then he turned toward me, a smile on his lips. He winked. *What the hell?*

The hostess gushed. "You are such a talented woman, Marilyn.... This is what I'm talking about. Something new." She glared at the audience. "Something that hasn't been done to death."

I flicked the GPS app on my cell, and keeping to the edge of the stage, I cleared the counter. There, behind a soaring glass cabinet, was a towering tree sculpture. It revolved slowly, and its branches swayed as though there were a breeze inside the cupboard. On the tip of each limb hung a cell phone. Mom's was high up in the branches, its screen illuminated with my picture and name.

"Think of it as a kind of tile work," my mother said. "And aren't we all sick of that broken pottery stuff?" As the words left her mouth, she winced.

A frog croaked, the hostess's smile broadened, and the numeral one beneath my mother's picture shifted to a two. *Rule one*, I thought, *ask no questions.*

"So true," the hostess said. "Broken china, glass beads, sick of it all. Your pill art, Marilyn, is fabulous and highly personal. It says something about the person and the things they're putting into their body. Of course, one does need to be careful with that...." The hostess winked at the mirror.

I felt the lip of the cabinet, wondering how I could get Mom's phone out of there. I also had this sense of dread. *Why had Nimby left me?* Considering the effort I spent trying to make her disappear, you'd think this would be great. It wasn't. It added to the pit in my gut. I remembered her pleas to not go into the mulberry tree. She'd been screaming when I fell through. Her not being here was significant, like another rule I had to understand. Nimby was always there; she was a constant of my life. Yes, I could make her vanish. It didn't mean she was gone, just that she wasn't visible for a bit. This was different… and I suspected important. My fingers pried at the edge of the cupboard. The door was sealed, and I couldn't find a lock or catch.

The band had started to play again, and Mom's dance partner swept her up in his arms. The hostess was displaying a beautifully detailed portrait of herself made entirely out of pills. "We'll be right back." Her tone dropped, and there was earnestness in her words. "It's a promise."

The ogre relaxed his hold on the mirror as Mom took to the floor with her guy. I let go of the cupboard and ran after her. "Mom!" She didn't hear me. "Mom!"

The music swelled as they waltzed across the stage, the floor bathing them in swirling color. "Mom, stop! Please stop!"

I pivoted at the feel of a hand on my shoulder. "What the?"

A frog croaked, the number under my picture changed to a two, and I was face to face with the hostess.

"Marilyn can't hear you," she said.

I struggled to steady my breath. My pulse pounded in my ears. This woman, or whatever she was, stood not two feet from me, her eyes gold as a cat's, her smile broad and cold and creepy. "Mom has to come home," I said.

"Interesting." The hostess glanced at the mirror.

I turned to see what she was looking at. Bright lights struck me in the face. I winced, and by slitting my lids could see the wavering surface of the water mirror. "She has to come home," I repeated. My voice sounded breathless and uncertain, more a question or a plea than a demand. I swallowed. "Mom has to come home, now!" I watched the two of us framed in the mirror, just like TV. Me, tall and thin and freaking out. Her, calm, with a hazy golden light dancing over her dress that was no longer red and white, but a shimmery forest green. She reached a hand in my direction. I recoiled.

She purred and ran a finger through my hair. I froze as her cool fingers slithered down my face, her touch like the muscular undulations of a boa constrictor. I stared back, trapped in her eyes. There was a hunger in her gaze. "You are a beauty," she said. It did not feel like a compliment, but an assessment. "I hadn't realized." Her head tilted to the side as she studied my face. Her hand dropped, and she stepped back.

I felt defenseless. Waves of vanilla wafted across the inches between us. She smelled like candy, my stomach growled, and through the terror, other emotions stirred. Hunger… but not like "gee, I'd like to eat something." More than that, and two words screamed in my head. "*I want!*"

I couldn't move. Her gaze raked up and down my body, like a used car buyer searching for concealed flaws. "The brother," she commented. "Not what I'd thought… always the sister. It's good to be a girl."

She was talking about Alice. *This is bad. So bad.*

Her hand inched up my back. Strong fingers pressed along my spine, vertebrae by vertebrae.

My knees felt like they could buckle. "Don't touch me."

Her body pressed against mine. She cooed in my ear. "You have little power here. Your thoughts are so confused. I feel your struggle, your fear, your excitement."

"What do you want from me? Shit!" *And why can't I move?* The latter I managed to keep to myself. But why couldn't I move? *So maybe this really is a dream… but a few seconds ago you could move—not a dream, Alex. So either going nuts or….*

A frog croaked again, and what was clearly some kind of scoreboard dinged, and the number below my image popped to a glowing three.

"So many questions." She chuckled. "Fine, fine, fine. I'm happy to answer." Her words carried on icy breath. Her mouth was an inch from my ear. "Dorothea," she called out. "Read the boy's questions."

A tiny… woman, I guess, in a dark-brown suit emerged from the shadows. She walked with a labored gait, something wrong with her hips as they shifted up with each step, her torso held forward, her arms bent like mantis pincers. She carried a steno pad in one gloved hand, and the other clasped a pencil. "Of course, your highness." She adjusted a pair of half-glasses. "Three questions." One of the birds in the band tweeted. "And they are.... 'What the hell was that?' 'What the…?' and finally, 'What do you want from me?'"

The hostess, having completed her inspection of me, clucked her tongue against the roof of her mouth. "A beauty, yes, but not the brightest bulb in the box. Here goes. For question number one, 'What the hell was that?' the answer is the scoreboard—fool." She shook her head, "Question number two, 'What the…?'"

The tiny woman cleared her throat.

The hostess turned at the noise. "Out with it, Dorothea."

"Your highness, the judges and I believe that was not a question, but could be considered an expletive. The final judgment is yours."

"Ahh." She smiled and placed the flat of her hand against my cheek.

I shivered. "Get off me."

"Such lovely skin, yes, fine, question two is not a question… although. No, it's fine. Onto question three… or in this case, we'll now call it two. 'What do you want from me?' Really, that's the only one of interest. So many ways to answer, so many levels of want. 'What do you want from me?'"

As she repeated my question, I listened for the croak of the frog. There was silence except for the scratching of the little woman's pencil on paper.

"First, let me explain the rule. Questions cost. It's simple. I'll answer each… for a price. For the first, I've given you the answer, and to be fair, you weren't aware the game was afoot. Admittedly, fair is a mortal delusion and has no bearing in reality, fey or otherwise. As to the second." She threw back her head and laughed. "I do amuse myself. You still weren't aware it was a game, but you will pay. Because this is a question of great value. The cost must be commensurate. The price is your name. You will give me your name, and in return I shall answer your third… excuse me, your second question."

I stared into her golden eyes. "You know my name."

"Of course I do. But you've not given it to me."

I bit my tongue to keep from asking the obvious—*then why do you want me to say it?* I needed to watch what left my mouth. And unlike the game show *Jeopardy*—answers in the form of questions were a bad idea. But that's what I had, questions blooming on top of other questions. Still, the one on the table, 'What do you want from me?' covered a lot of ground. But this was a trap. Nothing here was what it seemed. A glance at her little assistant proved that, as even heavy stockings and thick gloves couldn't conceal she had the arms and legs of an insect.

I weighed her words…. "*You will give me your name.*" There could be multiple meanings, from "Hi, my name is Alex," to a bride taking a husband's name. There was a twist here. I thought of Sifu William, who preferred to be attacked rather than be the first on the offensive. I mentally flipped through chapters of one of my favorite books—Lau Tzu's *The Art of War*. "The cost is too high," I answered. "I will not pay."

"Clever boy. Not a moron after all." Her smile never wavered. But there was something in her eyes, a flash of rage.

I held my breath, wondering if I was about to get stabbed with something.

"Then yes," she said. "Keep your name… for now. Still, you want your question answered. Your desire is like the waves on the beach."

"I take back my question," I said, not knowing if that was in the rules or not. "I don't care."

The frogs and birds in the band let loose with a horrible ruckus, like something being attacked.

Dorothea's black eyes widened in apprehension.

The hostess giggled. "Oh dear, that won't do."

I felt her fingers in my scalp; they played like worms. Suddenly, she clamped two fingers together and pulled from behind my left ear.

I screamed at the sudden sharp pain. I both heard and felt my skin rip.

She held a tuft of black hair—my hair, I could see the roots, bits of my scalp, and droplets of blood. "You can't change the rules, and lies, sweet boy, do you no good. Next time you don't want to pay, it could be a finger or a toe, much as I'd hate to damage such a lovely vessel. Please, don't make me hurt you. And here, a free gift without purchase, I will never lie to you. But I tire of this game, come…." She held out her other hand.

Like a switch had been thrown, I could move. I stumbled. She grabbed my elbow and kept me from falling on my face. Her strength was unexpected. Call me sexist, but outside of sparring, I'd never hit a woman. Right then, I wanted to punch her. But then she gazed up. Her beauty was undeniable and hypnotic. I thought, *What's the harm in giving her your name?* Sure, it hurt behind my ear, but not bad. She reminded me of Alice and how people would just do things for her.

The thought of Alice slapped me back to my senses. This woman—or whatever she was—was evil. She'd just murdered without hesitation and would have no remorse over pruning my body parts. I needed to get Mom and get us far away from here.

"I do so hope we'll be friends, Alex Nevus." Her tone was gentle. It pulled at something inside of me.

I didn't know what to say, her words carried hidden meanings. She scared the hell out of me. I spoke carefully—no interrogatives, no raising my tone at the end of a sentence. "Friends know what to call one another." It was a statement of fact.

"So true." She smiled over gleaming white teeth. "You may call me May." Her fingers applied pressure to mine. "I hope you realize that the answer to your question was a doozy."

"I can imagine." Having confirmed that, I'd now broken two of the three rules Nimby had warned me about. I suspected losing some hair and scalp was getting off cheap.

"Yes, I suppose that's true. But imagination only takes you so far. It's the flesh that matters."

I shuddered, still feeling the way she'd manhandled me. She was talking about my flesh… and the way she'd talked about Mom in that introduction. I felt connections just beyond my reach, and if in fact May did not lie, then…. "*The woman who will make the world mine… the fabulously fertile.*"

"Enough!" May shouted. She pulled her hand from mine and clapped three times. "To the dance!"

# Seven

THE darkened side of the TV studio blazed into daylight. What I'd thought was an auditorium turned out to be a clearing in the forest surrounded by a circle of mossy boulders. I turned in place trying to recognize landmarks. There were none. *Is this Fort Tyron?* The trees created a dense backdrop. Even May's kitchen had vanished. But appearing through the trees were dozens of fantastic creatures. Some, like Dorothea, were a mixture of insect and human, others nearly human but with pale-green, blue, or purple skin. Some had feathered wings, some like butterflies, still others with translucent dragonfly wings.

There was music—a harp and a flute. I searched for its source, the tune almost familiar, like Pachelbel's "Canon," the harp laying down the melody and the flute repeating two bars behind.

"You have no partner," May said.

I gasped when I saw her. She'd shed her previous outfit and was now dressed in layers of diaphanous silver. Her feet were encased in crystal slippers, and threads of tiny diamonds glittered in her unbound hair. "You look beautiful," I said. I felt a trickle of blood from behind my ear. It actually helped. It reminded me that no matter how pretty the wrapping, she was dangerous and evil.

"True," she said. "Still, you have no partner." Her eyes scanned the assembly as more creatures emerged from the woods and formed pairs. "Yes."

I followed her gaze. My breath caught. There, through the trees, coming toward us, was the most beautiful man I'd ever seen. For a heartbeat I thought of Jerod, and his smile and his brown eyes, but this….

"Close your mouth, Alex," May whispered. "He is lovely. I'll give you his name. Liam."

I did not need this. I swallowed as he approached, not wanting to stare but unable to take my eyes off him. His hair so blond it was almost white, it fell loose to his broad shoulders. As tall as me, he moved gracefully through the dancing couples. His white linen shirt was open at the neck, revealing a smooth chest, and then he looked at me. His eyes were a shocking violet beneath silver lashes. This was another trap, and as I stared, I knew it would be an easy one to fall into.

"Liam," she said, the syllables of his name like grace notes off her tongue.

"Hi." His cheeks dimpled. He reached an upturned hand toward me. "Dance with me."

A part of me resisted. But the bigger part…. I took his hand and felt a jolt at the connection. He pulled me close. "Look at me," he whispered.

"Not hard to do," I said. "I've never met a boy with purple eyes."

"You're pretty cute yourself."

"I don't know how to dance."

His hand snaked around my waist. "It's easy, and it's free."

My heart pounded. The feel of his body against mine made it hard to think. I glanced down.

"Don't look at your feet," he instructed. "Look at me."

I fought back the impulse to say I liked his deerskin boots but imagined they'd be impractical in downtown Manhattan. Which, as we picked up speed and began to spin, I realized was where I needed to be. "Alice," I whispered.

"Your sister," he commented. His voice rumbled through his chest and sent something squishy to my belly.

I nearly said, *How the hell do you know?* But didn't. I stopped dead. This was wrong, horribly wrong. What the hell was I doing dancing with this beautiful boy when I needed to get Mom out of here and get back to Alice?

Liam seemed perplexed as I pulled back. "Dance with me," he urged.

I turned and looked at the couples spinning by. It was like a fog. Liam's violet eyes, the music, the beautiful dancers. I reached back and touched behind my ear. I rubbed a finger over the exposed nerve endings. The pain and the sticky blood helped me focus. And there, not thirty feet away, held in the tight embrace of her romance-novel partner, was Mom.

"Alex." Liam's hand sought mine out. "Dance with me."

I stared at him and his dangerous beauty. Something in his expression—longing, desire, hunger—muddied my thoughts. "I can't." I broke away and pushed through the dancers toward Mom. I stumbled, trying to see her through the twirling bodies. "Excuse me… sorry… pardon me." The faster I moved, the quicker Mom and her partner waltzed away. "Mom!" I shouted. "Wait! Mom!" I screamed over the music.

A thought popped into my head—*try and block things out. Like you do with Nimby…. May's a fairy, these are… whatever they are, but certainly not human.* Right…. I tried to steady my breath. I pictured a red-clay brick and began to construct a mental wall against the music. Brick by brick I pushed it away, and brick by brick I shut down the intoxicating smells that wafted from the dancers. Brick by brick my vision narrowed to where all I saw was Mom and her handsome partner. And then brick by brick, I walled him out.

I thought of something May said: "You have little power here." Interesting, little was not the same as none. Perhaps walling fairies out was my super power. "Mom!"

Her red ball gown was gone, replaced by a familiar floral print she'd pulled from a bin at the Goodwill. Her black hair was a tangled mess, a strand caught in her mouth. Her expression was wide-eyed.

"He's gone." She spun in circles, her hands clutched at air. "He's gone."

"Mom, we need to get out of here. You have to come home."

"He's gone," she wailed, and turned faster.

"Stop it!" I grabbed her hand.

"Bring him back!" she demanded and pulled away. Her gaze met mine and then bounced from the ground to the stone circle that still remained. "Bring him back, Alex!"

"No." A dull pressure pounded at the base of my skull, as brick by brick I built my wall. "They're not coming back." I gripped her hand. The throb in my head grew stronger, like a vise being turned.

I focused on where we were, deep in the woods. Much as I didn't want to give up the hope that this was a dream, I knew it wasn't. And maybe I wasn't mad either.

"You can't make them go," she said.

"Apparently I can." I scanned the trees overhead. To my right I heard traffic… good, healthy New York City traffic. Figuring we were still in Fort Tryon Park, that would have to be the Henry Hudson Parkway. "Alice needs you," I said. "You can be crazy as bat shit next week, but, Mom, we need you. I'm not kidding. You've got to snap out of this."

She pulled against my hand. "You don't need me, Alex. Don't lie."

I was scared and angry, and the pounding in my head was awful; it completely obscured the residual pain from May's hair grab. I looked at her. "Shit!" She was crying, tears streaked down her cheeks, her nose was running.

"I'm so sad… all the time." She was sobbing. "Don't make me leave. Bring him back."

I pictured her dance partner. Moments ago she'd been beautiful and… in love? In thrall? But now…. "Come on. Please, Mom. This is serious. It was your DSS hearing today, and you weren't there." As I spoke, I searched for landmarks. Where was the weeping mulberry? This wasn't where things had started.

Whatever nightmare… or hallucination this had been was receding. My rational mind wanted to argue. *Alex*, it said to me, *if that was a hallucination, how come your mom had the same one? And how come you're missing a chunk of your scalp?*

"It doesn't matter," she said and wiped her nose on the back of her arm.

I felt rage and fear. I wanted to scream at her, *What do you mean it doesn't matter?* I bit it back and, patting my pocket, was relieved to find my cell. I powered it up. The GPS screen flashed, and I could see we'd moved a couple hundred yards from her phone. I thought of going back to hunt for it, but no. Too risky. The pain in my head pulsed, and if I focused on it I could hear a voice—May's voice. "No," I said aloud, and visualized a pallet of bricks being mortared into walls. I pressed *My Location* on the iPhone and stared at the map on the screen. "It does matter," I said. Trying to keep my tone calm, knowing how easy Mom spooked, not wanting my fear to infect her.

"Bring him back," she pleaded.

"Maybe later." The minutes those words left my lips, I regretted them. What I'd meant was *hell no. Never. Are you out of your mind?* Gripping her hand, I dragged her down a narrow dirt path. I felt a wave of relief as we came to a paved walkway. *This is real.* A bicyclist zipped past, and the pounding in my skull started to ease. I wouldn't let myself think about what we'd just gone through. We just needed to get away.

Like throwing an on/off switch, Mom's expression changed. Her voice was dull and flat. "Was Lorraine mad?"

"Yeah, and worried." I glimpsed The Cloisters on our right. The pounding in my head was gone.

"She worries," Mom said. "You worry, Alice worries, everyone worries. It makes you old and gray, all that worry. Worry lines, worry warts. I'm not a frog, you know. I don't need warts." She held her free hand in front of her and turned it from side to side. "Nope, no warts on me." She tugged back on my hand. "Stop. I need to look."

I desperately wanted to get away from there. Just get to the subway and get home. I pictured my brick walls. The pounding was gone and no trace of May's voice. "Fine." I stopped and let Mom examine my blood-smeared hand. I knew that if I didn't, she wouldn't let up. She held it in front of her and spread my fingers.

"And the other one," she said. I did as she asked and watched with relief as a pair of young women jogged past. I followed their retreat, making certain they had no pointy ears, wings, or other inhuman anomalies. "No warts. Good to go.... So Lorraine was mad and worried."

I grasped at the moment of near normalcy. Sometimes, if you snagged her into a real conversation she'd stick with you. At the very least, it was a distraction, and we had a long trip ahead of us. "You can't go running off like this, Mom. I need to know where you are."

"You found me. You are a clever boy, Alex. And the truth—we know the difference between truth and lies. You tell a lot of lies—you don't need me."

I bit back my fury. Clearly my crazy mom had been keeping a thing or two from me. But I knew from painful experience getting mad with her would either shut her down, bring on a crying jag, or trigger something so bizarre we'd spend the rest of the day in Bellevue's psychiatric emergency room.

Down the sloped path, I saw the park's entrance. "Thank God."

I pushed past my annoyance with her. The distant voices of well-intended therapists and social workers reminded me—schizophrenia is an illness, she doesn't mean to say or do these things to upset you. Or Sifu's wisdom, when I'd be at my wit's end, *"Embrace your reality, but only the moment. Let go of what's been, and don't grasp for what's to come. Find the moment; it's here and it's everything."*

"Truth isn't that simple, Mom." I gripped her hand, suspecting that if I let go, she'd run.

"True," she answered. Her tears had dried. She smiled as we emerged from the shadows of the trees and the park and came out in the normalcy of Washington Heights. "There are many truths that run together. Like children."

"Yes," I agreed, having years of practice in understanding her craziness. If schizophrenia could be considered a language, I was fluent. “So one of the truths, Mom, is that right now Alice and I need you. It’s no lie.”

“I disagree. You’ve done everything without me.” A throb entered her voice. “In spite of me. Ergo, ipso, you don’t need me. Liar, liar pants on fire.”

Her agitation was ramping up as I spotted the 190th Street subway entrance. I searched for words to calm her. “You’ve done okay. We’re safe now. We have an apartment and food and we’re together. Those are important things. If you hadn’t shown up when you needed to… when I needed you to, none of that would have happened.”

She pondered my words and let me lead her down the subway stairs. “Good things come to those who wait,” she rambled. “And you waited, and worried… but no warts. That’s good too. So what did Lorraine say?”

I fed our MetroCards through the machine—I always carried a second. And while our trip to fairy land was a first for me, tracking down my mom through the five boroughs—and beyond—is common. “The DSS hearing is important.” I wondered how much to share. I was torn between making her understand and not wanting to tip the apple cart that was Marilyn’s grip on reality. “Here’s the deal.” And I waited as our train roared to the platform. I found two seats, and I took the one closest to the door, just in case she tried to run. “Everything the three of us have—our apartment, your disability check, the fact that we’re not in some God-awful foster home, everything is tied together. You not being at the DSS hearing is bad. Because you’re our legal guardian.” I watched her face, checking for the impact of my words. “The people at DSS need to know that you still qualify for disability. But….” And this is where things got tricky.

“There’s nothing wrong with me. I’m not crazy,” she said.

I picked my words carefully. Mom truly believed there was nothing wrong with her. Whenever the disability paperwork came in the mail, I grabbed it. Too many times I’d found it shredded and in the garbage. “You qualify for disability, Mom. You deserve it. We need it to survive.”

“I don’t have schizophrenia. That’s insane.” Her voice was loud and high. “I’m not insane. That’s why I didn’t go to the hearing. They tell lies about me. They call me names. It’s not nice. Sticks and stones may break my bones, but names are for calling.”

“If you’re not there, Mom,” I said in a soft voice, aware that other passengers were watching us, “we’re in a world of trouble. It’s not just the money. They need to see you. And….” This was the kicker. “They need to know you’re able to look after children.” The nut of the problem was this, the folks at DSS needed to know my mother was crazy, just not too crazy to be the legal guardian of two minors.

“Children!” she snorted.

A woman across from us cast a worried look at Mom. I glared back at her. “Yes, Mom. Alice is eleven, and I’m sixteen.”

“You’re going to college in a year. You’re no child.”

“By law I am. Come on, it’s 14th Street, we need to get the L.”

“You think I’m crazy, don’t you?”

I gripped her hand, probably with more force than was needed. But I was tired and scared and pissed off. I needed to get her home, and I regretted the words the moment they left my mouth. “Yes, Mom, I do.” But she wanted the truth, and there it was.

# Eight

SHE said nothing on the L train and continued with the silent treatment as we transferred to the downtown Express. She was revving, and it did not bode well. This was my fault. I needed to keep my emotions to myself. I thought of May's weird game of questions and answers. Every question has a cost, and clearly my mom asking me if I thought she was crazy carried a hefty price tag.

Nearing our station, she finally spoke, "I'm not crazy."

"Fine."

"You don't believe that."

"It doesn't matter."

"Another lie, Alex. Of course it matters."

It was an argument I would never win. I checked the time on my cell—a little after two. It seemed later. Maybe I'd been drugged, maybe that's what happened. I thought back through the morning when Alice and I handled Mom's pill art. Maybe some of the drugs got absorbed through my skin, and I'd hallucinated the whole thing. I felt the raw nerves behind my ear—*and that could be from falling.* "I need to pick up Alice."

"She's a big girl," Mom replied. "She doesn't need to be carried. I don't need to be carried."

I glared at her. “Look, we’re picking up your daughter so no one messes with her on the way home. ’Cause you know what, Mom? We live in New York, and sad to say, Alice shouldn’t walk home alone.”

“See.” She sat back, not meeting my gaze. “You prove my point, over and over, pointy Alex. Alice has you. I’m not needed. I could have stayed at the dance.”

“Who was that guy?” Thinking how that was another question… but man, how does someone make it through the day without questions?

She giggled and blushed and let loose with a head-turning snort. “He was a she… that’s how they say it, only they spell it S-I-D-H-E. Which, speak of the devil so she may appear, what’d you do with yours?”

Okay, maybe I wasn’t fully fluent in schizophrenic, but I had a feeling she’d just dropped a bomb or two. “What are you talking about?” The train pulled into the station.

She giggled, wiggled her thick eyebrows, and said nothing.

“Fine! Just forget it!” I was pissed off and just wanted to get Alice, get home, and yes, lock Mom in her room.

“You lie a lot. There sidhe is,” Mom said.

I felt a familiar flutter over my right shoulder. I glanced and caught Nimby’s red-eyed face. Admittedly, I wished the damn thing would vanish, that I didn’t have a black fairy hovering over my right shoulder. But in that moment… seeing her, it’s like a piece of me was back. I did something I rarely do. “Coward.” I spoke to her.

“No,” her tinny voice spat back. “Smart. Smarter than you. Pay attention, Alex. The danger is real.”

“She’s right,” Mom said. “It was a stupid thing. Which makes no sense… you’re smart… and you did something stupid. Does that make you smart or stupid?”

A man in a suit glanced at us. I wondered which part of our conversation had prompted his perplexed expression. “You see her?” I asked Mom.

"Of course. She's as plain as the fairy on your shoulder." She giggled.

In the world of dream logic, this made sense. Sadly, this was not a dream, so how the hell could Mom see Nimby? She'd never mentioned it before.

I shadowed close behind Mom as we headed up the stairs to Houston. From there it was a quick walk through the fishmongers and fruit carts of Mott Street to the iron gates of Alice's school. I glanced up at the statue of Mary, her arms extended as though bestowing blessings on the children in the yard below.

Mom followed my gaze. "That's what May wants," she commented.

I spotted Alice's blonde head in the sea of mostly Asian children. She was with her best friend Tia, who lived with her grandparents over their restaurant on Henry Street. She was laughing. Her head turned, as though sensing my presence. She waved and then saw Mom. Her expression darkened. She shrugged and put her hands together as though praying.

I laughed. If she only knew.

Mom stood transfixed by the statue staring down at us.

"May wants to be the Virgin Mary?" I asked.

"Like the virgin," she said.

"Huh… that kind of makes sense." And of course I started the Madonna classic running through my head.

"Alex!" A male voice caused my head to whip around to the left.

"Ouch! Jerod." My pulse quickened as I saw him not twenty feet away. My stomach lurched. This was too much. As he approached, I tried to enlist my rational mind to put the brakes on things. Okay, I had a crush. I was sixteen years old, and this was supposed to happen. Was it just that he's so good-looking? Or what his voice did to me or how he moved or those eyes or the way dimples popped in his cheeks when he smiled or…. *Alex, chill.*

"So…." He smirked. "You went home sick."

"Yeah… migraine."

Mom snorted, "Liar."

Jerod looked at her and then back at me. "What happened there?" he asked, pointing at my ear.

"I fell." Thankfully my hair was long enough in back that I could mostly hide May's vicious grab. Even so, there was a visible patch of raw flesh behind my left ear.

"Lie," Mom said in a flat voice. I did not want to introduce her, and was given a reprieve by a younger version of Jerod running toward us, his book bag bouncing on his back.

"Hey, Clay, how was your day?" Jerod asked his brother.

"Homework," the nine-year-old wailed.

"Yeah, well, it only gets worse." Jerod turned to me. His expression was hard to read, worried, concerned. "We have to finish the chapter, and Mr. Flaherty says we can either turn in the questions at the end or have a take-home test."

"I'll do the problems," I said, actually looking forward to the black-and-white logic of chemical reactions.

Alice had worked her way through the crowded schoolyard. She looked at me and then Mom. "Things are good?" she asked.

"Yeah."

"Hi," she said to Jerod. "I'm Alex's sister, Alice."

"Jerod," he said. His smile was dazzling. "And this is my brother Clay. So where do you guys live?"

"In the Village," Alice said. She looked at Jerod and then at me. "East Village."

"You want to walk with us?" Jerod asked. "We're on the way, right across from St. Pat's." He glanced at Marilyn, who was staring at the statue of Mary.

"Mom," Alice said. "We're leaving." And then she did her Alice thing. "I love that church, the windows… how at the bottom of each one it says who gave the money for them."

"I study in the churchyard," he said. "It's quiet." He looked at his brother, who was hanging back with a couple of his classmates. "Clay, leaving! Now!"

I tapped Mom's arm. "We've got to go."

"Of course, dear." She looked away from the statue. She saw Jerod. "What a beautiful boy." She giggled, "But he's not a sidhe."

This was bad.

Alice interceded and took Mom by the arm. "So what did you do today?"

I didn't want to hear the response and said a silent prayer as Alice pulled Mom out of earshot.

"That's your mom?" Jerod asked. His long legs matched my stride.

"Yeah." I hoped this topic could end fast.

"Never seen her here."

"I do the pickup and delivery. So your au pair's still sick?"

He paused. "Not really. I just felt like picking up Clay. Like to see who he's hanging with. Make sure no one's bothering him."

"Same," I said. "Not the au pair part. Just me and Alice… and Mom." I needed a quick deflection. "So what about your folks?"

"We live with my mom," he said, his expression serious. "My dad's uptown."

I knew I was supposed to say something in return. This was what you were supposed to do in normal conversation. But I didn't feel up to offering information on the crap fest that was my life. And not to be greedy or creepy, I wanted to know about him. Everything…. "How old were you when they split?"

"Eleven. It sucked. Still does. What about your dad?"

Shit! I did not want to say I didn't know who, or where, he was. And weirdly, I flashed on Mom's drop-dead dance partner. "Not in the picture."

"So you know what I'm saying."

"Yeah." But I didn't. I remembered how he'd winked at me; maybe he wasn't my father, but he could have been Alice's… if he were even real. I thought about what she said: "*He's a she. S-I-D-H-E.*" Which I knew from sophomore history was the Irish word for fairies.

Jerod's shoulder brushed against mine. "You don't say much, do you?"

"No." The contact startled me.

He snorted. "No kidding. What's going on inside that head? You're the smartest kid in class, and you hardly talk to anyone."

"It's a mess in here," I said, feeling strange and exposed… and almost happy.

"Really? I wonder. So, like this weekend you maybe want to get together and do something?"

I was on overload. Of course I would love to do something this weekend. I glanced ahead at Alice and Mom as they crossed Canal. "Sure," I said, figuring I'd probably have to back out. But at least for the moment, I could pretend.

"There's a free concert in the park, some hippie music." He looked back at his brother, who was entranced by a battery-operated Godzilla in one of the Chinatown stalls. "Clay, now!"

"It's only five bucks," his brother whined. "I've got the money."

"Now," Jerod said. And then to me, "I love the little brat, but sometimes…."

"Yeah." I watched him retrieve his brother over the objection of the store owner. I thought over the morsels of our conversation. His parents were divorced. He kept an eye on his brother. But the part that was screaming in my head: *he wants to do something together. Like a date—no, you moron, not a date. Like two guys in class doing something together, in the park... like a date. He has a girlfriend... he's taking her to the prom.*

When we made it across Canal, Alice shot me a warning glance as Mom headed toward us. My stomach lurched.

"You never introduced me to your boyfriend, Alex," she said.

"Mom!" Alice shouted after her.

Jerod blinked and extended his hand. "I'm Jerod Haynes."

"I'm Marilyn… Alex is my son." She looked at his extended hand and clearly did not want to take it. "He's great. That's why I named him that."

Jerod pulled his hand back and looked at me. I could see his thoughts as he tried to piece together my mom's odd pronouncements and weird expression. She was staring at him. I shot her a look, and if looks could truly kill it would have made me an orphan.

"He is great," Jerod said.

"I said that. I don't need you to say that," Marilyn said.

"That's it, Mom. We're going home. Jerod, I'm sorry."

"But we're on for this weekend. Right? I'll Google the details. You going to be in school tomorrow?"

"Yeah, of course." I wondered if that was true. I needed to get Mom home, call her social worker, Lorraine, and fix the mess at DSS. Which might mean my migraine would be continuing for another day. "Yeah, we'll talk in school." I couldn't stand seeing his expression; it was pity, like poor Alex. But something else too. At least I thought there was, but I was probably just seeing what I wanted. "Bye." I turned back to Mom.

"I'm sorry," Alice whispered. "I tried to stop her."

"Not your fault."

"So I'm the bad guy." Marilyn seemed perplexed. "I tell the truth, and I'm the bad guy. I named you because I knew you'd be great. And Alice… just look at her, it's obvious."

"Come on, Mom." I took the hand she wouldn't shake with Jerod, and Alice took her left. And walking three abreast, we escorted Marilyn Nevus home.

# Nine

IT WAS bad. I knew it the moment we walked into the 10 a.m. DSS review. It was me, Mom, and her short and stocky mental health caseworker, Lorraine Needleman. This was a catastrophe in the making and why I cut school to be here. No way I could leave something this big to chance, even though I did trust Lorraine as much as I trusted any adult, which wasn't a lot. But it had less to do with Mom's well-intentioned caseworker and everything to do with the crapshoot of my mother's illness. I was here for damage control. And between three cups of coffee, walking Alice to school, trying to get some pills down Mom—and I have lots of tricks—and then praying she wouldn't make too much of a fuss when I'd locked her in her room while I was out—my anxiety was through the roof. I tried to steady my breath. *Just be cool, this is going to be okay.*

As we waited on a bench outside the hearing room, I tried to gauge Mom's state of mind. "You look nice," I told her. Her black hair in a thick braid, her outfit a kind of trendy—and very Mom—mishmash of an ankle-length skirt, white shirt, and vest, with strands of clunky wooden beads around her neck.

She shook her head; she was not happy with me. "That doesn't mean anything."

A security officer called her name. I looked up.

"You can go in now," he said.

*Just breathe*, I reminded myself, and slipped into the kind of head state I use when sparring at the Dojo. *Stay in the moment, don't freak. This is going to be fine.*

Inside, there were three DSS reviewers behind a long table. A dark-suited woman flanked by two men, one with a gray beard, and all three with Department of Social Services picture IDs around their necks. The woman glanced up. Her face was all angles, and her hair was tightly pulled back in a bun. Something about her was familiar.

"Ms. Nevus." Correctly identifying Mom, either by her outfit, her rapidly darting eyes, or the paper name tag on her vest. "You sit across from me." Her expression was pinched as she stared at Mom over half-glasses. She gave me a questioning look and nodded at Lorraine. She quickly rattled off her name—Clarice Carlton—and those of her colleagues.

Without waiting for a response, she pushed her glasses to the edge of her nose and flipped through a thick file. It started okay, basic questions and answers, with her and her two subordinates filling out forms that would add to the bulk of Mom's dossier. *Where do I know her from?*

"In the past two years, how many times have you been in the hospital, Ms. Nevus?"

Mom didn't answer.

"Ms. Nevus?" the woman persisted, her gaze fixed on Mom as she slid the chart to the man across from me.

"Marilyn," Lorraine said softly. "You need to answer the questions."

"Why?" Mom said. "There's a question for you."

Realizing we'd get nowhere fast, I supplied the information. "She was at Bellevue last September for ten days, then again in February… just about two weeks."

The man on the right recorded the information.

"Why did you need to go into the hospital, Marilyn?" the woman asked.

"Why aren't you wearing earrings?" Mom replied.

I looked at the woman's name tag—Clarice Carlton, LCSW. The name meant nothing… but something about her…. "Ms. Carlton, is it okay if I answer?"

"I'd rather hear it from your mother, but go ahead." She was annoyed, or maybe that was just the resting point of her face.

"She needed med adjustments."

"Liar!" Marilyn said. "I didn't go to the chiropractor." Her arms shot forward and landed hard on the table. Her jaw clenched, and she glared at the reviewers. "My son is a liar!" Ms. Carlton cast a worried look to the bearded man on her right.

"It's okay," I said, recognizing the woman's fear and seeing similar looks of alarm in the two men. I'm so used to Mom and her outbursts, I forget how they scare people. Even those who supposedly know about mental illness. "She gets loud, but not violent."

"Never?" Ms. Carlton asked.

"No."

"It says she's hurt *herself* in the past. Clutching the thick file, she flipped through her record. "There have been at least three suicide attempts. I'd certainly call that a form of violence."

"Nothing recent," Lorraine said.

"Hmm." The man directly across from me pointed to something in Mom's record. He slid it across to Ms. Carlton.

"Interesting…." She looked from Mom, to Lorraine, and then her gaze landed on me. "It says here that her psychiatrist wanted to pursue involuntary outpatient commitment. Were you aware of that?" The last bit directed to Lorraine.

"Yes," she said.

"What happened?"

"The judge ruled against it," Lorraine said. "She felt that Ms. Nevus was taking care of her basic needs and that forcing her to take medication was an infringement on her civil liberties."

Ms. Carlton snorted. "And the children?"

"What about them?" Lorraine asked.

"Her parental rights were never terminated?"

"No," I answered, and tensed for what I knew was to come.

The man across from me gave me what was meant to be a compassionate look. I knew it for something else, the prelude to bad news. "I'm assuming the Office of Children and Family Services has an open case."

"They did," Lorraine said, before I could answer. "The case was closed."

"Why?" The man glanced at Mom, his tone incredulous. "Obviously she's in no state to care for children." He looked at Lorraine. "You are a mandated reporter. We all are."

Lorraine did her best. "I'm in the Nevus apartment at least once a week. It's clean, there's adequate food in the refrigerator. There is no evidence of neglect or abuse. If I felt there was, I would contact OCFS."

Mom turned to Lorraine. "Of course there's food in the refrigerator. I don't put food in the toilet. That comes later. What a stupid thing to say."

I felt the meeting spin out of control. Keeping my emotions in check, I had to say something. "I go to Stuyvesant High School," I started. I let that sink in. New Yorkers know what that means. I was in the most prestigious magnet school. I got there solely based on my exam scores. "Alice is getting straight As at the School of the Transfiguration. My mother may have… an illness, but we're doing okay." I looked first at Ms. Carlton, and then to each of her flanking subordinates. "Every time OCFS has gotten involved, bad things have happened… to me and to my sister. I know they mean well, but…."

Ms. Carlton interrupted me. The corners of her mouth twitched, it might have been a smile. "Mr. Nevus, I can appreciate your concern.… We have no choice in this matter. I can see that your mother's disability benefit should be continued."

That was the good news. I waited for what was coming next.

"But I have no choice based on today's presentation. Your mother's schizophrenia...."

Oh no, I thought, as the S-word left her mouth. *You did not just say that.*

Mom shot up. She banged her fist on the table. "I do not have schizophrenia!" She was livid, her lips drawn back, her eyes bugging. "Who do you think you are? You're no doctors! There's nothing wrong with me! You're sick. You're all sick. Trying to paste names on me. I'm no poster child."

"Mom, it's okay." I tried to take her hand. She yanked it back.

"And you. With your locking doors and your secrets and your pills, pills, pills. You should have left me with Cedric."

I didn't need to see the pair of armed guards entering the room to let me know someone had pressed the panic button. Ms. Carlton and her two colleagues had pushed their chairs back from the table, the three of them staring wide-eyed at Mom as spittle flew from her lips and she raged. And that's when it hit me... the bug-eyed look on Ms. Carlton's face, her half-glasses, the odd angles of her wrists and hands; she was like the human twin of May's Dorothea.

"You need to calm down, ma'am," a female security guard said as two more officers entered the room.

"I'm calm. I don't have schizophrenia. I'm a mother, and mothers aren't supposed to take pills. It's bad for the baby. And I'm not Katharine Hepburn!"

"What?" I pushed up from my chair, looked at Mom, and then at the guards coming from either side of her. "Mom, Mom. Please, just look at me."

Her eyes met mine, and something shifted. She started to cry. "You should have *left me there*, Alex. Can't you *see*?"

Her tears ripped me apart. I hated it when she got like this, like the pain inside of her was too much to bear. "Are you pregnant, Mom?"

She let out a deep groan, like a wounded animal, and nodded.

The female guard approached, her tone gentle, and for a moment I thought maybe we'd make it out of there. "Ms. Nevus, would you like some water?" she asked.

But just as I thought the emotional storm had passed, Ms. Carlton's voice cut through the room. "She needs to be evaluated in an emergency room." And then to Lorraine, "I'm calling OCFS today. I will follow that up with a written LDSS-221A. Clearly, with two minor children… and the possibility of an infant. And Ms. Needleman"—glaring at Lorraine—"I will be in touch with your supervisor. What were you thinking?"

In its own way, what happened next was as surreal as yesterday's romp at The Cloisters. The guards surrounded Mom, clearly prepared to take her down, even Taser her or use the pepper spray holstered on their belts.

Sobbing, she offered no resistance as a pair of EMTs entered the room with a stretcher. "I'm not a schizophrenic. I'm not a criminal."

"I know, Mom. You haven't done anything wrong." She let me take her hand as they strapped her to the orange mattress on the gurney. "Is it okay if I go with her?" I asked a female medic. "I know all her history and stuff, and what meds she's supposed to be taking."

"Sure," she said.

And leaving Lorraine and the three DSS workers to wreak havoc on my family, I went with Mom.

# Ten

THEY wouldn't let me into the psychiatric portion of the emergency room. I had to wait in triage with a couple dozen sick and injured. I wasn't the only one dealing with bad stuff. Although, considering how the morning's hearing had gone… *what am I going to do?* I knew what was coming, and with Mom in the hospital I had to find a responsible adult who could serve in loco parentis so that OCFS didn't toss Alice and me into emergency foster care. I needed someone fast, and didn't have many options. Out of necessity, I let few people know about our lives because of crap like this. The only adults who knew the truth were Lorraine and Sifu William. My only other hope was to convince whatever doctor and emergency room workers were with my mom to let her go. I wished Alice were here—not because I wanted her to see any of this mess—but maybe her blue-eyed innocence could get Mom released.

I glanced at the triage nurse as she directed a man with his arm in a blood-soaked bandage to a chair. I heard the exasperation in her voice. "They'll call you as soon as they can. You need to have a seat."

I watched and waited. I'm good at reading people, and when folks are pissed off, asking for favors does not work. I needed to stay calm. I pulled out my cell and dialed Sifu. He picked up on the third ring. "Yes, Alex?"

“Sifu, I need a huge favor.”

I laid out the broad strokes. And ended with, “Would you be willing to say you’d be responsible for me and Alice… just for a little bit.”

There was a silence, and I wondered if we’d been disconnected.

“I can’t,” he said. “I would like to, but my citizenship status will not allow it.”

I knew Sifu had left China during the Cultural Revolution in the 1960s. Some nights, when most of the students had gone home, he would talk about it. His parents had been physicians and were made to leave their practices and work as laborers on a collective farm. Sifu had a wife and grown children; I’d just assumed somewhere along the way he’d become a citizen. “It’s okay,” I said.

“No, Alex, it is not okay. Let me talk to my son Thomas. I’ll get back to you.”

“Thank you.”

“You must not let them take your sister and your mother, Alex.”

“I know.”

“You should come back tonight after this is settled. We’ll talk then.”

After I hung up, I felt a tiny bit better. Sifu’s son Thomas was a physics professor at City College. He was also a highly skilled martial artist who would occasionally run class when his father was held up with patients in his thriving herbalist and acupuncture practice. I didn’t know how much Sifu would have told Thomas about my situation, but right now I needed help from any direction.

I looked at the triage nurse. There was no one in front of her window. I seized the moment. “Hi,” I said. “My mom—Marilyn Nevus—is back in psych being evaluated. Is there any way you could call back and see if they’d let me be with her? I have all her information.”

She looked up. Her expression was unreadable, as was her name tag, which was turned around.

"Please." I thought of Alice, and what she would do. I tried for my best puppy-dog-lost smile.

"How old are you?"

"Eighteen," I lied.

"Let me see." She picked up the phone. "Okay to send back Marilyn Nevus's son?" She nodded to me and hung up the phone. "Someone will get you."

"Thanks."

"You're welcome." And her attention shifted to a young mother approaching with two toddlers in a stroller.

Five minutes later, a redheaded man with a receding hairline and wire-rimmed glasses appeared through the ED's double doors. He called out, "Mr. Nevus?"

I resisted the impulse to raise my hand and stood up. I walked toward him. "I'm Alex Nevus."

"I'm Kevin. I'm working with your mom. You sure you want to come back?" he began, hand extended. "She's not making a lot of sense."

I shook his hand and tried to get a feel for him. He held a clipboard and had a pen wedged behind his ear. "That's her baseline," I said, slipping into the psych jargon I knew well. "She makes sense… in a way, but she functions."

"It can't be easy," he said. He pressed a button, and the doors slid back. I trailed behind, never having been in this particular emergency room. Mom's go-to place was Bellevue off First Ave….

"It's not that bad," I said, knowing that an OCFS report was already in the works. I needed to be careful and not give them any more ammunition to pull us into foster care. I had one objective: get this Kevin and whatever ED doctor would see my mom to agree to let her leave with me.

"Anyone else in the home?"

"It's Mom, me, and my sister, Alice."

"Your father."

"MIA." I offered. "Mom has a caseworker with DOHMH."

"Good to know." We came to a locked door with a small rectangular window. He pressed a buzzer and waited. "It's been a busy day."

*Good to know*, I thought. *Maybe I can move things along.*

He pressed the buzzer a second time. There was a pause, and the latch clicked.

Kevin held the door for me. It closed behind with a decisive click of the lock. Looking around, there was a nurse's station behind a curved Plexiglas wall. There were five closed doors with tiny windows—two on the right and another three to the left.

"She's in four," Kevin said. "I get the feeling you've been through this before."

"Yeah."

"Okay, we had to give her a shot to calm her down."

"Is she awake?"

He rapped on the tiny window. Inside, I glimpsed Mom in a hospital gown, her legs bare, her face to the wall. She didn't move, and Kevin turned the handle. "Ms. Nevus. I brought your son."

She rolled back slowly. Her eyes met mine. I could see her struggle to stay awake. "I'm sorry," she said. "You should have left me there. Did you see him? Did you see me dancing?"

I shot her a look. This was not a conversation to have here. What I needed to do was convince Kevin that my mother represented no threat to herself or anyone else. I'd been on this ride before. The ED doc and Kevin the Crisis worker had to believe Mom was safe to leave, and that they wouldn't see her on the nightly news or the front page of *The Post*. "It's okay, Mom. We'll get you back on your meds. This will be okay."

Kevin's expression brightened. He pulled his pen from behind his ear. "Do you have her current med list?"

It was going well. Almost like taking an oral exam—I had all the answers. I gave him Lorraine's card. He called her and then tried to get through to Mom's most recent psychiatrist—Norman Katz—at the Mental Health Center where Lorraine also worked. All the while, Mom dozed in and out. They'd given her a stiff helping of the tranquilizers Haldol and Ativan. As we zipped through Kevin's many paged forms, I had the growing hope that Marilyn would come home with me.

And then the doctor entered. She wore a starched lab coat and an eager expression. "So who have we got?" she asked.

Kevin glanced at his clipboard. "Marilyn Nevus, thirty-eight-year-old single woman—mother of two, brought by EMS on a police hold." He glanced up.... "This is her son, Alex."

"Alex." The doctor extended her hand. Her dark eyes were bright. "Doctor Cynthia Goodman, Nice to meet you."

I shook her hand and wondered what made her so happy.

She smiled at Kevin. "And?"

"And she was at her DSS hearing and apparently lost it. The police paper says: 'Became threatening and assaultive.'"

"Really?" the doctor said. "That's not good."

"It's not true," I said. "I was there. She got loud. She banged her fist on the table, and they freaked out. Her social worker was there, she'll tell you the same thing. People who don't know my mom misinterpret when she gets loud. She's not violent."

"Okay," the doctor said. "Did she hit anyone down at DSS? Push? Any putting her hands on someone else?"

"No, she doesn't... ever."

"Good." She looked at Mom, whose mouth was mashed into the pillow. She was snoring. "Marilyn... Ms. Nevus." She touched Mom's shoulder. "Ms. Nevus." She gently shook her. "Marilyn. Marilyn. I need you to open your eyes... Marilyn."

My heart sank; they'd overmedicated her. I knew from experience that even if they thought she was okay to leave, they wouldn't let her out the door until she was awake. Before I could ask the obvious question, Doctor Goodman beat me to it.

"How much did they give her?" she asked.

"I'll tell you in a second." And Kevin left.

"You think she's good to go home?" the doctor asked me.

"This is nothing. People push her buttons and then they act surprised when she reacts. She'll be okay."

"You take care of her, don't you?"

"It is what it is. She's an okay mom, just has some problems."

The doctor smiled. "You're a smart kid. What grade you in?"

"Junior." I regretted saying it the moment it was out of my mouth, but she probably knew my age from the DSS paperwork. It would have been a stupid lie.

"Which school?"

"Stuy."

"Really? That's where I went. I loved it. Absolutely loved it!" Her face lit up further, and I wondered what could make someone so upbeat in a place like this.

"You like your work, don't you?" I asked.

"Love it! It's always different, interesting people… like you and your mom."

Kevin returned. "Ten and two," he said, indicating the number of milligrams of the two medications the ED nurse had injected into Mom. "But there's something else you need to know." He glanced at the doctor and then at me.

"What?" the doctor asked.

Kevin hesitated. "She's pregnant."

Doctor Goodman stared at him and then at Marilyn. She shook Mom's shoulder, a bit more aggressively this time. "Ms. Nevus… Marilyn."

Mom rolled onto her back, her eyes were glazed, and saliva had caked in the corners of her mouth. "Wha?"

Dr. Goodman's smile brightened further. "Ms. Nevus, did you know you were pregnant?"

"That's nice," Mom said. "You're a nice doctor."

She was stoned on the meds. *Crap!* There was no way they'd let her out this sedated. I also couldn't predict how her being pregnant would complicate things.

"Marilyn," the doctor continued, "how far along are you?"

"All the way," Mom muttered, and she closed her eyes and rolled back to the wall.

My cell strummed.

"What a pretty ringtone," Doctor Goodman commented.

I looked at the readout. At first wondering who J. Haynes was. I felt a flutter in my stomach—Jerod. I picked up.

"Alex, you okay?" he started.

I looked at the smiley doctor, Kevin with his clipboard and forms, and my pregnant and overmedicated mother snoring in the background. *Okay? Not so much.* But hearing Jerod's voice. "Things are kind of crazy right now."

"You're not in school."

"Duh," I said.

"Fine, that was stupid to say. Are you sick?"

Something flitted over my right shoulder. Nimby's high-pitched voice was in my ear. "Alex has a crush." She giggled and kissed me on the ear. Reflexively, I threw down several mental bricks and blocked out her chatter. If she'd offer me some useful information—like whether or not Jerod… was gay or straight—I'd be willing to listen. But then I thought of his girlfriend Ashley and the prom.… *He's just a nice guy who's being friendly.* "I'm not sick," I admitted as I watched the doctor put her stethoscope on Mom's back and then on her chest.

"Okay." He didn't press for more. "I can pick up your schoolwork if you want and bring it over to you?"

"Thanks… but I don't know how long I'm going to be here."

"And that would be… where?"

"You don't want to know," I said. More importantly, he'd already seen my crazy mom. On the off chance that maybe this boy liked me… even if just to be friends… did I really want him to know how messed up my life was?

"I do want to know," he said. "You don't have to tell me, though. I'll pick up your school stuff. Call me when you're done with whatever secret thing you're doing. I like a mystery. I'll figure it out. You're probably not really sixteen but some kind of undercover cop. You're a nark, right? OMG," he said, mimicking his girlfriend's Valley-girl routine.

"Yeah… that's it."

"Call me when you can. Okay?"

"Yeah."

And he hung up.

"Has she seen her gynecologist?"

I looked up at Dr. Goodman. "I doubt it."

"What about her… boyfriend?"

I didn't know how to respond. These were normal questions. But in that moment I couldn't figure out the lies I'd need to get Mom released. Was I supposed to create an imaginary boyfriend, or go with the Prince Valiant hallucination she was waltzing with at the Fairy Ball? Like a bullet piercing my mental brick wall, Nimby shot out and shouted, "Ta da!"

I bit the inside of my mouth to keep from screaming at her to go away. That would be all I needed, to let this happy, smiley doctor know I had a little bare-breasted fairy chattering in my ear—like mother, like son. "I doubt he knows."

"So she's seeing somebody regular?"

I pictured the two of them waltzing—apparently, there was more than dancing going on. "I'm not sure how serious they are… or if she'd want him to know." Or if he even exists… although a pregnancy would indicate there was someone with a penis.

"Got it," Dr. Goodman said. I saw her struggle. "She's really out of it. Alex, I hate to say it, she's going to have to stay the night. I can't let her go like this."

And that was that. From the doctor's tone, I knew this was not up for discussion. I had no power here. Although even with crazy May I had some. So I made the attempt. "What if she woke up?"

"Sorry." Her smile replaced by a look of concern. "It's not just that. I'll need to have OB take a look at her, make sure she has a follow-up appointment with someone when she leaves."

I shrugged, not wanting her to see the depth of my fears… it would only make things worse. "Will you be here in the morning?" I asked, knowing there was every likelihood I'd have to go through this whole thing tomorrow with a different doctor, who might not be so willing to let my crazy mom out.

"All day." Her smile returned. "I come on at eight thirty."

"Great," I said, realizing I'd have to skip another day of school. If it went any longer, I'd need a doctor's note. I glanced at the clock over the nurse's station. It was just after one. The DSS worker's report would have gone in to the Office of Children and Family Services, and based on experience, I could expect a caseworker at our apartment by the end of the afternoon. This could play out a number of ways—none of them good--including calls to my school and Alice's to check up on us. My going AWOL would look bad, and staying here was pointless. Dr. Goodman's decision was made. She was giving Kevin instructions, and that was that.

"I can pick her up in the morning?" I asked.

"Hopefully," Dr. Goodman said. "But you know I can't promise anything. It'll be based on how she's doing."

"Right." I stuffed my emotions back. It did no good to let people see how bad you were hurt. And I was. Mad at Mom for… just about everything, mad at myself for screwing this up. More than anything, I was scared. I thought of Alice, and of what could happen… had happened, in the past. *Shit!*

# Eleven

FEELING like I might puke, I wandered out of the hospital. I had to stop thinking about all the "what ifs?" and just do whatever I could to get us through this. It was still too early to pick up Alice from school, so I got on the subway and headed home. Nimby chattered constantly. "May wants to rule the world, but she can't. She needs a bridge… or she'll go mad, really mad, like your mom. Whole creatures can't cross the divide without getting split."

It was interesting, and for once I resisted the urge to wall her out and listened. The subway was packed, so as much as I wanted to ask questions, one Nevus family member in the psych ward was enough for the day.

Out on the street, I whispered, "Is that what happened to Mom?"

"Oh yes!" Nimby said. "Like a wishbone, the big half is in Fey and the short end… barking mad."

"And is that why you didn't follow me?"

"Yes, yes, yes. You don't need a crazy fairy. No, no, no. Bad, bad, bad."

"So maybe it can be undone," I said. "Like maybe put Mom back together."

"No, no, no," Nimby said. "Once broken, never mended. Alex has two mommies. Or he could." She giggled.

"That makes no sense," I spat back, looking at the fairy on my shoulder. "What did you mean by that?"

I caught a worried glance from a woman on the street as I ducked into the grocery on Fourth. Interesting as Nimby's revelations were, I had to focus on the immediate danger. I used the rest of the food stamps to make certain we had staples in the fridge—milk, butter, eggs, OJ, a loaf of bread. It was a food pantry day, so I figured Alice and I could get a bag of whatever they were giving away, which usually included a block of decent cheese and some fruits and vegetables. In my not-extensive range of cooking, I could make a respectable mac and cheese, and depending on the choice of vegetables—hopefully there'd be some turnips and sweet potatoes—I could make a stew. From experience, when the OCFS people dropped by, the first place they looked was the fridge.

"No Mommy," Nimby sang. "Two little children, all alone. Ain't got no Mommy. No Mommy." I briefly listened and realized she was using the tune "Just a Gigolo." "You ain't got no Mommy. No Mommy… cares for you."

"Shut up," I murmured as I wheeled toward the checkout.

My cell vibrated against my leg, and then the harp strummed. I pulled it out. The caller ID showed STATE OF NEW YORK. So it began, wondering if I'd at least have time to run home and vacuum. What if they were already at Alice's school? What if they'd already hauled her off to some emergency foster home? I took the call.

"Alex?"

"Lorraine," I said, not expecting my mother's caseworker.

"Where are you?" she asked.

"Gristede's."

"They're keeping your mom overnight," she said.

"I know."

"I couldn't stop that woman from reporting to OCFS."

"I figured."

"I think I bought you a reprieve."

"What?" I fished out my wallet and handed over the last of the food stamps.

"I'm at your place. Do you mind if I let myself in?"

"Go ahead. I'll be there in a couple minutes." Her words had ignited that most dangerous of emotions—hope. I hung up, grabbed my bags, and sprinted home.

WHEN I made it up the stairs and keyed in, Lorraine was in Mom's room. She was pulling a blouse and skirt out of the closet and packing them into a knapsack.

"You want some tea?" I asked.

"That'd be great." She emerged from Mom's room, her hand on the knob. She looked at the deadlock I'd put on the door. "You need to ditch that."

"Good point. So…." I put away the groceries and got out mugs and tea bags. "What kind of reprieve?"

"I called OCFS right after that woman from DSS. If it were just you, this wouldn't be a big thing."

In spite of my funk, I cracked a smile. I looked down at Lorraine, who stood maybe five feet tall. "I know, after fifteen they don't care."

"They have too many cases," Lorraine said. "It's the younger kids."

"Alice," I said, realizing Lorraine's good news wasn't that good.

"Yeah. Eleven-year-olds are another story. I talked to the woman who got your case—her name's Lydia Green."

I poured hot water into the mugs. "Got it. When should I expect her?"

"By statute, she can come any time," Lorraine said. "I don't think she will, at least not till your mom's out of the hospital. I told her that you had a responsible adult in the house."

I put Lorraine's tea on the table and looked at her. Her hazel eyes met mine.

"Thank you."

"She will come, Alex. You need to make sure everything is the way it's supposed to be. I'll do what I can with your mom, see if I can twist her arm into taking the meds."

"She's pregnant."

"So it's true?" Lorraine's eyes bugged.

"They tested her at the hospital."

"I didn't know she had a boyfriend. What's been going on?"

"Don't know. She hasn't brought anyone home." I wasn't about to mention my visit to the enchanted kingdom.

"She'll keep it, won't she?" Lorraine sipped her tea, her eyes roaming over the small kitchen.

"Yup," I said. My mom's views on reproduction were in lockstep with her Irish Catholic upbringing. Abortion was not an option.

"Wow… that's a game changer. I'll have to tell Dr. Katz."

"Will they try to keep her on meds?" I asked.

"Probably. But they change them around if someone's pregnant. Not that she's been taking much of anything anyway."

"She'll refuse." I sipped my tea. My thoughts ran in half a different directions. "If OCFS gets involved will they take the baby?"

"It depends on how she's doing. On how you're all doing. For starters, this apartment is too small. I'll see what I can do with the housing people." Lorraine shook her head. "This really complicates things." Her lips curved into a half smile. "I wouldn't mention this to the OCFS people."

"It's going to get bad, isn't it?"

"Probably. Once she starts going to the OB clinic, they'll watch her closely. When she delivers, they'll either let her take home the baby… or not. At the very least they're going to want in-home visits. Your mom is erratic. Even a few years back, they'd never let her keep the baby. Now, they'll at least make the effort. But a lot of people want babies. If they think your mom's a risk, they'll yank him or her fast and have no trouble terminating her rights and getting the kid adopted."

"She did okay with Alice and me."

"She wasn't psychotic back then. She changed. That's the whole problem."

"I know. She's schizophrenic." But was that really it? Nimby's weird explanation about Mom's craziness ran through my head. But what did it mean? And why had Mom gone into Fey in the first place? And…. "She wasn't always schizophrenic," I said. "I can still remember her being normal. Artsy, but now… she doesn't make sense."

"And you never knew your father?"

"No." I felt Lorraine's gentle prodding. Much as I wanted to have someone… like her, to unload to, it wasn't safe. You tell people too much and they'll turn around and hurt you. "The line for father is blank on my birth certificate. Same with Alice's. So what do I do if this Lydia Green shows up?"

"I'll stay till five," Lorraine said. "I'll go through your mom's room and try to neutralize the crazy. I don't know what the hell to do with all those pill pictures. We have to get them out of here."

"She'll go ballistic."

"I know, but if any caseworker catches a glimpse of those…."

"Right."

"It's unlikely anyone will come off shift. My guess is she'll come tomorrow. Both you and Alice should be in school then." She looked me dead on. "Skipping is not in your best interest. She could show up there."

"Got it." I was torn between relief at having an adult step in and make some decisions, and wondering if I could trust her.

"My plan is to try and get your mom released in the morning, and then do an end run around OCFS and get them to close the case."

"What are the chances of pulling that off?" I asked.

"Fifty-fifty, as long as they don't know she's pregnant." She gave me a searching look. "The OCFS people don't want to take your case, you know that, don't you?"

"I know. No one wants to touch alumni of the McGuires' Little House of Horrors."

"It was a horrible thing. Alex, no child should ever have to go through something like that."

"But we did."

I looked at Lorraine. She'd entered our lives four years back. I could still hear Nimby's words in my ear that pivotal morning: "Push him, Alex. Push him hard." I did. Sean McGuire's eyes were forever burned into my memory as his arms flailed, searching for something to grab onto. His fall broken by the crack of his skull on the cement floor.

The days and weeks that followed were a blur. Endless interviews with counselors and doctors. Batteries of tests where I'd been given dolls with genitals and asked prying questions. Had anyone ever done this to me? The worst part was being separated from Alice. I knew what had happened and that she needed me. I'd wanted to kill them all. They'd segregated the boys and the girls in two safe homes. Then more interviews with cameras and one-way mirrors, and a woman judge, and lawyers. At first I thought it was about my having pushed Sean to his death. But that wasn't it. I'd lied and said he'd slipped on the stairs and fallen. That went unquestioned. It took me awhile to understand the fuss was about something bigger. In the safe home, they didn't want us to see the news. But it was everywhere—The McGuires' Little House of Horrors. Dozens of children and young adults coming forward, alleging molestation over more than a dozen years. Film clips of federal agents removing computers filled with child pornography. He'd never touched me; it was little girls—like Alice—that he wanted.

"Alex?" Lorraine's voice. "You okay?"

"Sure," I said, far from okay. I stared at my empty teacup. "You want some more?" I glanced at the clock on the stove. "I've got to pick up Alice. And then I was going to hit the food pantry… maybe stop by the farmer's market."

"I'll be here," she said.

I didn't mean to be rude, but I had to ask, "Why? I really appreciate this, but why are you doing this? It's not part of your job."

"I know." She got up from the table, took my teacup and hers, and brought them to the sink. "I couldn't live with myself if I didn't do something. You take better care of your sister than anyone else ever could or would. I've seen the things you do, Alex. How hard you work to keep this family together. It's not fair." Her voice cracked as she ran the hot water and rinsed out the mugs. "If I can help even a little… that's all."

"There is no fair," I said. "It's just a made-up thing."

She looked at me. There were tears in the corners of her eyes. "I know that, but someone your age shouldn't."

# Twelve

I WAITED outside the iron gates at Our Lady of the Fig—as Alice called it. I stared at the doors that would soon burst open, spilling out hundreds of navy-and-white uniformed kids. I thought about Lorraine waiting at the apartment in case an OCFS worker showed up. She'd stirred up awful memories. Alice never spoke about what happened to her in that house; she said she couldn't remember. But she had night terrors, sometimes they'd be so bad and so frequent that she'd refuse to go to bed. But no matter how hard she'd try to stay awake, sleep eventually found her… and with it, the terrors.

I stared at the statue over the stairs. The virgin watching over the children.

"Migraine better?"

My pulse quickened as I turned and met his golden-brown eyes. He pushed his hair off his forehead—it looked so silky. I wondered what it would be like to touch it. He'd probably punch me if I did. *Get a grip. He's got a girlfriend. He's going to the prom. You have a crush on a straight boy—deal with it.* I chuckled, thinking how next time Alice and I played "What's Wrong," I could add that to my list.

"What's the joke?" Jerod asked.

"You know I don't have a migraine."

"Duh… one more day and you'll need a doctor's note."

"I'll be there tomorrow."

He looked down. "So you didn't forget about Saturday."

"No." I said, wondering what catastrophes would occur between now and then, and realizing I'd probably call and cancel. But right now… it was kind of fun to think maybe I wouldn't.

Nimby fluttered at my shoulder. "He's dreamy," she chattered. "Look at those eyelashes, so long. Look at how he looks at you, Alex. He likes you. He really likes you."

I bit the inside of my mouth. But I wondered—something crazy May had said—"We don't lie." Was Nimby right? Was she mocking me, or did my fairy have better gaydar then I did?

"Alex? You okay?"

"Yeah, just a weird day."

"Weird good?"

"If only."

"So? What happened?"

And then the bell rang and the doors burst open. A navy-and-white army poured out, their laughter and end-of-the-day excitement deafening.

"You're not going to tell me, are you?" he said. "Then you know what…."

I braced for the worst. My life was too complicated to have friends. Not to mention I was seriously crushing on Jerod. A clean break might….

"I'll make things up."

It wasn't what I'd expected. The smile that went with it, straight teeth and something about his lower lip, full… what would those lips feel like? It was him in my dream. Crap!

Nimby kicked my ear, her little foot having the impact of a cotton swab. "Say something!" she shouted.

"Like fill in the blanks?" I felt the air grow heavy, and the chaos of hundreds of excited children seemed far away.

"Just like that." His gaze fixed on mine. "Let me see… you're a superhero with secret powers. Clearly you can't divulge this to just anyone."

"Clearly."

"Alex Nevus is the alter ego of…."

I waited for it.

"Avenger Boy."

"Really? What are my powers?"

"How should I know?" he said. His expression was unreadable, his lips gently parted, half smile, half serious. "But it's the costume that makes the whole thing," he added.

"Tell me."

"I'll do better than that." He slipped a backpack strap off one shoulder, and swung it around to his front. He unzipped the top and reached in. He glanced up as he pulled out a spiral-bound artist's pad. He hesitated. "Here." He flipped the book open and handed it across.

"Holy shit! You do anime. Really good." And then I saw me—or the anime me—a really handsome version of me. "Black jeggings, really?"

"They're bulletproof." I felt him watching me. His upper teeth biting his lower lip.

"Good to know." My anime self had a flaming "A" on his chest, broad shoulders with bulging muscles, and shiny blue-black hair that fell in front of the black mask that covered his… my… eyes. Beside him, facing down a circle of thugs, was Alice, only she was dressed like the Lewis Carroll Alice, with a blue dress and white apron with big pockets, from which she was pulling throwing stars. I started to flip pages, watching me—Avenger Boy—and his sidekick—Precious Alice—defeat the bullies who'd been torturing a frightened little boy. "These are amazing," I said. "Jerod, you are really talented."

"They're not that good," he said.

"Are you crazy? These are like professional work." It was no lie, each frame filled with action, the characters beautifully drawn and inked. The story was good. The band of thugs was merely the tip of a much more sinister plot by an underworld demon plotting mankind's overthrow. "So like you're secretly recording my life?"

"Trying to."

I flipped back to the book's beginning. "Really, really good. You do this stuff on the computer too?"

"Yeah…." His voice was pitched low, and I had trouble hearing. "It's what I want to do… you know, be an artist."

"My mom's an artist." I could have kicked myself. He'd met crazy Marilyn. This was not what he wanted to hear about his chosen profession.

"I know."

His response floored me. But as I tried to respond to that, Alice raced over, followed by Jerod's little brother, Clay.

"How did it go?" Alice asked. Her expression was anxious.

I felt Jerod gently pull his book from my fingers. I didn't want to let it go, and for a moment, the two of us were connected by the now-closed artist's pad. "Can I show Alice?" I asked.

He shook his head. "Not now… not here. I don't know why I showed you."

"Your anime?" Clay asked. "They're awesome!" The little boy was clearly impressed by big brother. "He gets in trouble for them."

"Clay, shut up," Jerod said. "They don't need to hear that."

"So what happened?" Alice was punching my elbow. "Tell me."

I felt Jerod watching us. "Not now," I said. But the look on her face….

"Alex, I'm dying. Please… it didn't go well, did it? I can tell. I could feel it."

Surrounded by screaming kids, I felt exposed, like something under the microscope. No superhero at all, just a scared kid with a more scared little sister.

"Tell me," she pleaded.

"Let's get out of here." I grabbed Alice's book bag and we all headed north on Mott. I needed a change of subject. "So why do you get in trouble for drawing?" I asked.

Jerod's easy mood had vanished. His voice sounded ragged. "Tell you what... you answer your sister's question, and I'll tell you."

"Please, Alex," Alice pleaded. "I've felt sick all day. What happened at DSS?"

I looked at Jerod and then at Clay. "We should go," I said.

"So you don't even want to walk with us?" Jerod said. He sounded hurt and a little angry.

"It's...."

"You don't think we can be trusted." He filled in the blank. "I get it...." He kicked the ground with the tip of his high-top. "I showed you my art. I don't do that. Not ever."

"He doesn't," Clay said. "My mom and dad say it's a waste of time."

"Shut up, Clay," Jerod said.

"Alex." There were tears in Alice's eyes.

I needed to get her alone before I could tell her. *But... why the hell is he looking at me like that? Like he actually cares.* "Alice, you don't care if they know?"

She looked at Jerod and then at Clay. "No. They're both good with secrets."

Clay's mouth gaped, and Jerod gave Alice a questioning look. The little boy blurted, "How do you know that? It's true, but how do you know?"

Alice seemed perplexed, as though he'd asked her why she had two hands or blonde hair.

"She just does," I said. I looked at her, knowing that when she made these odd pronouncements, which she'd done ever since she could form words, they were true. Like when we'd been taken from Mom's custody and put into the McGuires' House of Horrors. The first thing that came out of her five-year-old mouth when we'd walked up those front steps with our garbage bags full of belongings—*"These are bad people."*

"Mom's in the hospital," I said. "The lady at the DSS meeting called the ambulance on her when she got loud."

"There's more, isn't there?" Alice asked.

I felt Jerod's eyes on me but couldn't look at him. "They're opening an OCFS case. Lorraine's at our place in case a worker shows up."

Alice started to tremble. We were on the south corner of Canal, surrounded by hundreds of people and four lanes of snarled traffic inching forward with the sluggish changing of the lights. She knew what this meant, and there was no way to sugarcoat it. I hugged my little sister; she was shaking. "We'll get through this. I'm not going to let anything bad happen to you. Not now. Not ever."

She pushed her head against my chest. "You can't stop them, Alex." Her teeth started to chatter.

"I can. Listen, Alice, nothing is going to happen. Lorraine told them we have an adult in the house, and tomorrow she'll get Mom released."

"But they're going to come. They're going to see what she's like. They're going to say she's not fit. And there's no one else. They're going to take us… they won't let us stay together."

I had to stop her. "That's not true… we've got some time. I called Sifu, and he thinks that maybe Thomas would be willing to help out. You've got to pull it together, Alice."

She nodded but couldn't stop trembling. "What do we do?" she asked.

The walk signal came on. "Come on," I said, and caught Jerod looking at us. He was holding Clay's hand. We crossed the street in silence, the two of them a couple feet in front of us.

On the north side, Jerod turned back. "I'm sorry, Alex. I didn't know."

I wondered how much he understood. He looked so sad. "Glad you asked?"

"I am.… I think you're amazing."

I didn't know how he'd arrived at that. I just felt desperate and had the familiar sense of trying to run through quicksand.

Alice squeezed my hand and wiped her face with the back of her cardigan sleeve. I thought of Jerod's anime version of her—Precious Alice—and realized he wasn't far off. I could see the effort as she pushed away her fears, kind of like the way I could block out Nimby. "We have our own reality show," she said.

"Really?" Clay asked.

I shook my head at her. "Don't. They think we're weird enough."

She laughed, and like clouds swept from the sky, her blue eyes lit over a smile. "Yes, it's called *Sadly*."

"Don't." I was relieved that she'd managed to hold it together but not sure how I felt about sharing one of our twisted little games.

"Today on *Sadly*—" She looked at Clay and then at Jerod. "—we find Alex and Alice having to deal with their crazy mother being hauled off to the nuthouse."

"Can we be on your show?" Clay asked.

"It depends," Alice said. "Our viewers insist on a steady stream of bad news. So what you got?"

Clay pondered as we meandered through the touristy restaurant-lined blocks of Little Italy. He looked up at his brother. "Today on *Sadly,* Clay and Jerod have to go to dinner with their dad and his new girlfriend, Amber."

"That doesn't sound too bad," Alice remarked. "At least you get to go to a restaurant."

Jerod shook his head. "She's twenty-two, my dad is fifty-four…."

"Still," Alice said. She looked at me. "You shouldn't judge who people choose to love."

"Fair enough," Jerod said. "Today on *Sadly,* Jerod will have to deal with his father's twenty-two-year-old girlfriend after she gets drunk and tries to stick her tongue down his throat."

"Ew." Alice made a retching noise. "Okay, you can be on our show."

I knew they were trying to lighten the mood, but talking about reality shows…. I pictured May and her Technicolor kitchen and Mom with her demo spot on pill art. It fell under the header of "speak of the devil." My cell phone buzzed, and then the harp.

I let go of Alice's hand, gave her back her bag, and pulled the cell out of my front pocket. I checked the caller ID "It's the hospital," I said.

"Maybe they're letting her out," Jerod offered.

I took the call. "Hello?"

"Is this Alex Nevus?"

I recognized Kevin the crisis worker's voice. "Yes."

"I don't know how to say this, other than we're really sorry."

I braced for it. "What's happened?"

"Your mother left."

"What? How? She's in a locked room, inside a locked ward."

"They wanted to see how far along she was in the pregnancy. They took her for an ultrasound. There was a sitter with her, but… she got off the table and left."

"How long ago?"

"Half an hour."

"You're certain she's not there. Maybe hiding."

"Security filmed her leaving through the front door. She was wearing scrubs and a lab coat."

I stood frozen. I thought of the hurriedly put-together plan that had a chance in hell of working. Get her released, Lorraine would vouch for us, and I'd do the song-and-dance I did so well to keep them from taking Alice. With a single—and very typical Marilyn Nevus move—that had been shot to bits.

"Alex?" Kevin's voice in my ear. "You still there?"

"Which way did she head?"

"I don't know."

"Ask security, then call me back. Please."

"Of course.… I'm really sorry."

"Not your fault," I said, knowing they'd seen my mother, passed out from their medications, and never considered she could make a run for it. I hung up.

"She's gone." Alice was searching my face.

I nodded.

"We have to find her," she said. "You did it yesterday. You can do it again, Alex."

"I tracked the GPS on her cell phone. She doesn't have it with her." I pictured the revolving tree sculpture in May's kitchen. Mom's cell phone and dozens of others, slowly rotating. I'd not told Alice about yesterday's trip down the rabbit hole. She had enough to worry about. Having her brother follow in Mom's footsteps was not something I'd add to her list.

Jerod and Clay had heard it all. I felt a hand on my shoulder. Jerod's voice was in my right ear where Nimby normally hung out. "Where did she go yesterday?"

"Fort Tyron," I said, hyperaware of the gentle pressure of his hand.

"You think she'd go back there?"

"It's possible." I actually thought it was the odds-on favorite. Unless....

As though reading my thoughts Alice said, "Maybe she went home."

I pressed our number. "Lorraine?"

"What's up, Alex?"

"Is Mom there?"

"No. What's happened?"

I told her.

"This is bad. She could be anywhere."

"I know," I said. "But I think there's a chance she's hanging out in one of the parks. I'm going to look for her."

"How good a chance?"

"I don't know."

"Alex, I was willing to do this for today. But after going AWOL from the hospital. Do you have any adult who can step in?"

"I'm working on it," I told her, thinking of Sifu's son, Thomas.

"I could be in so much trouble here. I could lose my job over this, Alex. I feel bad for you guys. But I just can't."

My gut twisted. "What are you saying?"

"You're sixteen, Alex, they're not going to care if you stay in the apartment alone. Not for a while, anyway. Alice is eleven. They're going to want her in an emergency shelter."

I saw the fear on Alice's face as she overheard.

"When?" I asked.

"They'll come by and pick her up when you come home. I have to do this, Alex. I'm so sorry."

I disconnected. Just like that, the number of adults I sort of trusted went from two to one.

Alice's lip trembled. "I can't, Alex. Don't let them take me. Please."

Jerod's hand was still on my shoulder, it felt solid. "You can stay with us," he said.

"What'll you tell your mom?"

"She'll barely notice. I'll say your place is getting exterminated, and your mom wanted you to stay with friends."

"We could hide them," Clay offered.

Another voice: Nimby's. "No, Alex." Her tiny teeth chattered. "Don't go back. No. No. No."

"I've got to find her," I said. "And somehow drag her back."

"To the hospital or home?" Alice asked.

"Don't know. Home, at least there I can keep an eye on her."

"Okay," Alice said, and she dug through the zip compartment of her backpack for her MetroCard.

I turned to Jerod, regretting the loss of his touch. "Can she stay with you? At least for now?"

"Alex, no," Alice said. "I want to go with you."

"Me too," Jerod said. "Let me help you find her."

My thoughts were back at the weeping mulberry. There was no way I'd bring Alice or anyone else. And what was that shit Nimby had said about whole creatures getting ripped apart? I still felt like myself… but maybe it was something that would creep up on me. No way in hell I'd risk that with Alice… or Jerod. And hallucination or not, there was something dangerous there, and it drew my crazy mother like a moth to the flame.

"I'll find her." I looked at Jerod. Could I trust him? I barely knew him, and crush or no, I needed help. "Can you keep Alice safe?"

"Of course. But let us go with you. Four can find your mom a lot easier than one. Fort Tyron is huge." His voice was low, his tone serious. "Let me help you, Alex. Please."

I felt like screaming. I was scared and tired of not being able to tell anyone the truth, the whole truth, and nothing but the truth. But I knew that the second I did, beautiful Jerod, who turned my belly to mush, would run. Mom was right: I was filled with lies. Everything out of my mouth—whether out of necessity or not—was bull. Right then, my usual ability to string plausible fibs together had abandoned me. I pried my fingers from Alice's. Gave her what I hoped was a firm look. "Stay with Jerod and Clay. If you need me, call." Then to Jerod, "I'll be back before dark." Before they could react, I turned and ran.

# Thirteen

I RACED from the 190th Street Station back to Fort Tyron, with no plan. The quicksand was thick beneath my feet. One second I'd get an idea, the next I'd see why it wouldn't work. I felt desperate and frightened and furious at Mom. Ever since I'd managed to get our family reunited, trying to keep tabs on her had become increasingly impossible. Her running off with the fairies was just a sick new twist. To keep people out of our business, we needed to stay below the radar. Of all the things Mom could have done, getting pregnant was the worst.

As I sprinted north, I thought about what Lorraine said. At sixteen they'd let me slide, and if I could keep them off our backs for a few more years, they'd let Alice slide too, but an infant… no way. Whether or not I found Mom and got her home or to the hospital, we would be dealing with OCFS for the foreseeable future.

I pulled out my cell and went to the GPS app. Sure enough, Mom's cell was still on and still here. At least that part of yesterday's hallucination was real. I jogged down the footpath and from there to the dirt deer run that cut through the yew hedge, and from there….

"No!" Nimby hadn't let up since I'd left Alice, Jerod, and Clay. I'd tuned her out. But when we came to the clearing and the towering mulberry, she shrieked.

I stopped. I studied the tree, with its heart-shaped leaves and twisted cascade of branches that swept the ground. Nimby's wings beat fast as a hummingbird's as she wailed, "*Nooooo.*"

I turned, and she hovered in front of my face. When I was little, I liked having her around, didn't think there was anything wrong with it. She was fun, and I just assumed everyone had little black fairies only they could see. In kindergarten and elementary school, people thought I had a run-of-the-mill imaginary friend. When I described her, they'd think it was cute that my imaginary friend was mostly naked, covered with gold tattoos, and coordinated her loincloth with whatever butterfly wings she'd appropriated. In third grade, that changed. My imaginary friend got me sent to the school psychologist. There, I spent long afternoons filling out tests and answering her questions. Did I hear other voices or just the one? Did it come from inside my head or outside? Could I see things other people didn't see? Did I just see the fairy? I never knew what those reports said. I imagined they were still in my files. What I did realize was that other people did not have little black fairies, and I'd best shut up about mine.

Now, I stared at her. Her fluttering slowed, her red eyes were fixed on mine. Tiny creases formed in her forehead. "No, Alex."

"Why not?"

She shuddered. "No questions. Ask no questions."

"Crap." I looked from her to the Mulberry. It had been no hallucination. The weird scoreboard, May's delight every time Mom or I had asked a question. The pain in my scalp still real. "Okay. Tell me why I can't ask questions."

"You can't afford them."

"But I can ask you questions?"

"We're not in Fey. Here yes, there no."

"So what does May want?"

"Everything," Nimby said. "She wants everything."

"Not helpful. Be specific. Tell me what May wants from Mom."

"A child. A haffling… a bridge. Alice or you or the bun in the oven."

Her answer stopped me cold. “What?”

“Nooooooo!” Nimby darted back, her eyes fixed on the tree.

Something moved inside the mulberry. I smelled Mom’s patchouli and… donuts, just-baked donuts. My cell was in my hand, I was on top of the X for Mom’s phone. The mulberry’s branches rustled, and like a curtain being pulled back, a slender opening appeared.

“Noooooo!” Nimby flew in frantic circles.

I remembered what she’d said and why she didn’t follow me. I paused. “Mom’s crazy because… she crossed into Fey… only she’s not crazy there. So… why aren’t I changed? Or am I? Or…. Wait a minute. You just called me a haffling. What does that mean? What….”

The smell of donuts was like a drug. It clouded my thoughts. *I was thinking something important, about to make a connection. What was it?* I stared into the opening. This was foolish… dangerous. I had no choice. I touched the branches. It was dark inside. But there was something light too—at an impossible distance for it to still be under the tree.

Nimby’s screams grew fainter as I passed through the opening, and the branches closed behind me. And as I stepped from one world into another, the thought came: if humans and fey can’t cross without paying a heavy price, and I could, the only explanation was that I was neither human nor fey—I was a bridge. I thought of Alice and our game of *Sadly—haffling? Really? Today on* Sadly, *Alex is still gay, has never been kissed, has a crush on a straight boy, is going to get pulled into foster care, is probably going to lose limbs to a crazy fairy, and just learned that he might not be human.*

# Fourteen

LIKE a switch had been thrown, lights blinded me. I squinted as my pupils shrank, and I confronted the unimaginable. I'd braced myself for *Cooking with May* in her upscale fairy kitchen. But not for this—some kind of fair. People—okay, not exactly people—all around me. Lots of children… possibly elves. A family of green-skinned folk was headed toward me. The mother wheeled a three-seat stroller, with a trio of green heads looking in different directions. As they passed, the mother, who came to my waist, gazed up at me. I had the sense she found me as weird as I found her. Instinctively, I said, "They're beautiful."

She shot me a dazzling smile with teeth as sharp as needles. "We'd hoped for a bigger litter."

"The more the merrier."

"So true." And she and her clan crossed the dirt path to a merchant's stall on the other side.

I felt a question bubble to my lips… actually, a few dozen, and bit them back. They started with, *Where the hell am I? To….* Taking a note from Sifu, I stood and let my senses explain the inexplicable. *Just breathe, Alex.*

I started with the visuals. I was at a fair…. No, looking at the booths that lined both sides of the dirt road, a market. The stalls were tightly packed with a car, truck, or painted caravan behind the booths.

The elf family had stopped in front of a jewelry merchant whose tables were covered with exquisite flowers arranged in the shades of a rainbow. Elf mom was holding an iris that was purple on top and green on the bottom.

Elf dad, at least that's who I thought he was, was negotiating for the flower. "Tell me the cost, and make it small." He sounded angry.

The pointy-eared merchant, who was twig thin, translucent green, and over seven feet, responded. "Tell me the price you wish to pay." His long-limbed movements were fluid as he pointed at the iris being admired by elf mom.

"I wish to pay nothing at all," elf dad shot back.

Elf mom kicked him viciously as she held the iris to the light.

"It's glass," I said.

"It's perfect." She flashed me a smile and glared at a towering female ogre, who was also eyeing the sparkling flower.

"If wishes were cupcakes," the merchant replied back to elf dad, "you'd be covered in icing. Make me a true offer, or have your wife step away." He smiled at the eight-foot-tall ogress.

"Just looking," she said, her eyes fixed on the iris.

"Of course." The merchant bowed in her direction. "There is no cost for that."

Elf mom stamped her foot… on top of elf dad's.

He winced. "Tell me the going cost, and not a penny more." He glared at the merchant.

"One dollar."

"Impossible!" Elf dad's face grew dark. "Thief! Scoundrel!"

"One dollar," the merchant repeated. "You will find no other like it. It is rare, and it is mine. It could be yours for one hundred cents, or ten slender dimes."

Elf dad turned to his wife. "I don't have a dollar, dear. Not for this."

She nodded, stared at the herd of children that surrounded them, and kicked him. "It is precious," she shrieked. "It should be mine. I'm with Cheapskate, who says I'm not worth ten dimes."

The babes in the stroller started to bawl like cats being tortured. I dug into my pocket. A dollar seemed ridiculously cheap. I fished out change and pieced together three quarters, two dimes, and a nickel. Keeping any question from my voice, I stated, "It costs a dollar."

The merchant's gaze shifted from the scene of domestic abuse to me. "It's true that is the cost. You will find no other."

Elf mom's dangerously pointed slipper stopped midkick. She looked at me, her eyes a muddy red. I handed my change to the merchant, wondering as I did if this wasn't a huge mistake. *What is the road to hell paved with, Alex?* I thought as I handed over the change.

I told elf mom, "It's yours."

Her mouth gaped. "I can't take a flower from a strange man. I'm not that kind of woman…. And in front of the children!"

Elf dad turned toward me, he shook his head. "This is wrong." He glared at me. "Men who throw flowers at women they don't own…. We will fight till the ground is drenched with your blood."

*Oh crap!* "I'm sorry, I didn't mean to offend." My words were drowned by the screaming of the babies.

The elf child, whose hand he'd just released, clapped. He was joined by his siblings and a gathering crowd of elves, trolls, things that were part human, and a few of the graceful silver-haired people.

I backed away, thinking the best option was to run. But a tight circle had formed around us. Elf dad shed his tunic. His khaki-green torso was corded with muscle and covered with dark fur. His fingers ended in sharp black nails that curved like a bird's talons. He toed off his shoes, revealing six-toed feet that gripped the dirt like a second pair of hands.

On my end, I had height and reach, but one well-placed kick from those toes and I'd lose a hamstring or a knee. "I meant no harm. I meant no disrespect."

"Human," he scoffed. "Words cost nothing. Words are cheap. The mother of my babes is not!" He leapt like a cat, launching himself toward my face.

I pivoted back and away, observing his graceful movements as he tucked into a somersault and landed. So much for the height advantage. "I don't want to hurt you."

He grinned. "A tall bag of meat like you doesn't need to worry… about that." He attacked again, but this time low, his feet and hands like a crab's on the packed dirt. He was fast, and I barely managed to feint back and avoid a disabling swipe to my ankles. His hand ripped the air where my leg had been and landed in the dirt. His fingers tore deep grooves in the hard earth.

The crowd chanted, "Blood, blood, blood."

His back was to me; I knew what needed to be done. I spun fast and low. I shot the blade of my right foot into the side of his knee. His head whipped around on impact. He grinned, and as my foot should have connected, tearing the ligaments of his knee apart, his body shot ten feet away. I had no time to respond; he curled up tight, inhaled three big breaths, and seemed to inflate. Then, like a bowling ball, he barreled toward me, the talons on his hands and feet sticking out, ready to slash and rip.

"Blood, blood, blood." And from where his family stood. "Kill, kill, kill."

I darted to the right. He adjusted his trajectory. He was closing fast, a rolling green juggernaut filled with the kind of energy Sifu loved in an opponent—forward momentum. I stepped in front of the barreling elf. In less than a second he was on me, and as collision seemed imminent, I twisted back and to the right. Keeping my eye on the ball… er, elf, I kicked hard. I'd hoped that using his momentum would do some injury, maybe slow him down, or rattle him to where I could apologize for buying the damn flower.

What I'd not expected was to launch him like a helium-filled balloon into the air. I'd judged his weight wrong, his bones or something had to be hollow… or else the laws of physics were on holiday. The force of the impact reverberated through my body as I watched the angry elf shoot up into the sky.

"Holy…." My mind sought an explanation—he shouldn't be flying that high or far. Where was friction and shear stress… and good old gravity? The crowd watched his flight, a few pointed to the sky. Coins passed between members of the audience.

I looked at elf mom and her brood. “I’m sorry,” I told her. “I had no choice.”

She shrugged and pinned the glass iris to the yellow scarf around her neck. “He bounces,” she offered. “And don’t you tell him this….” She winked. “It feels good to have a strange man give me a flower. Makes me tingly…. Children, let’s go find your father.” She muttered as she left, “I used to get flowers all the time, now I just get children.”

“And you love us,” a little elf girl replied.

“Of course. Let’s find your father and tell him how brave he was in battling the hideous monster.”

“Daddy’s going to be mad.” The elf girl clutched her mother’s skirt and stuck out her tongue at me. It was green and forked like a snake’s.

“Yes,” elf mom replied. “Maybe next time he’ll think before denying my desire.”

The crowd parted and drifted off. I looked to where I’d kicked the elf. Would he come back? I was glad he bounced but hoped he’d be damaged enough to stay away. Judging by his wife’s response and the dissipating onlookers, that seemed a good bet, but still…. I needed to focus, and whether it was adrenaline from the fight or the smells—*where are those donuts?*—my head was fuzzy. *Alex, you have got to pull it together. No more buying flowers or giving unsolicited gifts.* On the other hand, it was good to know elves had bones like birds and weighed next to nothing.

I scanned the sprawling market, catching glances from elves with skin shaded from khaki to bright kelly. There were taller versions, with more delicately formed faces, possibly sprites or sylphs in sparkly outfits. Then families and couples of winged pixies about twice the size of Nimby, and here and there graceful human-sized men and women with hair the color of corn silk or silver. The merchants, at least the ones in the packed stalls, were tall. Some skinnier than me, and others heavyset ogres—possibly trolls—with overhung brows and Frankenstein jaws. As a biology geek, I wondered how many different species were here. If this were the Museum of Natural History, how would they be related?

A pair of hedgehogs stood in front of a booth that sold cell phones—hundreds of them. I approached, reminding myself to say nothing. The merchant loomed over his horseshoe-shaped tables.

"Fascinating devices," he growled. "This one, a classic," he said, picking up a shoe-sized flip phone from the nineties. "It starts big and better and then gets small and smart."

One of the hedgehogs pointed to a Motorola in a glass case. "That one… tell me the price. Tell me the things it does."

"Just so." The merchant flipped through a chain of keys dangling from a leather sash. His fat fingers felt the tip of one, selected it, and opened the case. "It does many things. Let's you listen in, and this…." He set the phone on top of what I first took to be a tree limb with the nubs of several broken branches. Apparently, those were rechargers. He pressed the phone on, and it blasted Radiohead's "Creep." He let it play, watching the hedgehogs, and shot a nervous glance in my direction. He glowered at me. "You are trouble. If you do not intend to purchase you should leave."

Despite my beginner's luck with kick-the-elf, I had no interest in discovering the blind spot of big green… whatever the hell he was? "Fine."

I was about to head to the next booth, when one of the iPhones in his case caught my attention. I pulled out my cell. The GPS app opened up, and sure enough…. To be doubly certain, I pressed Mom's number. The iPhone in the case rang.

"That's mine."

He glared at the ringing phone…. I could tell he was about to say one thing, and then reconsidered. "So it was, and now it is mine… it has a cost. Once paid, it could be yours again."

"Where is she? Where is my mother?" The instant the words shot from my mouth, all conversations stopped—dead silence. The merchant's expression shifted from surly to panicked. He sunk back into the shadows of his booth. All the merry shoppers scurried away.

All but one.… My breath caught as he approached. The beautiful blond boy, like something from a dream, but more likely a nail for my coffin. "Liam."

His full lips parted over sparkling teeth, the canines too sharp but otherwise perfect. His violet eyes were fringed with golden lashes, and he was dressed for a renaissance fair, but it looked good on him—a loose linen shirt over tight buckskin pants, his long hair tied back.

"I just screwed up," I commented. My gaze darted from him to the fairgoers who had pushed back to the periphery.

Liam's smile spread; he shook his head. "Perhaps. You asked questions. It comes at cost. I will give you the price for your answers… and the answers as well.… Dorothea."

My eyes blinked as the space between cell phone booth and its neighbor shimmered, and the half praying mantis, half human appeared. I stared at her face. If it weren't for the fact that she was clearly not human, she could have been the sister—almost twin—of that horrible Clarice woman at the DSS meeting. She held a feathery notepad and peered over half-glasses at what was written on the page.

"Two questions," she said, her gaze on me, and then she scanned the onlookers.

The fairgoers seemed frightened, some of the smaller creatures had run off, but curiosity—and probably bloodlust—held the remainder rapt.

"Two questions," Dorothea repeated. "Mockingbird, speak."

Her notepad flipped open. The top page flew out and twisted and folded into an origami bird. Out of its beak came my voice: "'Where is she? Where is my mother?'"

The crowd gasped.

Liam shook his head and stood next to me. His face was inches from mine. "Don't be scared. You'll be okay."

I swallowed, imagining how easy it would be to lose myself in his eyes. I felt myself getting aroused… but different from how I felt around Jerod. Something about this boy was like a drug. I needed to clear my thoughts. "You're beautiful." The words spilled like a line from bad Internet porn. This didn't seem the time to flirt… but. "Tell me the cost."

"May wants you to give her your name. In exchange, you can have both answers. Although they seem connected. It is a fair price. Just give her your name."

I strained to hear the conversations on the periphery. It's what she'd wanted before, and from the frightened expressions and the overall wackiness of upside-down world, I wasn't so sure the price was right. Clearly she knew my name, but there was something bigger involved in my giving it to her… like the weirdness with the flower.

Liam's gaze held mine. He whispered. "It is fair. And I would make no bother, beautiful Alex, if you gifted *me* with a flower."

For one of the few times in my life, I wished Nimby were here. I got the message that a flower was more than the sum of its petals. "You watched that," I stated, catching myself at the last instant from making it a question.

"Through the dark glass, I watched. Silly cow, to make such a fuss." His tongue darted across his lower lip. His expression was almost shy. "You don't know our ways… our customs. Know this, Alex Nevus, any time you offer, I will take your flower." He held out his hand.

Admittedly, what he'd just said sounded pervy. But the way he said it…. I reached for his extended hand. His fingers laced through mine and he lifted our joined hands, examining them in the light. "You must pay her price, Alex. May will not be stopped."

I kept my lips pressed together as my brain reformatted questions into statements. "Tell me the consequence for not paying."

Tears welled in his eyes, and like diamonds they sparkled and fell to the ground. "Blood."

I remembered the ease with which May had stabbed her blue-faced assistant and then ripped off a two-inch chunk of my scalp and threatened worse. He wasn't kidding. I was in deep shit.

Strange music wafted over us. It grew louder, a mix of ice-cream truck bells and a circus calliope. A woman sang. I caught snippets of lyrics, something about a bear being tortured.

"It's a fair price," he said, still holding my hand. He pressed it to his lips.

The feel of his flesh on my skin was electric. My knees buckled, and I stumbled into him. He caught me in a close embrace. Our faces inches apart, his eyes on mine. I let my fingers touch the silk of his hair… his cheek. Unlike the elf, Liam was solid and hard. There was an ache inside of me. Never had I wanted anything so much… the purple in his eyes, his pupils wide, the flicker of his tongue against his too-sharp teeth. My fingers in his hair, my palm against the strong pillar of his neck. I felt a hunger unlike anything I'd ever known.

A woman's long fingers clamped onto Liam's shoulder. A musical voice laughed. "Not yet."

Liam pulled back, regret, and a flash of anger, in his eyes.

I gasped at the loss of his touch. But the expression on his face… like a dog losing its bone. I thought of Jerod, and of Alice. I needed to pull it together. *Find Mom*, I thought, *and haul her ass out of here.*

My pulse raced as I followed the hand on Liam to May. It was as though we were on a stage and the curtain was being pulled back to reveal the fairy queen and her entourage. But not exactly a curtain, as I stared at the shimmery edges of the hole in reality… or unreality. May was dressed for a safari, her hair in two tight braids coiled beneath a straw hat. She was in a camouflage hunter's outfit covered with pockets. Behind her was the same hulking ogre with the dark water mirror. And next to him….

"Mom!"

"Hello, sweetheart." She, like May and the handsome silver-haired man holding her around the waist, was dressed in camo.

"And there we have it!" May's face smiled into the water mirror. "Questions asked and questions answered. I believe this covers both." She pointed toward Dorothea, who was still holding her notepad, the origami mockingbird perched on the edge. The insectile secretary tapped the bird's head; its beak opened, and in my voice repeated, "'Where is she? Where is my mother?'"

May swung her arm like a game show hostess toward Mom. "There she is… and now… time to pay. Every question has its answer and its price, which must be paid. Give me your name, Alex Nevus, give me your name."

My legs wouldn't move. I stared at Mom, her expression terrified. She was shaking her head "no." And when I looked down… how the hell had I missed that? She wasn't a little pregnant—her belly was huge. Yes, I'd thought she'd been putting on weight, but she'd done that before, and it usually meant she was taking her medication. Her partner's arm gripped her around the waist. She shook her head. "Don't."

"Give me your name, Alex Nevus," May sung into the camera. "Two questions answered, got to pay the price."

I looked from Mom, to May, to Liam…. *Why are his teeth so sharp?* The creepy music played softly in the background. I still smelled donuts. Thoughts flooded my head. I pictured Mom's paintings—many of them were portraits of creatures in this world. She wasn't crazy here. She was hugely pregnant. She knew about this place. She'd been here before… I suspected quite a lot. And she was clear—don't give May your name. I looked back at Liam… who wanted my flower… ick… yum. Oh crap!

I opened my mouth. "No."

May's head shot around. "Oh my!"

Gasps from all sides. Then pandemonium. That one word, "no," like the shot from a starter's pistol. The fairgoers sprinted away. Their expressions panicked, as mothers grabbed their children and merchants fled their stalls.

May raised her arms, her fingers stretching like a ballerina's. She began to spin, and darkness fell.

The world turned black, my feet still frozen. I braced for what was coming. Liam had said that to not pay would mean blood. I believed him. I also believed Mom didn't want me to give May my name. I thought of Alice… and Jerod. And then the darkness lifted. We were still in the fairground. I was still alive, and I could move. Slowly, I turned, seeing Liam, May, pregnant Mom, and… a very dead, cell-phone selling ogre.

May glanced at the merchant and then at me. She shrugged. "But you've killed before. I should have known… ah, well. Something else to like about you, and why this time, and only this time, I'll leave your charming vessel intact." She looked over the stalls that stretched as far as the eye could see. She turned to the camera. "Well, we're here, we might as well."

A dainty sprite with a bright-pink face in a lime-green dress spoke up: "Your majesty, it's a good concept."

"Fine," May said, clearly not convinced. She waved her hand at the cameraman and turned toward me. "Considering all the trouble you've caused, I expect you to play."

I glanced at Mom. She rolled her eyes and nodded.

"Fine." I was relieved that I was still breathing and had all my appendages. One thing was certain: I would ask no more questions. At the first opportunity, I'd grab Mom and figure a way out.

May spun to the camera, her smile assured, as a squadron of foot-high pixies hoisted and carted away the dead ogre. "Welcome," she gushed, "to *Tchotchke's Challenge*." Her arms flew high. "The rules are simple, we give each player a roll of dimes and set them lose on the grounds of Flotsam Fair. They have just one hour to be savvy shoppers. Then we take their purchases to auction, and whoever gets the highest price gets to keep the cash."

"That's *Bargain Hunt*," I blurted.

The bright pink pixie paled to the color of lemonade.

The change in May was instantaneous. She was livid. As the pink pixie opened her mouth, a snake leapt from the ground and flew down her throat. The pixie's eyes bulged as she clutched her neck. She couldn't breathe. Her pink pallor shaded to blue as she writhed on the ground. Her legs kicked, her arms spasmed, and she died.

"Nooooo!" May shrieked. "Tell me!" Her yellow eyes narrowed to slits. She glared at me. "Tell me *Bargain Hunt*."

What was wrong with me that I couldn't keep my yap shut? Then again, one of the underlying principles of Wing Chung is stillness, watch your opponent, and wait for the moment they lose balance or their momentum is out of control. May's fury was unpredictable and dangerous. *This is her off-balance*, I thought. Her violence was unlike anything I'd ever experienced, causing death at the flick of a finger. *Tread carefully*.... I felt Liam's gaze. There was no mistaking his hunger. And then May, who was struggling to regain her hostessy composure.

"Tell me *Bargain Hunt*."

I took a deep breath. *Chill, Alex*.... Donuts. Where were they? The smell, like a delicious fog, I had to shake off. *Bargain Hunt*. "It's a game show," I said. "It was on in England and then came to the US.... I don't think the American version did so well. But it's basically your Tchotchke thing. You're just copying it." The lines of her face shifted, her jaw twitched, and the corners of her mouth turned into a tight-lipped smile.

She trembled. "*Nooooo!*" She turned on her entourage. "You are pathetic... at best." She stared at a cluster of pastel-hued sprites. "In case I've not mentioned, this... imitation... of humans.... Unacceptable! I need the new, the now, the next. It's what they crave. It's the magic I need. You are all expendable."

As she ranted and had her "off with their heads" moment, I tried to focus. *You've been here before*, I reminded myself. *And you got away... it was the bricks. You shut them out. She knows you can do that, and so she's trying to confuse you. But you could shut all of this down. Grab Mom and run*. I glanced to May's right, where Mom, who was now in a gauzy floral dress, was leaning up against her gorgeous... whatever he was. Boyfriend? Husband? But *what* was he? Obviously the same race as Liam, close to human, just prettier and filled with something otherworldly and seductive.

The expression on her face as she gazed up at him, it stopped me. I couldn't remember the last time I'd seen her happy. Not forced happy, not the pretend smile she'd put on to get me—and everyone else—to leave her the hell alone. The two of them were beautiful together... the poster couple for "in love." Something else struck me—she seemed normal—or as normal as any pregnant woman could be at the fairy flea market.

Like it or not, this was real. Which put my notion of reality into a scary place. Going with that conclusion, other things followed. Like, if she ran back here once, she'd do it again. My other reality seemed horribly complicated. *What if you've gotten things backward, Alex?* Why not go back, grab Alice.... She'd love this place.

"Count off by three!" May shrieked.

The small throng—maybe thirty in all—of assorted creatures that comprised her retinue was terrorized. Their frightened voices squeaked off like choosing up teams in gym. I glanced toward Mom and her partner. They watched, concerned but detached.

"Dorothea!" May shouted. "Pick a number from one to three."

The little creature looked adoringly up at May. "I pick two, your majesty."

"Number two," May repeated, "come on down."

And every second creature dropped dead.

May sighed. She turned and spotted me. "A lot of death follows in your wake, Alex.... I really like that about you."

*No*, I thought, as the sky darkened and crows descended on the fallen. *This was not a place for Alice.* I held my tongue. My thoughts raced as I selected phrases, trying to decide if they were questions or not.... Best to avoid words like "who," "what," "when," "where," "why," and "how." One sentence formed. I turned it around, forward and backward... it could do. "Your Majesty, tell me your desire."

"Smart boy." Her camouflage gear and safari hat morphed into a silvery gown as she crossed the few yards that separated us. "Walk with me. I fear we started on the wrong foot, Alex Nevus." She put a hand on her chest. "We must be friends. Friends help one another." Her smile brightened. "Friends tell one another secrets, and I can tell that you'd like to know mine."

Up close, she was spectacular, her skin without wrinkle and smooth as porcelain. Her golden cat's eyes were filled with intelligence... and hunger. Of all the creatures here, she was closest to Liam and the one with my mother. Possibly the same species, although her teeth and ears weren't as pointed. She could pass for human. If supermodels could be considered human.

"Tell me a secret, Alex, and I will tell you a story. That is the deal." She held out a slender hand. She chuckled. "There are things better than flowers, and my hand is among them. Tell me a secret, and I'll tell you a story."

Caught in her gaze, I tried to fathom her request. Everything she said was filled with traps and misdirection, like a magician's sleight of hand. Nimby had said the fey could only tell the truth. She'd also said something about "neither a borrower nor a lender be," and I figured that had to do with maintaining balance, which seemed a major rule in this place. I had no doubt May was crazy and obsessed—but with what, I didn't know. My plan to grab Mom might get us through a day or two, but she was pregnant and in love. She was happy; she wanted to be here. So unless I was prepared to keep her locked in her room 24/7….

"So…." *Be careful*…. "I'll give you a secret, and you'll tell me a story." As someone who'd spent most of his life keeping his shit to himself, I had a lot to pick from. Like sorting through a deck of cards, I selected one, turned it inside my head, and decided it couldn't hurt me… not more than it already had. "I have no idea who my father is."

"Lovely!" She clapped her hands. "I know we'll be the best of friends." She stared at me too long, as though making some decision.

I shuddered.

Her tongue clicked against the roof of her mouth. "Closer even. And to show my good faith, I hold the answer to your secret. As one friend to another, I give it now." She raised her hand and pointed to Mom. But… not to her… to him.

Before I could respond; I bit my tongue to not blurt out, "*My father's a fairy?*" I stared at the handsome man…. She'd called him Cedric. *How is this possible?* As though sensing my attention, he looked away from Mom and toward me. His eyes were green like mine. He inclined his head and nodded. My mouth hung open…. This was the truth. The fey didn't lie.

May sang, "And now for my story."

And everything went black.

# Fifteen

LIGHTS blinked on. Flotsam Fair was gone, and I was in a dainty glass house seated in a wicker chair across from May. It was an indoor jungle, plants everywhere, lush flowers, climbing vines, and fruit-laden trees.

"It's my secret," May said, her amber eyes fixed on my face. She'd changed again, her hair short and spiky, her shimmery gown replaced by jeans, a white button-down shirt, and purple plastic clogs. To one side was a basket filled with gardener's tools.

"It's beautiful." Instantly on edge, knowing nothing was as it appeared, and still reeling from the revelation that my father… my father…. I'd seen my father. And he wasn't human… which meant I was… yup, a haffling, and all of this was starting to make sense. "You don't have pointy ears and teeth," I said as I took in my surroundings. A greenhouse, yes, with a thick glass ceiling and walls, the edges beveled, which caused the light to bend and make rainbows. But no matter how many advanced science courses I took—and I was in them all—things didn't add up. Lovely prisms… but the colors were all wrong, and even when they were right… not in the expected order—violet, blue, green, yellow, orange, red. Nope, not here. I threw out hypotheses as to why green was next to purple… some of the time, and pink was attached to yellow. "It's different here."

"Yes… that's truth." She poured tea, at least that's what it looked like, from an intricate silver kettle chased with thistles and bugs and pointy-eared creatures peeking from under leaves. She smiled, as though to give further proof to the statement. "I had a bit of work done." And she mimed a file to her teeth and made scissor gestures with her fingers across the tip of an ear.

I bit back the obvious—*why?* "Your tea service," I said instead, checking my words before they dropped from my mouth, "it's incredible. It's like stuff Mom used to paint."

"They say we can't tolerate different metals—iron in particular. It's odd how those stories arise. In case you get any ideas, metal has no ill effects on us."

"Tell me your story."

"Perhaps. Try the tea."

I stared at her, and then at the fragile pumpkin-shaped cup in front of me. Steam misted off the surface of a pale-green liquid. She gazed back, her head cocked to one side.

"It's not poison. If I'd wanted you dead, we wouldn't be here."

"Yes, that's true." *Not poison, but drugged?*

She chuckled and reached for her tea. She sipped it. Her eyes never left mine. "It's delicious."

*Glad to hear it, but what else?* When I was younger, before all the badness with Mom getting sick, I had a fascination with mythology. Everything I could get my hands on at the library… and not just the kiddy section. That's the stuff I needed now. The story of Persephone being dragged to the underworld and then eating something that made it impossible for her to ever be free. So maybe the tea wasn't poison and possibly not even drugged, but were those the only choices? Everything here was twisty. Mom was sane, rainbows came in different orders, and tea could be more than a delightful afternoon drink.

She grinned, enjoying my dilemma. "There's nothing wrong with the tea, Alex. It's tea. It's getting cold. If you don't want to drink it, I will take no offense." She sipped and watched.

It did smell good, and there was a plate of frosted pink, green, and blue cakes dotted with crystallized flowers. I picked up the cup, my finger testing the heat through the fragile surface. I sipped. It tasted like berries with a tang that clung to the tip of my tongue. “It’s good.”

“Yes, it’s delicious,” she repeated. “I enjoy your caution… your fear is pleasing, as is your face and your form. I did not expect you to be such a beauty.”

Sure, it was a compliment, but… it sounded like someone finding a car they really liked. I pictured my father—Cedric—and then I thought of Sifu. This little tête-à-tête with May was just like sparring.

“Have a cookie, Alex. They are trick free.” And she reached for the plate, selected a pink petit four, and held it toward me.

“Thank you.” *Okay, so maybe the tea’s fine, but these?* They looked so good. Everything about her, this place, beautiful Liam… she was trying to seduce me. *Is that what happened to Mom?*

“Now, I owe you a story.” She arched an eyebrow and popped a cake into her mouth. “Mmm.”

I sat back with my frosted treat and risked a nibble—so good. “I would like to hear your story.” Saliva filled my mouth, and I wolfed down the pastry that tasted like almond paste and raspberries. *So good.*

“Thank goodness. I’d started to think you didn’t believe me. Eat all you want. While I start at the beginning.” She pushed the three-tiered pastry tray toward me and settled into the cushions. “The fey,” she began, “were here long before humans. Some believe that mankind arose from the mating of fairies with creatures of the material world. The truth is unknowable. But fairy nature being what it is, possible, which means probable, which means that’s the way it happened. We like to touch, to feel. But more than anything, we need love and attention.” She sighed and gazed at one of the crystal panes to her right. Its surface turned opaque, and a scene appeared of a Grecian temple. “We need you, and I suspect that one of my ancestors created your kind as a sort of food. You would love us, worship us… and keep us strong.”

My attention went back and forth to her and the scene playing on the crystal. Priests were offering sacrifices of lambs and baskets of food. Blood seeped down altar steps, and apples burst as they were tossed into a roaring flame. The next window flashed, and a scene of a South American pyramid surrounded by jungle came into focus. The structure was capped with an elaborate stone crown and slab, where a dark-skinned priest in a feathered headdress slit the throat of a man. Other windows came to life, and with a shock I realized these were actual scenes from hundreds, thousands, maybe even tens of thousands of years ago.

The greenhouse had turned into a multiplex with hundreds of simultaneous features. The unifying themes were worship and adoration, some too awful to watch. Others were simple worshipers in stone circles or at altars in the woods. A child leaving a basket of bread and fruit at a tiny shrine. A woman praying, her face focused as she chanted to a female statue on top of her fireplace. She tossed a chunk of bread into the fire.

"By the time of my birth," May said, "things had changed. My parents and the other ancient ones said it was for the best. 'Things must run their course.' I was too young, as were my sisters, to understand how pathetic we had become. The world that was ours had drifted from our control."

The scenes shifted, and where they'd been crystal clear, they grew hazy, like a layer of gauze had been placed over a lens. Children playing games, skipping over cracks, women tossing bits of bread into a fire or out the back door. Their intentions not clear; was this a sacrifice, or crumbs for birds?

"Like you, Alex, they learned to shut us out. And what they couldn't see became unreal. The see became the unsee. And with it came the mist. And no one cared… but me."

"That's what's clouding the scenes," I said, keeping my inflection flat at the end of the sentence.

"Yes."

A fog rolled across the images. My attention was now drawn to isolated scenes where the mist rolled back. In one, men in hooded robes, their arms inked in swastikas and iron crosses, drank beer around a fire. Behind them, three men hung dead from a tree. Another scene of a concentration camp, the sky thick with black smoke. To my right, a window sparked with a scene of men running through a night jungle with machetes dripping blood. Another showed a buxom brunette in a tight sequined gown on a shopping show, displaying expensive fairy dolls. Words flashed beneath her screen, and a red warning indicated the Princess May doll was nearly sold out.

"We are misunderstood," May said. "We must be worshiped. The blood is not necessary. Yes, it's nice, shows the devotee is committed, but not essential."

The screens were all clouded now; here and there, one flashed an image. I focused on those, trying to figure the connections. Google and Bing searches for fairies, and words with confusing Gaelic spellings. One screen flashed a fairy figurine on eBay. The little statue looked like it could have been modeled from a relative of Nimby's, right down to her swirly gold tattoos.

"We lost relevance." May's voice sounded hollow. "No one cared. No one stopped it from happening. This, Alex Nevus, is all that remains of Fey. We are surrounded and hounded by the mist. It seeks our annihilation. My own sisters had no concern, as one walked into the mist, and the other…."

I couldn't tell how much of her emotion was an act. Still, this was information that might prove useful. "Tell me the locations of your sisters."

"They took veils," she said. "Lizbeta went into the mist with my parents and most of the fey. And Katye." May stared at me. "She crossed into your world."

The screens went blank and then back to their crystal state. Through the prisms I saw perfect lawns that stretched in all directions. I sipped tea and tried to make sense of… the senseless. She was scared of the mist, wanted to be worshiped, and missed her family. Okay, I could sort of get a handle on that. But there was more. An idea formed. It seemed ludicrous at first, but…. "You need a platform. That's what you're trying to do. And not a little one either. You need something massive. You want to bring back the fey."

"Yes." She clapped her hands. "You're not nearly as dumb as everyone says." She smiled, letting me know she'd made a joke. I heard harp music and wondered if it was coming in response to my brilliant deduction. I felt the vibration in my pant pocket: it was my cell phone.

"Don't answer it, Alex," May warned. "Leave them be."

"Tell me who's calling."

"I won't.... Leave them be. It's in their interest and in yours."

As she spoke, the buzz and strum of my phone pulled at me. I shook my head, stood up, and dug it out of my pocket. It said, "Missed call." Then a single strum of the harp and a text message appeared. "*Where are you?*" It was from Alice.

Then a second strum and another text message. "*Problems, come home now!*" Still Alice. Followed a couple seconds later by another message—Alice was a whizz with her thumbs. "*Not home home, but Jerod's.*" I stared at the screen, and the greenhouse shook. I braced. It wasn't unheard of for New York to get earthquakes—little ones that did enough to remind you how puny we all were. And when I'd been really young, I still remembered how the ground shook on 9/11.

"Put the phone down, Alex." May's smile was taut. She seemed tense and not quite solid. Even the smells of the cakes and the tea seemed distant, like in the next room and not a couple feet in front of me.

"Family comes first." I pressed the number for Alice's cell.

"Your family is here," May said with a warning in her tone. But something more, my thoughts were pulled... literally, like a war for control of my attention. I was holding the phone.... *Why are you holding the phone?* And then I pictured Alice and remembered. I pressed Alice's number. The phone rang.

"Alex." May's voice snapped like a whip.

"Alex." Alice's voice through the phone.

"Wha...." I caught May's delighted expression as I nearly blurted a question. I caught myself midsyllable. "... Tell me what's wrong, Alice."

"They're looking for us... me in particular."

Very little rattled Alice, or at least not to where she'd let people see. She sounded terrified. "Tell me." I didn't want her to know I was dealing with my own pile of shit.

"Lorraine called. She told me I have to go to a shelter. That it's temporary till they find a foster home. They won't let us stay together, Alex." She was sobbing. "You've got to do something. She said you're too young to look after me, and that they've been digging through our case...." She hiccoughed. "Alex... I can't go to that shelter. I can't... tell me you found Mom. Maybe if you got her back and...."

"I found her... I'll figure out something. Put Jerod on."

"He left," she said.

"Wha.... Whe.... Tell me."

"Tell you what?"

Crap.... "Jerod."

"When he left? Where he's going? What's wrong, Alex?"

"Tell me, Jerod, all the above."

"About an hour ago. He said he'd use his GPS to locate you. What's going on? You sound weird."

"He left you alone," I stated. I felt May's attention pulling at me. I refused to look at her. Things couldn't be worse. Lorraine, not just bailing, but actively throwing Alice from the boat. And now Jerod. I asked him to take care of the one person who meant the world to me... and he left her alone.

"We're not by ourselves," Alice said. "They have Blanca—she's their au pair. She doesn't speak a lot of English.... What are we going to do?"

I was about to admit that her brother—king of the improbable plans—had nothing, when a voice intruded.

"Alex, what are you doing in here?"

I startled at the sound of his voice. *This is not possible... and really bad.* Jerod had just walked through the wall of the crystal house.

"*No*!" I shouted.

May squealed in delight, "Wheeeee!"

The teahouse vanished. Lights popped all around us.

"What's going on?" Jerod asked. Confusion in his eyes, the beginning of fear.

"Shut up!" I shouted. I ran toward him, as painfully bright lights made it impossible to see.

"Alex?"

A buzzer dinged. The floor shifted, and the gorgeous glass mosaic reappeared. "Jerod. Listen to me! Stop asking questions." I ran into him, nearly sending us both tumbling to the floor.

He grabbed me by the shoulders to keep from falling. The closeness, the feel of his hands. My eyes burned from the lights as I scanned up from his red sneakers, to his jeans, and T-shirt, to those full lips, to his golden-brown eyes… which weren't squinting at all, but the opposite. His pupils were wide, as though he was in a darkened room. *How come he can see clearly, and I can't?* "Alex." His face was inches from mine. His hands weren't letting go of me.

I felt the whisper of his breath across my lips and cheek. "What's going on?"

And there was that damn bell, and the sound of the frog and bird band.

"What was that…? That noise. Did you hear it?"

Ding and another ding, and the band was going to town. "Stop asking questions, Jerod. For God's sake. Please, no questions." My hands went to the sides of his face. I didn't know what I was thinking. I just needed to make him shut up and stop asking questions. But I held him like that, staring into his eyes, feeling his bare cheeks against my palms. The touch of flesh on flesh sent shocks from my head to my toes. "Please. It's not safe here. Go back and look after Alice."

A hand landed on my back.

"Who the hell is that?" Jerod's eyes widened. His jaw dropped, and his pupils shrank to the size of a pinhead.

The bell rang again, the band swung into a raucous jig, and I saw May's triumphant reflection in Jerod's eyes.

His mouth gaped, and before he could blunder into more questions, I clamped my hand over it. The softness of his lips thrummed down my spine. Blue sparks danced around my hand.

"Finally," May said. "Look at all you've learned today, Alex. I can only imagine."

Still holding tight to Jerod… and he to me, we took in our new surroundings. A variant of May's dream kitchen, only this had the feeling of a game show set. There was a low-lying table to one side with three—judges? Contestants? In the middle was Dorothea. To her right was a lantern-jawed ogre in a red-and-green plaid suit, and on her left, a bearded man with goat hooves visible beneath the table. It was like the fairy version of Mom's DSS hearing.

May turned from us and spread her arms. Three ogres holding water mirrors followed her movement. She addressed the one in the middle. "Welcome," she said. Her clothing shimmered, as though trying to decide what it should be. Finally, a tight red dress painted itself onto her body, and her hair twisted up into a sleek French knot. She glanced at us. "We are so pleased to have Alex Nevus with us today, and the boy he's in love with…. Tell me his name, Alex."

My hand was still clamped on Jerod's mouth. His head turned from the crazy game show set to me.

I felt my cheeks flush. "You bitch!"

"As everyone knows." She winked at me. "I speak the truth… the whole truth… and nothing but the truth, so help me, me."

"Now, your young beau has racked up." There was a drum roll. "Seven questions. So many things your handsome swain wants to know. All questions can and will be answered, if…." A much louder drum roll, "*It doesn't kill you.*" A sign—saying just that—burst into life, its eight-foot letters made of tiny sparklers. Thunderous applause came from darkened bleachers behind the mirror-toting ogres.

"You have got be kidding." I let go of Jerod. I didn't want to think about what she'd blurted out and how this straight boy was going to deal with my having a huge crush on him. This was not the time for that. "It's no wonder," I said, advancing on May. "That the mist has wiped you out. This is boring, and this is dull. This—" I did my own TV show wave toward the set. "—has been done to death."

From beyond the water mirrors came worried shouts. "Not true," someone yelled. "He lies. Humans lie. It is well-known."

"We sure do," I said. "We also know bullshit when we see it. And this… you're just making cheap copies of stuff that's been done before. Stephen King did this in *The Running Man*, then we've got *The Hunger Games.* That should be this show's title, *Done To Death*."

May's smile vanished.

I'd scored a hit. I was frantically trying to piece things together. The mist that wiped out her world, these crazy TV remakes of things on basic cable. All those mirrors, even Jerod's appearance… he couldn't see her at first, as though his mind needed to be primed for this all-out whack fest.

May tore at her face. She stomped her foot, and the lights went on in the bleachers and behind the cameras. "Dorothea!" she shrieked.

The mantis woman made a tsking noise as she scurried forward on her jointed legs.

I braced for what was coming. In the audience I spotted the elf family, including the father I'd kicked downfield. They were clustered together, and I knew if they had to count off by three or whatever…. I caught the eye of elf mom, shear panic on her face as she looked over her brood.

"Stop now!" I shouted. "This is getting you nowhere."

"Fine." May turned on me. Her bun had unraveled and her hair streamed out. "Then give me what I want. Or I will take a life." She stared at Jerod. "His."

I felt Jerod's hand seek out mine. "This has to be a dream," he said.

"I wish," I replied, not taking my eyes off May and stuffing down my panic. There had to be a way out of this…. "You want me to give you my name… but that's not all you want. Not really." I needed time. I had to figure this out.

"Truth," she said.

I thought through everything I'd seen, all the weird fairy stuff. I knew she wanted to push back the mist that threatened her existence, but more… she wanted access to the human realm. And somehow, as a haffling, I was tied into her plans. Yet judging by her disregard for life—fey or otherwise—setting her loose in lower Manhattan… a bad idea. What I hadn't figured… what was with all these TV shows? "There's a purpose to this," I said, trying to read her face. And then it came… like kids at Stuy who have thousands of friends on Facebook or ridiculous numbers of followers on Twitter. "You want to be famous."

She nodded. There was a hint of a smile.

"You *need* to be famous."

"Worshiped," Jerod added. His fingers twined through mine. "She is May," he said. "Queen of the Fey. It's a children's book, Alex."

I nearly blurted, *What?* He was scared, but the look he gave me, with his mop of hair over his forehead. I wanted to kill May for outing me, for saying the thing I was too scared to admit. But yeah, this wasn't just a crush. Jerod was smart and kind and… going out with a beautiful girl named Ashley… and holding my hand. Oh God… and in May's crosshairs.

"I used to read it to Clay. It was one of his favorites." He looked across at her. "This is so weird…. In the story you have two sisters."

"More truth," she said. Her anger gone, replaced by rapt attention.

"Katie and Elizabeth," Jerod continued.

"Close enough," she said. "Continue." Her body, draped in webs of silver, started to sway. The frog and bird band played something soft and sweet on a flute and harps.

"In the book, there are three worlds," Jerod said. "One is lost, one is human, and the third where you are trapped."

"Yes. Tell me the story," she said. "Tell me how it ends."

"It doesn't," Jerod said. "It was meant to be a series, and I kept looking for the second book, but it never came out. The queen of the fairies… you stole a child. You raised her as your own, and when she was grown you tried to possess her as a way to enter the human world. It didn't work because she was human, and you'd have to give up your magic. You weren't willing to do that. The child escaped, and that's where it ended with a cliff-hanger. The girl knows she's safe, but knows you'll try again…. Oh my God!" Jerod clasped his free hand to his mouth. He looked at me; he'd started to shake. He whispered, "In the book… her name is Alice."

# Sixteen

MAY paced frantic circles, her progress followed by a mirror-cam ogre. I glanced back to the bleachers—mostly empty, the audience having fled from her homicidal rage. A small band of anxious, pastel-faced sprites, along with Dorothea, hung to the periphery. "That was good information," May said. She stared at Dorothea.

The mantis woman looked at her book. "It was, your highness. It cleared his debt."

"Fine." She smiled at Jerod. "It's in a book," she muttered. She stepped like a ballerina onto a pointed toe. She started to dance. "A book about me I did not write." Her movements were smooth as water. She kicked out a gauze-draped leg and whipped it around in ever-faster pirouettes. "Someone wrote that book. Books don't write themselves. Someone who knows May, Queen of the Fey."

The harp and flute played a jig. Her dance shifted, and she leapt gracefully from foot to foot. Her hands swayed from side to side. "There are answers here, sweet Alex." She skipped toward us and held out her hands. "Dance with me."

"I don't know how," I admitted, and was horrified to see Jerod's free hand make contact with hers. His other still held mine. I glanced at him and was horrified to remember what Nimby had said—"Whole creatures can't pass between the realms without paying a terrible price." For Mom it was her sanity. Jerod shouldn't have come. He shouldn't have followed me… and he had. *What have I done?*

"It doesn't matter," she said.

That was most certainly the truth, as the connection between her, to him, to me was instant and electric. Like a circuit being thrown, my feet were off the floor and moving fast. It wasn't just the movement… it was pure emotion. Joy. My jaw ached, and I realized it was from smiling. Jerod grinned like a maniac. May's head was thrown back. Her long hair was unbound and threaded with silver.

"I hate to dance," she said as we whipped around in circles.

The piper changed his tune, and May let go of Jerod's hand but held tight to mine. I thought he'd let go of mine, as well. He didn't. We were no longer a circle, but a line of three. Our steps were intricate, her dipping beneath our arms, pivoting around, me following behind, and then finally Jerod. Like a serpent turning back on itself, no end and no beginning.

"I hate to dance," she repeated, "yet it is necessary. At times you must dance." She let go of my hand and skipped lightly from side to side.

He and I, like escapees from *Glee*, gavotted back and forth in sync. My feet touched down and pushed back up again. My body felt loose and free. With every shift in the music, I had no hesitation, just followed along with the crazy jigs and reels. At times I was connected to May and Jerod, and then we'd break free, only to find one another again. Each time his fingers met mine, I felt a rush of emotions—joy, fear, and something I could only describe as recklessness. I was going to get my heart broken. It seemed inevitable. This joy was bad; it would get me hurt. If Nimby was right—and why wouldn't she be—it had already extracted an awful price from Jerod.

"You are so beautiful," he said.

I didn't care if it was drugs or fairy dust or a hallucination or whatever. The boy I was crushing on had just said I was beautiful. Was this the truth, or had May scrambled his brains?

As quickly as the dance had started, the music stopped, and May froze. Her right hand was overhead, as though she was reaching for something. She balanced on the toes of one foot, her gaze on the ceiling. Her fingers uncurled, and her arm slid down. "It's time to strike a deal, Alex Nevus. I shall start. You may keep your name… for now. You want to take your mother…. Clearly, she does not want to go. Still, you have your reasons. Stupid reasons, but reasons, nevertheless. You may not have her…. She's thick with child."

The giddy joy I'd felt vanished. She spoke fast, and I knew that everything out of her mouth was suspect. Yes, truth, but mined with traps. "Marilyn needs to come home to her children," I said.

"Ridiculous! And, yes… children should be with their mother," she parried. "Bring your sister here, you can all stay. It's a better choice, Alex. Look at the trouble you're in. Social workers wanting to snatch precious Alice." Her expression shifted, her tone was warm.

"Like you care. No, the truth is you do care. Too much." I thought of the book Jerod had described. Was that the plan, inhabit Alice and then invade New York? Only, in the book he said it didn't work; the fairy queen couldn't possess the human child, not if she wanted to keep her magic. I stared at May, her golden eyes unblinking.

A woman screamed from the distance.

"Mom!" I shouted.

She was running toward us, followed by… my father the fairy. "Marilyn, don't! Stay away from her!" he shouted after her.

Mom, her flowery dress billowing in the breeze, planted herself between May and Jerod and me, like a pregnant human shield. "You cannot have Alice," she said. "My child is human!"

"Half human," May corrected. "She is a haffling, as is Alex. Alex, it's time you formally met your father, Cedric Summer."

Ever since I could form thought, I'd imagined my father… my dad. Who he was… why he didn't stick around. Here he was. My height, green eyes… like mine. Blond like Alice, pointy ears like neither of us—thank you, God. Not human, and dressed like a glam rocker in a purple-and-gold brocade overcoat, white pirate shirt, and tight canary-yellow britches. My throat was dry.

"Hello, Alex." He stepped forward, his expression solemn. He extended his hand.

"You're not what I expected." Not prepared to touch him, I felt a shiver of repulsion. *What are you?*

He nodded, not taking his eyes off me. As we stood sizing each other up, I felt a tingle along the back of my neck; *he's trying to speak directly into my head.* I heard his voice: *"Careful... say little... or say nothing... listen to her words... look below their surface."* And then something else: *"I love you, Alex. I have always loved you... and your sister... and your mother."*

I lost it. "You have got to be kidding."

He shook his head. "Guard your tongue, Alex. Hate me if you must, but now is the time to think of whom you love. Protect them. It's what you do."

It was too much. This handsome… no, not handsome. There weren't really words for how gorgeous Cedric was. Stick him in a Prada suit, fix the ears, and he'd be on the cover of *GQ*. But he was pissing me off. *Keep the people I love safe?* For sixteen years I'd had a fairy father off cavorting in the woods—or whatever it was he did. Did he even have a profession? Did he ever wonder what was happening with his two kids…? Did he care that someone had done horrible things to Alice? Or that I'd had to kill the bastard to keep her safe? Or that right now we had OCFS wanting to haul her away? Or that this whacked-out fairy queen wanted to hijack Alice… or me… and rule the world while making bad reality shows?

"I do care," he said.

"Get out of my head!" My hands balled into fists. I wanted to punch his perfect face.

"As you wish. But I do care, Alex. It is no lie."

"Touching," May said. She glanced at Mom's belly. "Your mother stays. Bring Alice, Alex. You can all stay." She glanced at Jerod. "Even your boyfriend. It's simple here, but not back there. He has a girlfriend, Alex. It's truth. She's pretty, and people won't call him vicious names if he's with her. She's bought a lilac dress, and he has a tuxedo with a matching cummerbund. He intends to give her a flower.

She intends to return the favor." May ran her tongue lewdly over her upper lip. "It's a simple choice. All that waits on the other side is pain and heartbreak."

Mom was frightened and angry, and I heard Cedric inside my head. *"Keep Alice safe. Keep her from May."* And then Jerod… what was the cost for him following me here? There was a dazed expression on his face, as though he was still in the dance. In that moment I realized several things, and suspected a couple more. I needed to get Jerod out of there; maybe it wasn't too late… although—*the fey don't lie*. Mom was looking and doing a hell of a lot better here than in the real world. Yes, I needed her, desperately. But the OCFS wheels were in motion, and having a raving lunatic of a mother wouldn't keep Alice out of foster care. Her pregnancy also complicated things. The instant OCFS realized she was pregnant, they'd be relentless. They'd watch her like a hawk and snatch the baby and say it was in their best interest.

I didn't have a plan B…. I grabbed Jerod's hand. "We're leaving." I yanked hard.

He blinked. "What's going—"

"No questions." I clamped my hand over his mouth.

Cedric shouted, "Alex, wait!"

And in my head, his voice. *"I can help… some."*

He turned on May. "My queen, balance must be restored. You have taken the boy's mother. You have left a hole on the other side."

I stared back, clueless at his intent, but his words were like Nimby's. May's face was red, and I knew her looks could kill. I felt frightened for this father I never knew I had… and kind of proud. He was standing up to her. He was doing it for me.

"She came of her own will!" May spat back. "You know that."

Cedric looked down, and then at Mom. "She has left a hole on the other side." His voice was as persuasive as an attorney arguing in court. "It must be filled."

"Lawyers and bean counters!" May shrieked as she advanced on Cedric and Mom. He stepped aside, leaving Mom in front of the enraged fairy queen.

I started to run to protect her, but Cedric shouted inside my head, *"Hold back!"*

"Fine!" May raised her hand and raked it down Mom's side.

It was unexpected and brutal. May's movement too fast, her fingers like eagle talons. Mom screamed as May's claws tore her flesh.

"Help her!" I shouted toward Cedric.

He shook his head. "Watch," he said.

I couldn't.... *What the?*

Mom screamed as May's fingers pulled back, clutching what at first appeared to be a meaty slab of Mom's side covered in torn fabric… but it was moving… growing. May shook it off her hand, and hurled it to the ground. "Disgusting!" She wiped the blood on her shimmery gown.

Jerod stood close. His words gave a name to the blob of meat as it grew, shooting out a leg, then a second. An arm popped out of a stumpy neck, and then its mate. "She's making a changeling," he whispered. And then a tumorous mass of slick tissue bubbled and surged. Black hair sprouted and twisted back into an exact replica of Mom's thick braid. A face formed; even the dress became a duplicate of Mom's flowery print.

May stepped back as Mom rubbed her side. She winced in pain but seemed physically intact. Even her dress was undamaged. "The ground upon which you walk, Cedric Summer, grows thinner by the year. Careful it does not break. And remember… I know your secret."

He winced and bowed his head. He spoke. "Your majesty, my every breath is at your whim."

"Yes," she said. "That is truth. Do not forget it."

I stared at Mom, as Cedric… my dad… wrapped an arm around her waist. From there I looked at the changeling, who was an exact duplicate of her… only her expression. Not quite dazed, as she stared at her feet and wiggled her toes from beneath the hem of her dress.

I felt Jerod next to me. "Wha…."

Before he could finish the word, I screamed, "Shut up!" I saw the hurt on his face… like I'd slapped him. "Please, no questions."

"Right." He shook his head, looking from Mom, to other Mom, who was playing with her dress, her expression wide-eyed and goofy.

I looked at Cedric. He was in my head. *"Take her and leave this place. Keep May away from Alice. Keep her safe."* And then something I'd never known I'd wanted: *"I love you, son. I'm proud of what you've done... and I'm sorry for the pain I've caused. But leave fast. Now!"*

In all of this insanity, his voice in my head was the only thing that made sense. It was time to move. I whispered to Jerod, "We're getting out of here. Stay close." Then, in a loud voice, "That's way cool, May!" I ran across the space, dragging Jerod by the hand. I stopped inches from my new duplicate mother. "Hi, Mom."

The changeling looked at me, her eyes on my face, her mouth moved as though uncertain what to do with it.

I smiled.

She smiled back.

I brought the corners of my lips down.

She did the same.

"You're my mom," I said.

"I'm your mom," she replied.

This could work. "Come on, Mom." Overcoming my revulsion at touching her hand. I expected it to be slick and bloody, but no, just a warm, dry hand. She was solid.

"You're not going anywhere," May said.

"Jerod." My eyes left hers to find his. "Block May out. It's easy. Imagine bricks being built around your thoughts, one on top of the next. Mortar them down, fill the cracks. Hold my hand." I grabbed his and closed my eyes. Time to build walls. I had a lifetime of practice, and he had none. "Thick bricks." Feeling his hand in mine, changeling Mom's in my other. I gripped hers, he gripped mine. "Just wall them out. None of this is real. It's make-believe."

"A dream," he whispered. "It's just a dream."

"Dream," she echoed.

"Exactly. And we're going to wake up soon." I spun bricks from thin air, laying them down inside my mind. I felt their hands in mine and willed bricks around them. It was surprisingly easy. So many years of blocking out Nimby, blocking out pain… memories. But I'd never thought to include others. I pictured the thick brick wall that surrounded the church across from Jerod's house. Like that. "This is make-believe," I said, spinning bricks into place, snapping them together like fairy-repellant building blocks. I pushed away doubt, and all the questions that could shatter my fortress. I held them tight as my walls grew thick and strong.

Something scratched my face… branches.

I cracked my eyes open. It was dark. The air was cool and moist. The three of us were under the mulberry tree. I took a breath and heard Cedric's voice in the distance. "Find Katye."

Jerod, still holding my hand, tripped on a tree root, and we tumbled through the wall of branches. Cedric's voice was gone, and the only sounds were our breath and the croaking of frogs.

# Seventeen

WE LAY winded outside the tree's canopy. It was daylight. Jerod's hand in my right, changeling Mom's in my left. He let go first. I felt an ache at the loss of his touch… and fear. He'd followed me into Fey and now…. Tears welled. He'd done something heroic, and according to Nimby, his selfless actions would be rewarded with a horrible cost. He was so beautiful, and now, it was like I'd broken him.

He pushed back on the ground, putting distance between us. "Shit," he said. He shook his head and tried to stand. He stumbled back and sat with a stunned expression. His mouth was agape. "Wha…." And then he shut it fast. "Questions," he stated.

"They're okay on this side." I stared at his face, trying to decipher his expressions. Would he be crazy like Marilyn? Was this the opening of a schizophrenic monologue?

He swallowed and nodded. "Too much." He stared at me, and the minute our eyes connected, he looked away. He squinted at changeling Mom, who was drawing circles in the dirt with her free hand.

This was bad. What did he mean by too much? Really bad. I didn't cry. I did not cry…. Tears were streaming. "I'm sorry."

"I'm sorry," changeling Mom parroted, her gaze now up on the branches overhead.

I couldn't stop crying. I wanted to wall out this reality as well. How pathetic. I struggled for words. Truth was, May was right. She'd ripped me open and let Jerod have a good look, which didn't really matter because he'd be too crazy to remember. "I'm sorry." And between the wall of bricks and trying not to look at Jerod, I realized I was about to lose the only friend I had outside of Sifu and Alice. I couldn't focus. I let go of changeling Mom's hand and I turned away. I couldn't look at him, like something was tearing inside of me. I stared at the ground. Maybe if I stayed still, he'd get up and leave. That would be best. But feeling Jerod sitting there.... *Please go away. Just leave me alone. Don't make this worse.*

"That wasn't a dream," Jerod said, not sounding crazy. His voice was deep. "As evidenced by… she's really real." He called to the changeling, "Marilyn."

Distracted by a stream of ants, she glanced at him. "Marilyn," she repeated, her tone parroting his.

"That's your name," he said. "Marilyn Nevus. Alex is your son."

She smiled and looked from him to me. "Alex is my son."

"Way out!" Jerod said. "She seems partially programmed… if that's even the right way to think about it."

A carpenter ant crawled onto her leg, pulling her focus.

He moved closer. His nearness made it impossible to think. And then he did the unthinkable… his hand found mine… again. "What are you doing?" I asked.

"Look at me, Alex."

Great, I had snot running, and I'd been crying like a five-year-old who'd just learned there's no Santa… and I felt that worst of all emotions… hope. Like maybe he was okay, which didn't make sense because the fey don't lie.

"Alex."

I looked at him.

His other hand was on my face, his fingers wiping my tears. I couldn't breathe. This was the dream, his eyes all I could see, brown and fringed with long lashes. His face inches from mine. His skin against mine, in my hand on my face. His breath… it brushed my lips. I've never been kissed. And suddenly…. The first touch of his lips was like a spark of pure joy. It shot through my body. My toes curled, and it wasn't him just kissing me, but my mouth on his. Our lips together. His hair against my cheek, my hands against the back of his head, twisting in his floppy mop… like silk. His lips parted, and the tip of his tongue tickled my mouth, and my tongue found his. His taste, his smell… like boy and spring woods and something sweet. I didn't hear the park ranger. Neither did he.

Everything outside of that kiss didn't exist. If that kiss could have lasted forever, it would have been fine.

"Boys!"

Okay, I sort of heard that.

"Boys, you can't do that here."

I felt Jerod pull back. Our lips parted. He smiled, and something lurched in my chest.

"Guys, you can't be doing that here."

I should have been mortified as I saw the park ranger. He shook his head and smiled. He looked at us and changeling Mom, who'd transferred the ant to her finger and was following its progress. "It's not a gay thing," he said. "It's just we can't have people making out in the woods. If we do, this place will turn into the Brambles."

Having Googled places where guys cruise in the city, I knew what he meant. But that was… not what we were doing. Although, looking to Jerod, his lips so red and delicious…. His cheeks were flushed. He was grinning, and those dimples…. If this was him being insane, I could certainly deal. "Okay, we'll stop."

"Okay then." The ranger looked down. "I'll give you a couple minutes to… pull it together. When I come back, you'll be gone? Ma'am, you understand."

He caught her attention. She smiled—*holy shit!* She really looked like Mom, only… not nutso. Her eyes were clear. "I'm Marilyn," she said. "Alex is my son. Jerod is his boyfriend."

"Okay." The ranger seemed amused. "You boys are cute, you don't want to be out here doing that stuff."

As he walked away, Jerod whispered, "Yeah, we do. She said I'm your boyfriend. You know what that means?"

"Tell me."

"It's got to be true."

I was speechless. Just taking it in, the crunch of leaves and branches as he stood, the way he held out his hand. He pulled me up. A breeze off the Hudson brushed over us. I still felt his lips, the taste of him, his stubble against my cheek.

He smiled, his upper teeth gently biting his lower lip.

"What?" I asked. I had a moment's panic.... No, questions were okay now. "What's so funny?"

"Everything.... I've wanted to do that for a long time, Alex."

"Don't lie," I said. "We barely spoke before a few days ago."

"And...." He stared at me. "I've wanted to do that for a long time. There's a lot more I want to do. I didn't know...." He looked away. "I was scared."

"You have a girlfriend," I blurted. *Why the hell did I have to bring her up? Alex, what is wrong with you?*

"Ashley... crap."

It was like a balloon popped. As Sifu said—repeatedly: "*The moment is now, you can't hold it. You can only be in it as it gives way to the next.*" Our moment had passed. "You don't have to explain," I said. Realizing that while I had my laundry list of problems, which now included a replicate mother, Jerod had his own issues. And maybe, just maybe, I hadn't broken him. *But how was that possible?*

"I'm a coward," he said.

"Are you kidding? You're not. A coward wouldn't have walked into that world, or stood up to May.... You did see all that, right?"

"Oh yeah."

I nodded and felt my breath steady. Just say it, Alex. "A coward wouldn't have kissed me."

"I didn't know… I didn't know if you'd want me to… or if you liked boys, or…. She said you liked me."

Of all the crap that had just happened, May outing me to Jerod had seemed the worst. Apparently, she'd done me a huge favor. I heard the crunch of the ranger's boots. "Come on," I said. "Mom… Marilyn, we have to go."

She bounced up, letting her summery dress swish against her legs. "Okay."

"Stay close," I told her. Finding myself actually believing she was Mom, and then….

"Are you mad about that?" Jerod asked.

"About?"

"The kiss," he whispered. "It does make me kind of a coward… or… an opportunist. Oh shit… and it's not like you don't have more important stuff to deal with. What the hell was I thinking?"

I didn't care that the ranger was a few yards away. His crossed-arm posture let us know that our welcome in Fort Tyron Park had come to an end. Yeah, I had lots of things to worry about. If Alice were here, it would be one hell of a game of "What's wrong, Alex." But in that moment, I had a single impulse, and I acted on it. I pulled Jerod close and mashed my lips against his. Not like the first kiss, but strong and delicious, and one word over and over in my head: *"Mine!"*

From behind I heard changeling Mom say, "Boyfriends."

When we pulled apart, Jerod was grinning. His eyes sparkled. "I got an idea," he said.

"I got a few myself."

He chuckled. "I'm not talking about that, but yeah. God, you're beautiful."

"Boys." The ranger's voice. "Time to leave."

"Time to leave," Marilyn repeated.

"Come on." Jerod grabbed my hand, and I grabbed… Mom's. We walked fast and then started to run like maniacs down the dirt path. From there to a paved walk, and then to the road that ran through the park. Dodging bicyclists as they headed to The Cloisters, we sprinted toward Fort Washington Ave. The daylight was blinding, like slipping into yet another world.

"Way out!" Make-believe Marilyn said.

I stopped, still holding her hand in my right and Jerod's in my left.

"Way out," she repeated, looking at the street, the cars and taxis, a women with a stroller, people on their cell phones, a bus shooting past. "Way out."

"She's like a blank tape," Jerod said. "Everything we say, only there's other stuff. She knows to change things. What's your name?" he asked her.

"Marilyn." She smiled. "You're Jerod."

"I am," he said. "You need shoes."

I looked down. Her feet were bare and filthy.

"I need shoes," she said.

We stood at the park entrance. My heart raced, and not just from the run. A woman wheeling a double baby carriage smiled as she passed. I couldn't focus.

"Your father said we need to find Katye," Jerod said.

"Yeah." My mind was spinning. "You heard that too." I'd just met my father. Turns out he was a fairy, and not in the "let's march in the Gay Pride Parade" kind of way. And Jerod said "we"… and *we* were holding hands. I didn't ever want to let go… except. *Crap*, people were looking at us. Maybe it was barefoot Mom, but…. I squeezed and let go.

"I think I know who she is." He was looking at me. "What the hell is that?" He raised a hand and pointed at my right shoulder. His eyes were wide, wonderment on his face, as he moved his forefinger through the air, closer and closer to my shoulder. "I'm losing my mind."

My gut lurched. "Don't say that."

"You are an onion, Alex Nevus," he whispered.

"What the hell does that mean?" I turned and saw Nimby on my right shoulder. She was staring, mesmerized, at Jerod. Lying on her stomach with her hands under her chin, her red eyes fixed on him, her black-and-blue wings beating slowly.

"An onion," he repeated. "Layer upon layer of pure amazing. Please tell me she's real and that I'm not losing my fucking mind."

"You can see her?" I asked, watching the space between his finger and Nimby close. Clearly he saw something.

"Thank God! You see her too," he stated.

"Yeah."

His finger halted with less than an inch between it and my dreamy-eyed fairy. "She's not new, is she…? I mean… I don't know what I mean."

I got a crick in my neck, twisting to watch Nimby and Jerod. "No one sees her but me. She's always been there." It felt weird watching my imaginary hitchhiker stare at Jerod and be so quiet. "She's usually impossible to shut up." Nimby turned toward me and stuck out her forked black tongue.

"What's her name?" he asked.

"Nimby."

"Hello, Nimby. I'm Jerod."

She giggled, and her wings fluttered. She flew off my shoulder and perched on his finger. "Hi, Jerod. You're dreamy!" She launched from his finger, kissed him on the cheek, and then darted back to her usual perch on my right shoulder.

"That tickles. How cool are you," he said, staring at her in amazement. He looked at me. "You're like the magic boy," he said. "Or I am losing my mind."

"Please don't say that. And I thought I was an onion."

"A magic onion. She's always with you, isn't she?"

"Pretty much."

"I'd watch you in class. And there'd be like a blur around you. That was her."

"You'd watch me?"

"Oh yeah…." His voice was gravelly. His gaze went back to Nimby. "You are the prettiest thing."

"Oh, Jerod." The curlicue gold tattoos on her cheeks and eyebrows glowed. She flew off my shoulder and landed on his.

Standing there watching him, it was like something I'd been carrying, something heavy, had just fallen away. If he could see Nimby, that was a convincing argument for her not being a hallucination. If she were real… maybe I wasn't headed toward a life as a mental patient… like Mom. Who didn't seem crazy at all in the whacked-out world under the mulberry. So how come her trips into Fey cost her sanity, and Jerod—at least for now—seemed excellent. "You said you had an idea about that Katye."

"Yeah. The book I was talking about, the author is Katherine Summer. That's the same last name as your father…. And Katherine… Katye, it's not that different."

"I don't know that book… it was strange how you did."

"Not that strange," he said. "I think magic onion boy lives under a rock. *May, Queen of the Fey* was a hit among the kindergarten set. It won awards. There were dolls and stuffed animals." He looked at changeling Marilyn and then across at a store on the other side of the street. "They've got flip-flops. We should get her some."

Holding her hand, we crossed to the stall that sold touristy T-shirts, postcards, and cheap shoes. "Pick a pair," I told her, and watched. She reached into the stack and looked down at her feet. She stared at her dress, which was a mix of turquoise and flashes of hot pink and purple flowers in a tangle of green leaves. She grabbed a pair of flip-flops that matched the green. I reached into my pocket.

"I got this," Jerod said, as if he knew I couldn't afford the five-dollar plastic and rubber shoes.

I broke the bit of plastic holding them together and watched changeling Mom put them on. I thought of real Mom's artistic abilities…. This one knew something about color. "Good choice," I told her.

"Yes," she said. "They match."

Jerod's cell rang. He pulled it out. "It's Clay." His finger slid across the screen. "What's up…? No!" He looked at me. "Two social workers are at our place. They're looking for Alice."

My stomach lurched. “Tell him to get her out of there….” I knew she couldn’t go back to our apartment. I wondered how’d they’d traced her…. “It’s got to be her phone. Lorraine must have given them her number, and they’re tracking her by the GPS chip. Tell Clay to have her ditch her phone and go to Sifu’s. I’ll meet her there.”

“Clay, did you hear that? Toss the phone, and go out back… yeah, down the fire escape. Be careful. No, do not let them take her.” He was about to hang up. “If you can do it quick, grab *May, Queen of the Fey* and take it with you.”

He hung up.

“I need to go,” I said. It was clear Lorraine had sold us out. I didn’t think she knew about Sifu, or not beyond knowing I was into martial arts. “Come on!” I grabbed changeling Mom’s hand and ran toward the 190th Street Station. I tried to remember if Sifu had ever met Lorraine. I didn’t think so. He’d met Mom a lot of times.... He knew about us. Alice would be safe with him… but for how long?

I felt Jerod behind us, and then at my side, keeping pace as we flew down the stairs into the subway station. I swiped Mom through the turnstile with my MetroCard. I grabbed for the spare, but I must have left it at home. Problem was, mine wouldn’t work again for thirty minutes.

“Take mine,” Jerod said.

I glanced up, knowing there were cameras. I heard the rumble of an incoming train. “No.”

I leapt the turnstile, grabbed Mom’s hand, and sprinted toward the downtown express. I looked back, half expecting a cop, but just Jerod a couple feet behind. The train pulled in, and we ran onto an empty car.

“Sit,” I told her. “This is bad.” I pulled out my cell. It was nearly four. Through all the years of dealing with Mom and the related agencies that tried to butt into our lives, I knew they shut down at four thirty. That was mostly true. But if they thought an eleven-year-old was in trouble…. “Crap!” They’d send cops after Alice.... They’d search for her.

Jerod’s hand was on my shoulder. “It’s going to be okay.”

I snapped. "How the hell can you say that? It's not okay! You have no idea what's going on? None of this is okay!" I couldn't stop myself. He recoiled as if I'd hit him. I backed away and stared down the empty train. And then at fake Mom, who was glaring at me.

Nimby scolded, "Bad Alex! Don't yell at Jerod."

"I'm sorry."

I started to hyperventilate. *Calm down. Think, breathe. This is what you're good at. This is what you know. You've gotten out of worse spots... far worse.* That was the truth. Getting Alice and me out of foster care, getting Mom on disability, our Section 8 housing, even getting Lorraine to turn a blind eye to our circumstances…. I was good at this stuff. I'd memorized state statutes to where I could cite chapter and verse and find the loopholes that kept our leaky ship afloat.

I looked at changeling Mom. She didn't seem crazy. I sat next to her and started to talk. *This has to work.* I felt Jerod at my back. He was about to hear things I'd never shared. "You have two children. Alice is eleven, and I'm sixteen. We were taken from your custody because you have schizophrenia and wouldn't take your medications. They put us in a home where bad things happened to Alice." I hesitated. "The man who did them had an accident and died. When the state came in, they found that this man had molested many children. There was a scandal, and I used that to convince people we were better off with you… crazy or not. You are now taking all of your medications, and you do not hear voices, and you do not see things that other people can't see." I watched her carefully as I spoke. Her gaze never wavered as the car filled at each stop. "Who are your children?" I asked.

"I have two," she said without pause. "Alice is eleven, and you are my son, sixteen. I hear no voices or see things that other people can't see."

I felt the tiniest surge of hope. *This is too easy.*

She continued with a bright smile. "Jerod is your boyfriend, you're his magic onion, and Nimby is your fairy."

# Eighteen

THE express zipped down Manhattan. At Fourteenth, Jerod's cell rang. "It's Clay."

Changeling Mom stared at him. "Clay is your brother."

He nodded and took the call. "What's up?"

Mom's gaze was fixed on him; her face mimicked his. It was like watching a weird kind of camera. Every twitch, the way his hand brushed his temple. "Don't panic," he said. "Calm down, Clay."

"What's wrong?" Stepping away from Mom, I was aware of how crowded the train had become. "What's going on?"

Jerod whispered, "It didn't work. There were cops in the alley. They're taking Alice."

"No!" The train was back in motion. I felt like punching something.... No, let it pass. Adrenaline surged. I couldn't look at Jerod, the concern in his face. Whatever feeble plans I'd pieced together were all shot to shit. "Is she still there?" I asked.

Jerod nodded. "They're in front of our house. Do you want to talk to him?"

"Yeah," I said, reaching for the phone.

"Be kind, Alex. He's only nine. This wasn't his fault."

"I know. Hey, Clay, it's Alex. Tell me what's happening."

The third grader was crying. "I tried to get her away. They were in the alley. I told them it wasn't Alice, but they had her school picture. They said if I lied to police I'd get in trouble. I'd go to jail."

I bit back my anger—what sort of twisted creep threatens a nine-year-old with jail? "It's not your fault. You're a brave kid. Where is she now?"

"She's in a blue Prius in front of our house. She's looking out the window. She's crying, Alex… I'm sorry." He was sobbing.

The train slowed. We were at Chambers Street. "Clay, we're on our way. I need you to do me some big favors. Write down the names of the social workers, the license plate of the car… anything that can help me track down Alice. We're on our way."

"Okay."

I handed the phone to Jerod as the doors slid open. "I'm going to your house."

I bolted out the doors and ran flat-out. I had no plan, only to get there fast. It was the sort of strategy Sifu hated. As I dodged the snarling rush-hour traffic on Canal, I imagined his warnings—*too much momentum... find your center... stay in the middle.* All useful when you're sparring, but now….

Pumping my legs and scanning for obstacles; there was too much foot traffic and touristy crap on the sidewalks of Little Italy. I swung into the road, nearly colliding with a bicycle messenger. Off to the right, I spotted the weirdly canted brick wall outside the church. And then I saw the flashing light of a police cruiser and a blue Prius as it turned on its signal light and eased away from the curb.

Alice was in the back, strapped in. She was straining against her seatbelt. I shouted. "No! Stop! Wait!"

In front of the house, I saw Clay being restrained by Blanca, the Haynes's Columbian au pair. The little boy's face was tear streaked, and he clutched a skateboard as he tried to free himself from Blanca.

"Let me go!" he screamed.

"Clay!" I called to him.

"Alex… I'm sorry." He was red faced and crying.

I watched the Prius and the cruiser, now at the end of the block, heading toward Houston.

"Give me your board." I grabbed it from his arms. I flipped it over, then dropped it to the ground, and with my right foot pumping asphalt, was in pursuit.

As I chased after them, Clay shouted, "I got the names of the social workers."

"Good work!" I screamed back, bobbing and swerving to avoid potholes and a double-parked delivery van.

At Houston, the cruiser took a wide left, and the Prius went right. The only thing in my favor was the time of day. It was rush hour, and traffic was going nowhere. Four lanes of vehicular sludge. Staying a few car lengths behind the Prius, I tried to catch my breath. The car had state plates and a sticker proclaiming the agency's commitment to energy conservation. From the outside, it looked normal, but having been hauled into protective custody, I knew the inside handles were disabled and the doors locked. I looked at the two workers in the front seat—a man and a woman—who took their jobs serious enough to go after an eleven-year-old near the end of their shift. It was nearly five, and there'd be hours of work as they got Alice settled.

Each time the lights changed, traffic inched a dozen spaces. My cell buzzed. *Where are they going?* I didn't want to think what would happen if they got on the FDR Drive, but that seemed the destination. I looked at the on-ramp five blocks in the distance.… It had no sidewalks, bicycles, pedestrians, and skateboards off limits. It wasn't going fast… but it was moving. They could take her anywhere.… My phone buzzed again, and then the harp came on.

I pulled it out, never taking my eyes off the Prius. "Yeah?"

"Alex." It was Jerod. "I'm on the computer. The two OCFS workers—Gary Osborn and Lydia Green—are out of an office in City Park." He gave me the address. I memorized it while staring at Alice's blonde head. She didn't know I was following. I couldn't think about how terrified she must be, although she'd never show them. She'd shut down, instead. They'd see a quiet little blonde girl who'd give them nothing.

"Where are you?" he asked.

"Houston. They're heading to the FDR.... There's got to be some kind of intake place or safe house."

"They don't give the addresses for those," he said.

"No, they don't want parents kidnapping their kids."

"Or brothers either," he added.

"No." And the light changed. Still holding the cell, I pushed off. I kept low and mostly hidden behind a boxy yellow cab. It seemed a lifetime ago when we'd been pulled from Marilyn's custody. In reality, it was five years, nearly a third of my life. "It was close," I said.

"What was?"

"The place they first took us... it could have been City Hall Park.... I was too numb to notice, but I know we didn't leave the island." The Prius was a block from the FDR. If they were going downtown, they'd have already turned. "I'm going to lose them." And then an idea came. "Jerod... do you have numbers for the workers?"

I heard the clicking of a keyboard. "Yeah."

"Here's what I need you to do.... You got a pen? It gets complicated." I watched as the Prius took the on-ramp for the FDR and headed north. The traffic started to flow, and I glimpsed Alice. It was all I could do to fight back my anger and my fear and tell Jerod what had to be done.

# Nineteen

MY RIGHT foot touched down, my knees soft like shock absorbers as I wove through traffic. There was a weird snippet in my head from one of the dozen or so psychiatrists I had to see when I was in OCFS custody. I think he might have been in training, and the only reason he stuck in my head was he had the most beautiful brown eyes.... Yeah, sucker for brown eyes. He told me I had trust issues. I remember looking at him and cracking up. His statement of the obvious had struck me as ludicrous. “No shit,” I’d said. And then I’d torn into him… like, of course I had trust issues. Yet here I was, flying like a maniac up Avenue B, depending on someone else to come through. That scared the hell out of me. I didn’t really know Jerod… and for all his words, and those kisses. But no, I had to get home and pull together a costume for make-believe Mom.... *But if it doesn’t work, if Jerod doesn’t do what he needs to*.... “Shut up, Alex,” I told myself.

I tucked into a sharp turn and shot for our building. I jumped off, flipping up the board and catching it. Then I keyed in and tore up the stairs. As I rounded the fifth floor, I wondered if maybe there’d be workers waiting for me. It seemed unlikely. Sure enough, there was no one there.

I thought about Lorraine… would she be inside? I hoped not. On the subject of trust and why it’s not something I did… she was a blinding example. To be on the safe side, I knocked. There was no answer. I turned the three locks, feeling the heft of the security bar and the deadbolts as they pulled back.

Inside, I flipped on the lights. It was home, and it felt empty and sad. Lorraine had tidied things up, and there was a bowl of apples and oranges on the kitchen table. The door to Mom's room was open, and most of her artwork had been taken down. The clothes were off the floor and stuffed into the closet.

I knew what I needed. I dug out a navy skirt suit I'd bought for her at a thrift store on Canal. It was from an upscale women's shop and had never been worn. I pulled a wrinkled white blouse out and a pair of low-heeled navy pumps. I hauled it into the kitchen, pulled out the iron from under the bathtub/kitchen counter, and went to work on the shirt.

The iron huffed, and I wondered where Nimby had gone to. I was so used to her incessant chatter amping up my anxiety. But no, my little fairy had gone AWOL. I suspected she'd left me for Jerod. Who could blame her? As I worked at the worst of the wrinkles, I wondered how it was that he was the first person who could see her. Yes, Alice believed me when I told her about Nimby, but she couldn't see her. So why Jerod? Was this the tip of the price he'd have to pay for traveling into Fey… for me? That was a whole other set of rules, and I sure as hell hadn't figured them out yet. I resisted the urge to check in with him. He'd either get it done or…. I didn't have a backup plan. *You have to trust him. Oh God.*

I held up the blouse, the front pretty good, the back and arms like the skin on a Shar-Pei. My cell buzzed. "Yeah?"

"We're in," Jerod said, his tone was incredulous. "How the hell do you know this stuff, Alex?"

"Someday… maybe a week when you've got the time, I'll tell you. So where did they take her?"

"It's an emergency youth shelter on Twenty-Second between Seventh and Eighth. That Lydia woman did not want to tell… your mom where they were taking her. If you hadn't given me that statute to cite."

"Mom had her full custodial rights restored," I said, zipping into what Alice called my lawyer mode. "Even in an emergency, they have to make reasonable accommodations for her to have contact with her children. If they don't, it's like kidnapping."

"So you've got these things memorized?"

"Pretty much. The important ones, anyway." I didn't want to share how I could cite entire chapters of state and municipal code. "Until a judge says otherwise, they've got to let her see Alice, even if it's supervised."

"She said we've got till seven. After that, it goes from being reasonable to unreasonable. She also said we should bring clothes... that it was unlikely Alice would be released without a full case review."

"Jerod, you did good." I glanced at the clock—five fifteen. "We don't have a lot of time."

"Tell me what to do."

My mind raced. Everything I'd built to keep Alice safe had just been blown apart. If I didn't tread carefully, this would get far worse. "Give me the address, and I'll meet you and Mom there." I glanced at the partially ironed blouse.... *No time*. "Try to tidy her up, and see if you can get some real shoes on her."

"I'll get something from my mom's closet," he said. "She'll never notice. Are you planning to break Alice out?"

"I wish.... Get there fast. At least Alice will know I'm working on this. It'll make her less scared."

We hung up, and I shifted into hyperdrive. I had an awful pit-of-my-stomach feeling as I filled a black plastic bag with Alice's clothes. The nightmare we went through five years ago was always with me. The car ride to the McGuires', our stuff in garbage bags, a feeling of helplessness. I swore this would never happen again. I also knew that OCFS had all the power. May's words popped to mind: "*You have little power here.*" Every word out of my mouth... out of Mom's mouth, was going to be weighed and potentially used against us.

I opened the filing cabinet next to my bed and pulled out copies of important paperwork—the signed order giving Mom her custodial rights back, our report cards with school attendance records for both

Alice and me—hers perfect, mine a bit fuzzy. A copy of our lease and Section-8 voucher proving we had secure housing. Bank records, copies of the utility bills—all paid on time. Then Alice's birth certificate and social security card, her medical records showing she'd been immunized and saw our pediatrician annually.

As I tore through my carefully labeled files, trying to think what obstacles they'd throw in front of me, it was like dealing with another version of Queen May. Right down to her wanting to take Alice.... *Not going to happen.*

I stepped back, my fingers over Mom's social security disability files. I felt sick. This had to be a coincidence. *Right?* Alice getting hauled in by OCFS was related to... dominos falling. My thoughts raced over the last couple days... the catastrophic disability hearing, the trip to the hospital, Mom going AWOL, Lorraine ratting us out. Dorothea's resemblance to that Clarice woman at the DSS hearing. Then all the rest of it.... *Something's going on here, Alex. This can't be coincidence. And if it's not....* I glanced at the clock—5:35. *Got to move*. I shoved the papers into a Manila envelope, tossed them into the garbage bag, and like Santa, hoisted it over my shoulder.

I tried to figure which would be quicker: subway, running, or.... I grabbed Clay's skateboard. Then down the six flights, back onto the street. Right foot pumping, the city blurred as I tore up Avenue A. Something fluttered over my right shoulder as I zipped past Tompkins Square Park. Nimby had returned. "You left me," I whispered.

She tittered. "Jerod has dreamy eyes."

"I'm aware of that."

"He kissed you."

"Also true." Realizing that if anyone looked at me, they'd see a gangly teen on a skateboard with a garbage bag over his shoulder, talking to himself. Something nagged at my thoughts. "You said whole creatures can't travel between the worlds. Jerod did... he seems okay."

She giggled.

"Stop that! Just tell me. Is he okay?"

"No."

My foot faltered, and I nearly took a nosedive over the curb. I corrected and tried to catch my breath. "What's going to happen to him?" In my head, all I could think was that I'd ruined this beautiful boy, who'd only wanted to help.

She giggled again. "Jerod is fine, and no, I won't stop. You're mean to me, Alex."

She was right. For years, I'd done my best to make her go away, and now.... "I need your help, please."

"Say you're sorry."

I whipped my head toward her and gritted my teeth. "I'm sorry."

"Like you mean it."

"Look, please." I was shouting. "I'm sorry, and I need to know the rules. You've got to help me."

Nimby startled. "Yes, truth. I am here to help you." Her tone changed to a scold. "About time you figured that out. Everyone says you're so smart, Alex, but you can be dumb... and blind."

"Enough riddles. Please, one straight answer."

"Ask the right questions, Alex. I tell the truth... unlike you."

"Yeah, weird fairy truth." And timing the light, I hung a wide left onto the north side of Fourteenth heading west. "How come Jerod is okay?"

"He was protected when he entered Fey."

"By what?"

"You."

This was worse than I thought. I wanted to scream. "How did I protect him?"

She muttered, "Really dumb. This is why you shouldn't look a gift fairy in the mouth. You love him, Alex. You protect those you love. It's what you do."

As she said it, something clicked. Yeah, I loved Jerod, and maybe... those kisses were real. Maybe he felt something for me. Cheesy love songs flipped to mind, all that crap about the power of love.... What if it wasn't crap? "But Mom's in love with Cedric. Why didn't that protect her from going mad?"

"He was a trap," she answered. "One you avoided."

"Liam," I whispered, remembering his eyes, his touch as we danced, the sense of something powerful and predatory.

I felt like my head would pop. Too much information and not enough. I swerved around a pothole and hung a left onto Twenty-Second Street. As I crossed Seventh Avenue, I spotted Jerod and changeling Mom a third of the way down the block in front of a gray brick building.

"You did good," I said, jumping off Clay's board. Make-believe Mom looked… normal. Her hair was pulled back, her floral dress replaced by jeans, a button-down yellow blouse and flats. She even had a pocketbook—something I could never get real Mom to carry.

"Blanca helped," he said.

"She's perfect." I was out of breath.

"Hello, Alex," she said.

"Hi, Mom. You look nice. This is what we need to do." I tried to think through all the ways this could go down. Everything was at stake.

"We don't have a lot of time," Jerod said.

"I know." And I rang the doorbell.

A woman's voice came through the speaker. "Yes?"

"It's Marilyn and Alex Nevus to see Alice." I braced for being told they'd changed their mind or that only Mom could go in—no way in hell that was going to happen. But instead, the door buzzed and clicked open.

With Alice's clothes over my shoulder, I held the door for Mom. "We have to go in," I said.

She smiled and looked back at Jerod, who was holding Clay's board. "Of course.… Your fairy's smitten with your boyfriend."

I let go of the door and grabbed her hand.

Her expression was startled. "Something is wrong."

"Two things you are not to mention—fairies, of any sort, and me having a boyfriend. Can you do that?"

"Of course."

The door slammed behind us. We were in a brightly lit corridor. In front of us was a horseshoe-shaped desk, and behind that a uniformed guard. There was a dome camera overhead, and I spotted another behind the guard. In front of the officer was an open logbook.

We approached.

He looked from Marilyn to me. “IDs, please.”

I pulled out my student card and Mom’s driver’s license and handed them over.

“I’ll need to go through that.” He pointed at the garbage bag. “… and your pocketbook too, ma’am.”

I pulled out the folder of documents and handed the bag to the guard. I watched as he pulled on gloves, patted the bag, and searched through its little-girl contents.

“Sign in.” He examined both our names, looked closely at make-believe Mom, and then at me. He handed back our IDs with two plastic visitor tags. “Wear these at all times and give them back when you leave. She’s on the third floor. Take the elevator. It’ll be on your right.”

I gave a polite smile, and Mom did the same. It was creepy, the way she mimicked me, but the guard didn’t notice.

I said nothing as we rode up. There was a camera in the elevator, and I knew everything that happened in tonight’s visit would be recorded. The doors slid open. “Come on, Mom… let’s go see Alice.”

“Yes.”

I had an awful thought, and clearly I was out of the running for son of the year, but changeling Mom was a hell of a lot easier than the real one. At least so far. We found the ward… or whatever they called it at the end of the hall. I read the sign over a telephone handset hanging on the wall. I picked it up, told them who we were, and the door clicked open.

“Alex!”

“Alice!”

She ran toward us. “I knew you’d come.”

Her face was tear streaked and she was still in her school uniform. I hugged her, smelling the shampoo we both used, wanting her to know that I'd figure this out.

"You're safe," I whispered, burying my face in her hair.

She sobbed against my chest. Which, considering how infrequently Alice let others see her emotions… I knew she was freaked. "It's okay. Everything is going to be okay," I said. We both knew that was a fat lie, but it sounded good. I felt Mom's presence and braced myself. If it were real Mom, she would have said something bizarre. But make-believe Mom was smiling up at a sandy-haired woman heading toward us.

"I'm Marilyn Nevus," she said. "Alice is my daughter."

The sandy-haired woman stopped and looked from Mom and then to Alice and me. "I'm Lydia Green…. I'll be your caseworker."

Mom extended her hand. "Pleased to make your acquaintance."

The caseworker seemed taken aback. "Likewise…." She shook Mom's hand.

"Alex," Mom said, "introduce yourself."

I let go of Alice. "Hi," I said. I tried to get a feel for this Lydia, one of the two who'd snatched Alice. Her eyes seemed tired, and I had the sense that we were keeping her from something. The other strong impression I got—she was suspicious.

"You know I can't let her leave with you?" she said, looking first at Mom and then at me.

"We know," I said. "We brought her clothes."

"This is a nice place," Mom said, taking in the homey surroundings. At least that's what someone had been shooting for, with child-sized furniture and a living room set in front of a bank of wire-laced windows with bars on the outside. The only other kid was a little boy staring at a TV, and behind him was a young aide chatting on her cell.

"We try," Lydia Green said. "Would you like to look around?"

"I would. Thank you," Mom said.

Alice gave me a funny look, and tugged my hand as the social worker took Mom for the tour. "What did you do to Mom?" Alice whispered. "It looks like her." She stared after them. "A pocketbook? She never wears a.... It's not Mom." Her mouth was agape. "Alex? Who... what?"

"It's okay." Continuing with my stream of lies. "Just go with it." The thought of explaining was more than I could handle. Alice couldn't even see Nimby, which had always added to my fear that I was a lunatic in training. She'd say she believed me... but right up there with Santa and the Easter Bunny—the fairy on my shoulder.

"Get me out of here," she begged. "I want to go home."

"I know." And Mom and the caseworker headed back toward us. I shot them a nervous glance, looking first at the worker's expression and then Mom's.

"Not what I was expecting," Mom said. "Clearly, thought has gone into making this feel like a child's home."

The worker's wariness was gone. "I could say the same.... You're not what they'd told me to expect."

"I know," Mom said. She was much more than a tape recorder. All the things I'd thrown at her on the subway ride, she'd taken in and put back together. "I have schizophrenia. It's a serious illness. I have to take medication every day."

The worker listened attentively. "You seem pretty together. They said you left an emergency room against medical advice."

I held my breath.... The fey didn't lie... it was apparently a rule. Like the rule that Lydia the OCFS worker did not have the authority to release Alice... but she would have input into the hearing for emergency custody that would take place in the morning.

Make-believe Marilyn smiled. "I let my temper get the better of me at a disability hearing. Alex was there.... They sent me to the emergency room, and then they over-sedated me."

Alice squeezed my hand as we watched and listened. I kept waiting for bad things to shoot out of her mouth... the Mom things, or something about me having a fairy... or God knows what.

"It's what happens to people with mental illness," Mom said. "But when I woke up and realized they were going to let me go anyway… I left. Those places take forever. I realize now it was a mistake. I just wanted to get home to my children."

"And you take your medication?" Lydia asked.

"Of course. It's not a cure for schizophrenia." She sounded like a public service announcement. "But it keeps my symptoms down."

I hated to break into Mom's stellar performance, but I needed information. "There'll be a hearing tomorrow?" I asked.

"Yes." The worker looked from me and then to Mom. "If you get here at nine, Judge Lawrence only has two cases.… Do you have a lawyer?"

"I have Alex," Mom said. "He goes to Stuyvesant."

The worker smiled. "Smart kid."

"He's a genius," Mom said. "Straight As."

"I brought copies of some paperwork," I said. "If you're going to be our caseworker, you might want these." I needed this woman to like us, to not break us up. I was having a hard time reading her.… She seemed less suspicious, but exhausted. "You'll be here in the morning?" I asked.

"Oh yeah." She took the thick folder and looked in.

It was nearly seven… great… a caseworker who took her job seriously. Her partner from earlier had obviously gone home. "You're working a double?" I asked.

"No." She stared up at me. It was an awkward moment, like being at the pediatrician. She was studying me. I never knew how to behave around these people, so I stood and let her look. I wanted to tell her how desperate I was to get Alice home… but that could work against you. I didn't know if she was friend or foe. Considering what had just happened with Lorraine, I wasn't going to risk it. Finally, she spoke. "You manage."

"Yes." I wasn't entirely certain what she meant by that.

"Okay. Then I'll see the two of you in the morning."

"*No*!" Alice gasped. "I want to go home!"

Her voice ripped into me.

"Please." She was begging the caseworker. "Please don't make me stay. Something bad is going to happen."

Her words were like ice in my veins. So similar to what she's said when we'd arrived at the McGuires'.

Make-believe Mom sank to her knees in front of Alice. She hugged her. "Sweetie. You have to stay tonight. I'm sorry."

I watched Alice tense, and then something gave way and she collapsed into Mom's arms, sobs wracking her little body. I put my hand on the back of her head and stroked her hair.

"It's going to be okay," changeling Mom said. The slightly flat tone to her voice was gone. She repeated my words… only from her, they didn't sound like a lie. "It's okay, Alice. Everything is going to be okay."

# Twenty

IT TOOK everything I had to leave Alice there. The Nevus children don't cry… and we were both doing more than our share. As make-believe Mom and I headed toward the door, I heard Alice beg, "Don't leave me here." She sounded exhausted and numb. I remembered her prophetic words our first day at the McGuires'—"*These are bad people.*" Just like then, there was nothing I could do.

And then we were outside, and Jerod was on the curb reading a big children's book, Clay's skateboard on the sidewalk. He looked up. Nimby was on his shoulder, staring at the open book. They turned and looked at us.

I couldn't speak, scared I'd start bawling.

"We'll come back in the morning," changeling Mom said. "There'll be a judge. Lydia said we'd go first. It's okay. It's going to be okay, Alex."

Jerod put the book on top of the skateboard and came toward us. He brushed his bangs off his forehead. He stared at me, and before I knew it, his arms were around my shoulders and he was holding me. He felt solid and safe.

"It's going to be okay," make-believe Mom repeated as she hugged the two of us.

I knew she was parroting what I'd said… but the fey can't lie… so maybe it was the truth. Or maybe changelings weren't technically fey. And I guessed the Nevus kids did cry… because I couldn't stop.

"Ssh." Jerod's breath was in my ear. He kissed the side of my face.

But something was off, and not just the fact that the woman who looked exactly like my Mom wasn't her, or that my fairy seemed to like Jerod best. Something shivered down my back. I batted away my tears and broke away. I turned toward the OCFS building and looked up. There was someone in the third-floor window watching us. It was Lydia. Our eyes met. *Okay*, I thought, *she's seen Jerod.* Big deal… she's just doing her job. I gave a small wave, which she returned, and then she vanished from the window. I couldn't read her, and it bothered me. Because I knew that in the morning, things could go for or against us. Having Alice's OCFS worker on our side would be huge.

"Let's get out of here," I said.

"Check this out." Jerod grabbed Clay's skateboard and the picture book. He showed me the cover. *May, Queen of the Fey.*

On the cover was a beautiful blonde fairy with a crown and wand against a background of lush foliage. On the bottom it read Katherine Summer, and there were three gold stickers for awards it had won. "It's a hell of a coincidence… but."

"I think we're catching a break," he said. "While you were inside, I checked out a few things. I went to the book's website, nothing's been added for years, but there was a link to another site. Katherine Summer is still writing, romances… lots of them."

"With the fey?"

"No, chick lit.… Secretaries, a nun who falls for the pizza delivery guy… who turns out to be a super-wealthy computer geek. That kind of stuff. She's got a Facebook page and half a million followers on Twitter. She's written a lot of books."

"Your mother is in love," changeling Mom said.

"Huh." I wondered where that came from.

"I feel it," she said, patting her hand against the skin of her other arm. "Your mother and father love each other." She was grinning.

She was no tape recorder. This was real thought; she was piecing things together. "What does that have to do with what we're talking about?" I asked.

"It's a romance. That's what you're saying."

I had no idea where this was going. "I guess."

"It's a big romance," she said. "Filled with drama and sacrifice. It ripples through her flesh… my flesh. It makes her whole."

"It ripped her apart," Nimby added, having settled on my shoulder, her butt pointed at my face as she stared at Jerod.

"Stop." I looked at Nimby and felt blood rush to my cheeks. "You said love protects." I didn't want to go further, still feeling the tingle of Jerod's embrace. He was being a stand-up guy, and maybe he kind of liked me in that way. "If Mom… and Cedric are in love, why didn't that keep her whole?"

Nimby stared back at me. A wicked smile crossed her face. "You'd think this was difficult to understand. Cedric was a trap set by May. He lured her into Fey with the promise of love. Yes, later he fell in love with Marilyn, but by then the damage was done. It binds him to your mother, and May uses it to her advantage. He is sorry, as much as any fey can feel guilt… and there's no turning back."

"I get it." I felt a weight and shame for all the bad things I'd thought about Mom. "So where's the break?" I asked Jerod.

"Katherine Summer lives in Manhattan."

"You found an address?"

"Not yet, but maybe better.… She's on a book tour and speaking at the midtown library… tonight. We can make it."

"Too easy," I said, already figuring the most direct route to the library. It would take us back by the OCFS building, and I didn't want to bump into Lydia. She'd probably think we were planning to spring Alice. Which, if that had been a realistic option, I'd be on it. Getting Alice home meant playing by the rules, playing smart, and playing better than anything and anyone they threw at us. So we turned up Eighth Avenue and doubled back on Twenty-Third Street.

Nimby hopped to Jerod's shoulder and said, "It's not easy. It's fey way."

I realized that, like Mom's gibberish, there was a logic in here, a different language, like knowing the OCFS statutes and being able to kind of speak schizophrenic.... "It's fey because it looks like a coincidence, but it's not."

Nimby flitted back to my shoulder. "Yes. Katherine Summer is waiting for you, although she will not know that. It's no coincidence—it's synchronicity."

There were layers of meaning... and a lot of garbage in Nimby's words.

"Let me tell you about the book," Jerod said. Holding it in front of us as we walked, he flipped the pages. The illustrations were gorgeous, and I could see why it had been popular. Lots of cute elves and pixies, a villainous queen who hid her evil behind a beautiful face as she plotted the overthrow of the human world. It ended as Queen May was foiled in her plot to possess a little blonde girl.... Alice, who looked like my sister. It was clear that it had been meant to be the start of a series. The fairy queen vowed to return, stronger and more beautiful. Her final words were, "You will worship me. You cannot vanquish me, for I am May, Queen of the Fey." In the end, she was imprisoned in a peanut butter jar and hurled by Alice into a frightening mist.

"That's not how it happened," Nimby said as she hovered in front of the book.

"Which part?" I asked.

"The jar... that wouldn't hold her. The fey love glass... and water."

"Why?" Jerod and I asked at the same time.

Nimby turned in midair and looked between us. "Good. Glass and water are transparent. You can slip between them and see into them."

"The ogres with the water mirrors," I said.

"Like the statue in Tompkins Square Park," Jerod added.

I looked at him.

"There's a statue," he continued. "A woman staring into a bowl of water." He looked at Nimby. "Is that what you mean?"

She kissed him on the cheek. "So smart. Yes, she is skrying." She turned to look at me. "It's how Cedric seduced your mother. It's an old story. She gazed into a mirror, and he was there…. Mirror, mirror on the wall…."

"Why her?" I asked, picturing the antique-looking glass on my mother's worktable. I had a memory of being a little kid and watching her stare into it as she was working on a series of self-portraits. Was that how all of this started? One day she looked in, and there was Cedric looking back?

Nimby pondered. "I do not know. Clearly she has the sight, but so do others. It is a good question, Alex. Perhaps we shall find the answer."

Our walk took us to Bryant Park. The historic library with the marble lions was on our left, and across the street was the newer and taller main branch. In the lobby, before going through security, was a poster on an easel:

Best Selling Romance novelist Katherine Summer

on

*Addicted to Love.*

The program was to start at eight…. It was ten to.

"This is creepy," Jerod said as he opened his book bag for the security officer to inspect.

"Yeah, not coincidence, but synchronicity…. Any clues?"

"How crazy do you want me to get?" he asked.

I stayed next to make-believe Mom in case she needed help. She didn't, opening her purse like she'd been dozens of times, and letting the security lady look in and then clicking it shut. "It's on the sixth floor," she said.

"You can read?" I asked.

A sandy-haired man behind her in line looked at me, and then at her.

She smiled back and shook her head. "My son thinks his mother is an idiot. He's making fun of me."

The man chuckled. "Kids. You can't live with them, and if you try to drown them they stick you in jail."

"So true. You have some of your own?"

"Three," he said.

"No wedding ring," she commented.

"Mom!"

The man, who seemed around her age and was kind of attractive, chuckled. He looked at me. "You're sixteen, right?"

"It's the voice, isn't it?" make-believe Mom asked.

"Absolutely. There's a tone that only sixteen-year-old boys can get when they're embarrassed by their parents."

"It is unique," she said. "Part whining, part complaining… and something else."

"It's the obligatory eye roll," he said. "I'm Jacob, by the way. Jacob Katz."

"Marilyn Nevus. That's my son Alex, and—" She shot me a wicked grin. "—his boyfriend Jerod."

"Mom!" I felt the color rush to my face.

"Definitely the eye roll." Jacob Katz smiled at me. Then looked at Mom. "Maybe something in the jaw too. Could I give you my card?"

"What for?" she asked.

I was stunned. She was flirting. But now she seemed confused.

"Maybe I could take you out for coffee… although… I didn't see a ring on your finger either. Have I just made an awful mistake… are you with someone?" His words were fast and flustered.

"Just my children—I've got two. Coffee sounds good, Jacob Katz." She took his card and tucked it into her pocketbook.

Jerod had gone ahead and was waiting by the elevators. "Mom," I said, "we've got to go."

"It was nice to meet you. Call me if you feel like," he said. "Nice to meet you too, Alex."

Great, fine, whatever…. My cheeks were burning. She did that deliberately… embarrassed the hell out of me in front of a stranger. I grabbed her hand and pulled her toward the elevators.

She laughed… not at all like real Mom, but easy and light. "Got to go."

I glanced back. He was watching us. He seemed like an okay guy, but I wondered what would happen if he knew the woman he'd been flirting with didn't exist before this afternoon.

"What a nice man," she said.

Jerod was holding the elevator.

"I should call him."

"Not now," I said, wondering what sort of catastrophe that would lead to.

"I should wait," she said. "That's what you're saying."

"Yes." I watched the numbers light overhead.

We got out on six and followed the signs and the people to a crowded room with rows of folding chairs and a speaker's podium with a microphone in front of a bank of windows.

"We should get started," a dark-haired woman with a library ID around her neck announced from the podium.

It was standing room only. We found a bit of wall space toward the back. There wasn't much, and the three of us pressed together, me in the middle, Mom on my right, and Jerod on my left. His arm pressed against mine, our legs touching.

I glanced around. The audience was comprised of mostly women. Jerod and I were the youngest in the room. I listened as the lady at the podium ran through Katherine Summer's writing credits.

"We all love being in love with Katherine Summer," she gushed. "From her contemporary romances to her New York Times best-selling Three Sisters series to… so many wonderful books. All of which I'm proud to say are in our permanent collection, and many in large print, audio, and electronic editions as well. Without more of my prattle, I am honored to present… Katherine Summer."

A couple things surprised me. First, no mention of *May, Queen of the Fey*—which according to Jerod had been a best seller. Was this the right person? And the second odd thing—Katherine Summer.

The announcer walked to the front row and offered her hand to a tiny woman with a snow-white bun fastened at the back with a pink crystal butterfly barrette. The old woman waved her away as she gripped her walker. On her right sat a much younger man with wavy dark hair in a Prussian-blue shirt. I couldn't see his face. He steadied the old lady's walker with one hand, and with the other guided her up. She glanced at him, shook her head, and smiled. Then, with careful movements, she eased up and hobbled on high heels embellished with pink rhinestones toward a wooden armchair next to the podium.

The three hundred or so attendees were silent as the tiny woman, who had to be in her eighties or nineties and clearly had a thing for pink, made it to her seat. Her getup was bizarre and way too young. A pink miniskirt, pink fishnets over matchstick legs, and dangerously high stilettos. Her top was a lacy camisole that revealed withered cleavage and arms with a banner crop of liver spots. She gazed over the audience as the announcer clipped a microphone to a gauzy scarf she'd draped across her shoulders.

A half smile formed on her crinkled lips. Her hands gripped the armrests. "Love is magic. The only magic left in this world," she whispered. "As a romance novelist, it's my job to capture that—lightning in a bottle." Her voice was younger than her body and had an Irish lilt.

Even from the back, I could see the intensity in her water-blue eyes as she spoke of love. My thoughts were fixed on Jerod and our tightly pressed bodies. My breath caught; she was staring at me. The room was dark, and it seemed unlikely she could see us in the shadows.

"Unlike anything else," she said, her eyes fixed on mine, "love transforms. It makes us better if we let it." She winked.

What the hell was that?

“It can also destroy.” She sighed and broke eye contact. Her hand fluttered up. “But what a way to go.”

The crowd tittered.

I felt Jerod’s arm against mine, our hips touching. Nimby was on his shoulder, watching the speaker. “Is she Katye?” I whispered.

Nimby’s gaze was fixed on the speaker. “She is fey. Or was.… She is broken.”

Jerod turned to look at Nimby, and then our eyes met. I couldn’t breathe. “Broken how?” he asked, not taking his gaze off mine.

A woman in the last row turned angrily. “Ssh!”

He looked at Nimby. “Is she Katye?” he asked.

“Yes.”

I stared at the withered woman. Her eyes were bright as she regaled the audience with how she came up with her latest story. Then she was taking questions, and I hadn’t realized, but my hand was in the air.

“Yes,” she said. “The handsome and very tall young man in the back. You have a question.”

“How come you never wrote the sequel to *May, Queen of the Fey*?” I asked. I heard gasps, and heads turned.

Katherine Summer stiffened. “Young man,” she said. “You have the impulsivity of your age.… It’s best not to speak of that book.”

“It was a best seller. It won awards,” I shot back.

“Enough,” she said. “I’m here to discuss romance. There will be no further questions.”

The librarian who’d made the announcements was by Ms. Summer’s side. She was joined by the young man in the blue shirt. Who, when he turned—he was like something out of *GQ* or Italian *Vogue*—with long black hair that curled like mine, caramel skin, and green eyes.

Hands waved in the audience. A woman called out, “Ms. Summer… Katherine, will you still be signing books?”

The ancient authoress was on her feet and gripping her walker. The young man had a hand by her right elbow. "I'm tired," she said. "Not today… thank you all for coming."

A woman in a red hat turned angrily. "Why did you have to do that? I wanted her to sign my *Hungry Heart*."

"Sorry," I said, hoping she was referring to a book title. My anxiety spiked as I watched the old woman inch toward the door.

Nimby tugged on my ear. "Lying fey," she said.

"Huh?" I stepped into the aisle as several others in the audience called to the retreating author for signatures. She ignored them as she neared the door. Jerod and make-believe Mom were at my sides. "What makes you say she lies?" I asked Nimby.

"She's not tired. She said that to give an excuse."

"We have to talk to her," Jerod said.

"I know," I said, trying to figure out why my question had kicked off her retreat. Clearly, a book as popular as *May, Queen of the Fey* would have people asking questions. "Why is she leaving?"

"I don't know," he said.

The disgruntled attendees were picking up their bags, some still calling out to Katherine Summer as she turned down the hall. Keeping to the wall, we trailed her. We weren't alone; other audience members were at her side, holding books and pens, begging for signatures.

Her handsome companion waved them away. "Sorry." His voice was firm. "She's too tired."

One glared at me as she passed. "Stupid boy."

The dark-haired man looked at me. I could not read his expression.

"He kind of looks like you," Jerod said.

"Yeah, right."

"He does. You in ten years."

Clearly Jerod was delusional, but if he thought I was in the same league as this guy, I wasn't going to argue. We followed Katherine's slow progress. I expected them to turn right toward the elevators. Instead they took a left.

We followed.

She took another left, and was halfway down the hall when she stopped. Her right hand tapped her companion's arm. He looked at her and then back at us. He nodded, left her side, and tried the handle on a door next to where they stood. It opened.

Slowly, moving her walker in tiny steps, she faced us. Her bright-blue eyes squinted. She shook her head.

"Why did you…," I started to ask.

"Ssh!" She made a jerking motion with her head. "You don't want them to hear you, boy. Now leave me alone."

"No… Cedric told me to find you."

"Go away. I don't know any Cedric."

Nimby shouted… which was more like a squeak, "She's lying! Lying fey!"

The old woman's eyes narrowed to tiny slits. "What was that? Who said that?"

"A fairy," I said, noting the white film across her eyes. She was practically blind with cataracts.

"No such thing, boy. It's a children's story. Make-believe."

"Lies, lies, lies." Nimby shrieked and twirled in angry circles on my shoulder.

She stared intently at the space above my right shoulder. "No. Leave me alone…. I'm old, and I'm tired."

"We have to talk," I repeated. Cataracts or no, I knew she could see Nimby. This was no ordinary woman.

She started to turn. Her broad-shouldered companion said nothing. He stood in front of an open door, looking at her and then back at us.

Katherine Summer repeated, "Go away."

"No. Cedric told me to find you."

She looked at her companion and shook her head. He bent down, and she whispered into his ear. She redirected her walker from the hall to the open door. "Then come along… and bring your Nevus fairy…. I've not seen one of those in… centuries. And black, to boot. My, my."

"What the hell is a Nevus fairy?" Jerod whispered.

Apparently, Katherine Summer had damn fine hearing for someone who was.... *Did she just say centuries?*

"She's been with you since birth." Her gaze fixed on me.

"Yes."

"Tell me what your name means, young Master Nevus."

Her directives made me think of May.... Warning flares went off in my head. "It means birthmark."

"Yes," she said, and her walker made tiny steps toward her companion, who stood by the open door. "Marked at birth, you were. The Nevus clan... still beautiful, one is black and one is blond. And the third—they come in threes—is the ginger child, hair of fire and skin like milk."

Her words sent a shiver. We followed. At the door, her companion seemed to be studying me.

I felt his hostility and braced for the worst. He was protecting her, but something more. His jaw twitched, and his fists balled at his sides.

"It's all right, Lance."

Like a slow parade, we followed Katherine Summer into a tiny librarian's office. There was a desk covered with papers, a row of filing cabinets, a wall of cluttered shelving, and two chairs in front of a table that were lost beneath an avalanche of books.

She inched her walker to a battered armchair, positioned herself, gripped first one side of the chair, then the other, and lowered down. All the while, her companion stood stiff as a soldier, his eyes fixed on her.

The way he stared at her.... Adoration... love.

"So," she said, looking at me. "You would ask me questions." She chuckled in a young woman's voice. Weird to hear it coming from a face like a dried apple doll. I had a sick pit in my stomach—this was not someone to trust.

"I would," I said... not really knowing where to start, but more than that. *Be careful*. "Cedric told us you'd help."

She grunted. Lance was at her back, he placed a hand on her shoulder. “I doubt that very much. Be precise, young Alex Nevus.”

“You’re right,” I said. “He told us to find you.”

“That rings true. He told you why?”

“No.” I noticed how she had no trouble asking questions… or according to Nimby, telling lies.

“Cedric plays dangerous games. Still, you have been to a place and seen things I would know of. We might trade.” Her head cocked to the side. “Your fairy is a puzzle… she shouldn’t be here… and she is. Quite a rare thing… a black Nevus fairy. Can’t recall the last….” She sighed. “She might be the last. Let me think… yes, sister May, how does she do?”

“Hungry,” I said, offering the first word that came to mind.

Katherine Summer laughed. Her face was a mesh of wrinkles. “Well chosen, boy. And mad as a barking dog?”

“You bet,” I replied. Counting that as her third question.

Her gaze narrowed. “I will answer the first question you asked. I did not write the sequel because it has not been.”

“It hasn’t happened,” I stated. “That’s what you’re saying.” Again, keeping the end of my sentences down. It seemed clear that while the rules had shifted, questions still cost.

“Perhaps.”

“I get another two.”

“Choose well.” Her hand reached back and found Lance’s. Their fingers interlaced. A dreamy smile spread across his perfect face… and I realized he had to be older than I’d first thought. There were tiny lines around his eyes and the corners of his mouth. I revised my estimate from twenties to late thirties… and gray around his temples… that hadn’t been there before.

“What are you doing to him?” Damn… not the question I’d wanted. But I couldn’t pull my eyes off of them. Gray spread through his long curls. Wrinkles creased his forehead and cheeks.

Katherine Summer inhaled and let go of his hand. “I’m showing you truth, Alex Nevus.” Her face was no longer that of a nonagenarian.… Maybe a woman in her fifties. She turned back and stroked the side of Lance's face. As she did, his hair regained its luster, and like shaking out the wrinkles on a sheet, his face was young and unlined.

Jerod gasped.

I looked at him and at Nimby perched on his shoulder. Then I looked at Mom… who wasn't really Mom. Something clicked. Almost like a law of physics, where every action has an opposite reaction, a body at rest tends to stay at rest, a body in motion tends to stay in motion….

"It's balance," Jerod said, beating me to the punch. "She's talking about balance."

"You're right," I said, turning back to the wrinkled woman in pink and her perfect… lover? Food source? "I have my next question.… What is Lance to you?"

"Interesting choice," she said. "He is everything." She looked at Jerod and back to me. There was intensity to her words. "He is everything."

It felt like I was swimming in Jell-O.

The old woman smiled. "So May is hungry and mad. Nothing new there. I would know what she's doing."

"Ask me your question, then," I said, knowing I was out and wondering if I could entice her into more.

"You are sweet…. I'm surprised she let you go." She glanced up at Lance and then at me. She took a sharp intake of breath. "But of course…. I should have seen it sooner."

"What?" I clamped a hand over my mouth.

"Goody!" she said with delight. "Another for me. You and Lance are cut from the same bolt. It's obvious."

"Told you," Jerod said.

I bit back the obvious question—"Same bolt"? I looked at Jerod.

"It means something," he said. "Don't ask me what."

"My turn," Katherine said. "What are my sister's plans?"

"Game shows," I said. "Although some are more like reality shows.... Cooking shows, a weird fairy redo of *Bargain Hunt*."

"Interesting...."

"I need another question," I said.

"Then ask.... I could use another as well."

I watched her. There were so many questions. "What does your sister May want from Alice and I?"

"Yes, *that* is a good one. May wants everything. She always has. She wants to rule the human world as well as what remains of Fey. Quite simply, my handsome young haffling, she needs a vessel to travel between worlds. A creature that is neither human nor fey, but both. It is horrible and spectacular. This world is not prepared for a creature of such magic. For as you've seen, my sister is mad. I cannot imagine the chaos... the death."

I felt sick. "I want another."

"I am waiting for it, Alex Nevus, but it is the last I will answer."

It was like a weird game of Hansel and Gretel.... If I could follow the crumbs she was dropping, maybe they'd lead me to someplace that made sense. Her answers were clues: love, balance, her crazy sister who wanted to rule the worlds. I looked at make-believe Mom, more evidence of the fairy laws of physics. If real Mom was under the mulberry tree, I got to take a fake one home. It was like those stupid bowls next to cash registers—take a penny, leave a penny. But more.... I looked at Jerod and Nimby. Katherine was surprised to see Nimby... and that sort of made sense, she did not belong in this world... and yet, here she was. Katherine Summer did not belong here... and here she was. Bits and pieces of the fey world had spilled into the human world, or been left behind, or.... And if that were true, and balance was so important....

"I have a question," Jerod said. His eyes met mine.

I nodded. "Do it."

"Why do you hate your sister?"

# Twenty-One

KATHERINE SUMMER gasped.

I stared at Jerod. "Awesome question." I watched the old woman in pink.

Her lips pursed, her breath was fast and shallow, she seemed in pain, and then she shrieked. "She tricked me!"

Lance sank to his knees. He pressed his forehead to her wrinkled brow. "Ssh, Katye… ssh."

The old woman's shoulders shook.

"It's okay," he said, his hand was on her shoulder and then on her back, inscribing gentle circles.

"No," she gasped. Her hand found his cheek. "This is not okay… none of this is okay. She took the thing I am, the thing that is my special, and made it wrong." With her hand still to his face, she looked at us. "I was tricked by my sister May, we both were."

"Your other sister…," I said.

"Yes… Lizbeta. May used our special against us."

Nimby, her gaze fixed on the old woman, jumped from Jerod's shoulder to mine. "Do not ignore me, Alex Nevus."

"Wouldn't dream of it," I whispered.

"Special is power. It is theirs, and it is unique. You'd do well to understand yours."

"Good to know… thank you."

Nimby lunged for my cheek. I flinched, my thoughts on her razor-sharp teeth. But she kissed me. A quick peck. "You're welcome, Alex." She launched from my shoulder and flew back to Jerod.

Katherine Summer gasped; her tears streamed as her fingers gentled down Lance's sculpted cheek and jaw. "Not fair… not fair."

"My love, we are together." His voice was tender. "If it's time… then it's time. No regrets."

And then it got freaky.

Her fingers trembled as they stroked his cheek. His lips found hers… the beautiful man and the withered hag. The kiss stretched. Streaks of white shot through his hair as the flesh on her face filled out. It was like one balloon being deflated while the other filled. Her hair shimmered, and the butterfly barrette on the back of her bun started to move. Its pink-jeweled wings flapped once, twice, and then it launched into the air. It hovered above the kissing couple, its wings gracefully flapping.

A blur pulled my eye, and the pink butterfly was gone. In its place was Nimby, who'd ripped the poor thing apart. She held its glittery wings while gobbling down its body. She grinned while savoring what was apparently a delicious meal.

I felt Jerod's hand. "You see this too?"

"Yeah." I was torn between Nimby's act of brutality and the kissing couple.

Katherine Summer's hair spilled down her back; it seemed alive as it cascaded to the floor, twisting and sparkling, the white replaced by lustrous waves of golden red.

Her lips, still locked to Lance's, were now full and candy-apple red. Her too-young pink outfit was suddenly just right for the voluptuous redhead. Lance, in his electric-blue shirt, was little more than a husk; his hands covered in spots, his back bent, his hair thinned to where I could see blue veins on his scalp.

Katherine pulled back from the kiss and rose from her chair. She took her walker and passed it to Lance. He nodded, and never once taking his gaze from the bombshell redhead, he shuffled toward the door. She followed at his side.

He turned to Jerod and me. "It's worth it." His voice was cracked and barely audible.

"Come," she said, her voice urgent. "We have little time."

I looked to Jerod and then to changeling Mom, who was crying. "You okay?" I asked.

Her gaze was fixed on Katherine and Lance. "Her special is love," she said. "She was tricked in love."

Katherine stopped, one hand on Lance's back, the other steadying his walker. "Yes. I was tricked… and my mirror cracked." Her tears flowed. "The thing is done, and we must hurry. Please."

Her sorrow was palpable. I wanted some clarification—*mirror cracked? Huh?* It didn't seem the time. But maybe…. "I know this story." And lines from a Tennyson poem we had to memorize in seventh grade came back: *The mirror cracked from side to side. The Lady of Shallot.*

Jerod nodded. "But she dies in that… and Lance… holy crap! He's Sir Lancelot—as in King Arthur and the round table, Lancelot."

Katherine gritted her teeth and urged Lance forward. With each step, it seemed he aged another year. Bald patches on his scalp, hands like bird claws clutched the walker as he shuffled.

We followed them to the elevators and down to the front of the library, back through security, and out to the street.

Lance's breath was labored. The air rattled in his lungs.

Katherine looked around the busy avenue, oblivious to the attention she attracted. Men stopped to stare at the gorgeous redhead, her curves on display in her pink camisole, fishnets, and mini. "There." She pointed toward a church two blocks north. "We must hurry… my love," she said Lance. "Hang on."

He didn't answer, just nodded, and with a determined look he made a step and then another. He faltered, his right knee buckled.

"Help him!" she pleaded.

Jerod grabbed Lance's arm.

"Please." Katherine looked at me. "Help me! Help him! Please." She was frantic.

"Tell me what to do," I said, careful to not get tricked into unintended questions.

"Carry him."

"We need an ambulance," I said.

"No. That won't help. Please, you must get him to the churchyard."

A man in a business suit, who'd been openly admiring Katherine, spoke up. "Is there something I can do?"

She glanced at him and then at me.

"No," I said, and went to Lance's side. Jerod and I lifted the surprisingly light man, and leaving his walker behind, headed toward the church.

Katherine followed, with changeling Mom bringing up the rear. "Hurry." Her voice choked with emotion. "Hurry! Run!"

I felt the fragile bones beneath Lance's shirt. The scraping of his breath was faint. We crossed the street, and I heard a sickening crack as the arm Jerod held fractured.

"Ooh!" Lance made a leathery gasp.

"Hurry!" Katherine was shrieking.

Jerod shot me a panicked look. Not knowing what I was supposed to do, I wrapped my arms around Lance and swept him up. For someone who'd just minutes before been a strapping six-foot-something hunk, he weighed nothing. Maybe thirty pounds… maybe less. His eyes were barely open, his lips cracked and dry.

"*Hurryyyyy!*" Katherine's wails drowned out the traffic.

Jerod raced ahead and pushed open the iron gate in front of the Norman-style church.

With the dying man in my arms, I ran through.

Lance grunted… actually… it was more like a croak. The churchyard was dark and filled with shadows. The square steeple was lit by a spotlight. I tried to make sense of what I was seeing in the dim light that seeped through the gates.

"Where is he?" Jerod asked.

I felt the bundle in my arms; there was nothing… no one. An electric-blue shirt, pair of black pants, a leather belt, red boxer briefs, and a pair of leather shoes that dropped one by one to the ground, leaving the socks dangling from the pant legs.

Holding the bundle, I walked into a pool of filtered streetlight, searching for any trace of him. Through the church gates I saw Katherine and changeling Mom.

The redhead was frantic, her hands wrung together, her shoulders shaking as tears flowed. She dropped to the ground.

"I can't go in there," Mom said. She stared at the gate and sounded surprised. "Neither can she."

Nimby, hovering over Mom's shoulder, nodded, her stolen pink wings flashing in the light.

"Great!" I gave into my frustration and confusion. "Isn't this the world where things are supposed to make sense?"

I startled at the sound of a frog. Something hopped on the ground. It jumped next to me and then up onto the knee-high cement wall, which provided the base for the wrought-iron fence.

Katherine looked at the frog. And then at me. "He croaked," she said, as if that explained it all.

Still holding an armful of clothes, I stared at Katherine and then at the frog, which apparently had once been her boyfriend, who had once been an Arthurian knight. "Jerod…."

"Yes, Alex."

"He's a frog."

"Yeah… he croaked." Jerod started to laugh.

I was trying hard not to.

Katherine glared at him through the gates… and then at me. Tears flowed down her cheeks. The frog hopped off the wall, and with an occasional ribbit, vanished into the cemetery next to the church. I couldn't hold back… it was too weird. "He croaked…." It felt like my gut would bust from how hard I started to laugh.

Katherine was angry… and then she smiled. "He croaked…." She chuckled and then laughed. "I do love him, though. He is my love. My Lancelot."

"That's your special," Mom said. "You are love, and you were tricked by love. This is why you hate your sister."

Katherine looked at changeling Mom. "Yes… and Alex Nevus would know the story."

"Please," I said.

"And Jerod Haynes," Katherine said, "is filled with questions. I am in his debt, and he asks good questions." She pushed her hair from her face and dabbed at her tears. "You may ask a good question, Jerod Haynes."

He shot me a look. "Okay." He stood still. "What do you want from us?"

"Yes," she said, "an important question. I want revenge, Jerod Haynes. I want to give May my sorrow. I want her to suffer…. I want her special."

# Twenty-Two

FOR someone… or something… that had just had her heart broken, Katherine—“call me Katye”—Summer walked like a queen, as the four of us—five, counting Nimby—were led to the back of a dark pub and restaurant.

Heads turned as she passed. Men wanting her, women wanting to know what it would be like to have her beauty. Even for me, who always knew I liked boys, it was hard not to stare. Light danced in the gold and fiery reds of her hair. Her eyes were bright blue… a lot like Alice’s. Her skin was like cream, and her figure—long-limbed and perfect. She held her head high, aware of the attention. She flashed a smile to a handsome diner as his mouth gaped, and he ignored his girlfriend.

We trailed behind. I still had Lance’s blue shirt, which was far nicer than anything I owned. I’d left the rest of his designer duds in the churchyard.

“Lovely,” Katye said as the hostess showed us to a quiet booth. I scooted in next to Jerod. Make-believe Mom slid down the other side, leaving the space across from me for Katye.

“I’ll have them bring appetizers,” the hostess said without us asking.

Katye gave the young woman a tender look as she pivoted and sank into the booth. “My boys are thirsty….” She looked at me and Jerod. “And… too thin. Stout, pints of stout. And shots of whiskey, a single malt with the flavor of peat.”

“Of course,” the hostess said.

Nimby whipped from my shoulder to Jerod’s. “You’re too young to drink, Alex Nevus.”

Katye pointed a finger at my fairy, with her stolen pink rhinestone wings. “And you should not exist,” she said.

Nimby shut up. She seemed frightened.

“A fairy mystery,” Katye said as she stared at Nimby. A candle in a red glass holder threw flickering shadows onto the rough plaster walls. Like a second table above us, even Nimby visible on Jerod’s shoulder. “A night of mystery.” She threw back her head and laughed.

I glanced at Jerod. He shrugged. It so wasn’t worth asking—*what’s so funny?*

She wouldn’t stop.

A pretty waitress with a ponytail returned with our drinks. She looked at Jerod and me and hesitated. While I was no big fan of alcohol—not that I’d had a lot of experience—I was looking forward to a little something to dial down my nerves. I watched the waitress start to say “IDs please…” or something to that effect. Her mouth opened, the words about to spill out, when she looked at Katye.

Even in the dim light, the change to the young woman was noticeable, a glassiness in her expression, a shift in her smile. Her mouth hung open with one question, and she changed it to another…. “What’s so funny?”

Katye’s blue eyes reflected the flame of the candle. Like there was a fire inside of her. “He croaked.” And she was overtaken by another round of musical laughter.

“We all got to go sometime,” the waitress replied, distributing shots of whiskey and pints of stout.

"Not all of us," Katye said. She smiled at the young server. "Do you have a boyfriend?" she asked, seemingly unconcerned by the give and take of questions.

"I don't," she said, her gaze fixed on Katye. "And right now… men are the last thing from my mind." She was flirting.

"Yes," Katye replied. "I can have that effect." She looked the girl up and down…. "Your last man treated you badly."

"He cheated," she said, her jaw tensed.

"And you were true. He must be punished."

"If only things worked that way," the waitress said.

"But they can," Katye replied. "They often do. You gave him love, and he repaid you with betrayal…. If you were queen for a day, what would his punishment be?"

"It really hurt," the waitress said. "Like he'd punched me. He did it with one of my friends…."

"Worse and worse," Katye said.

I noted the candle's reflection in Katye's eyes. But no, not a single flame, but the blue of her irises replaced with fire. I sipped whiskey and felt the cool burn on my tongue and down my throat. Jerod pressed his leg against mine. I snorted and started to cough.

Katye glanced at me and then at the waitress, who seemed rooted in place. "Tell me his punishment," she said.

"Pain," the waitress said. "The same as I felt."

"No," Katye said, and she reached up and took the young woman's hand. "His should be three times what he gave to you. It's only right, it's only fair… consider it done."

The waitress shook her head. "I totally zoned." She glanced down at Jerod and me, "Great… oh, what the hell. You're both over twenty-one…. Right?"

"It's fine," Katye said. "Bring us whatever is good and filling. It's been a long night, and there's many hours before the dawn."

"You got it… there's a brisket to die for… and…." She stared at Katye. "Why do men hurt us in love?"

"It depends on the man, dear. But the reasons are three. He does not love you, he only wants sex, or he is of faint heart. The trick is digging through the lies and liars and finding one who will accept your love and return it with his own. A man who will take you as you are, and find you precious." Katye sighed.

"Thank you," the waitress said, and off she went.

Katye looked between me and Jerod.

I wondered at her words to the waitress. I felt Jerod's leg pressed against mine. Maybe it was the whiskey, but all I could think was that I was in love—truly, completely in love with Jerod. His leg against mine was real.… Those kisses. He certainly wasn't faint of heart; if anything, his trip to the land of whack-a-do put him on the opposite side—he was heroic.

"Shingles," Katye said.

"Huh?" Jerod grunted, his hand on my thigh.

Changeling Mom nodded and said, "That's what she'll give the bad boyfriend. They're very painful."

"Yes," Katye replied. "Open sores are always suspect in young relationships. His new love will leave him."

The whiskey and foamy stout on an empty stomach made my thoughts zip. Suddenly I didn't care about the cost of questions. I wanted answers… and I wanted to be alone with Jerod. But then I pictured Alice… her tears, her fear, and this crushing sense that while we sat here, horrible things could be happening. Was this all a crushing waste of time? "Why is the punishment times three? It's like a wives' tale that whatever you do… especially bad things come back threefold."

Katye nodded. "Easy answer, Alex Nevus. The first is for balance, to set the scales straight. The second is for punishment, and the third is the fey portion… a bit of a sacrifice. Now I've a story to tell. Drink your whiskey, boys, more shall come, and the songs that I sing will dance in your heads. It's a tale of three sisters, of a world before mankind. In the beginning there was only dark, and then God struck a match, and the first fairy was born."

She was right about the whiskey. The things that spilled from her mouth went down better with a buzz. Kind of a cross between the Old Testament, complete with Adam and Eve, a flood, another flood, and then brutal wars between factions of the fey.

"Entire races wiped out…," she said. "Creatures of amazing size and abilities, one moment there and then gone… no trace. While we fought amongst ourselves, the children of Adam and Eve multiplied and spread. Puny, but quick-witted. By the time the Fairy Wars had ended, it was too late."

"For what?" I asked, and I felt a twinge of my earlier fear.

"Don't fret, Alex Nevus. We are deep in each other's pockets, ask free and drink well."

"Why are you trying to get him drunk?" Jerod asked.

"Not drunk," she said. "Softened, the both of you. For I've favors to give and favors to ask."

His hand found mine beneath the table.

"Why was it too late?" I repeated, squeezing Jerod's fingers. The two of us pressed together like conjoined twins, not caring if anyone saw us.

"Because the war had been won… by my father… but the bigger war had been lost. The world was no longer ours. It had been claimed by the children of Adam and Eve, and their vision of what was and what was not—the See and the Unsee—had taken root. Like you, Alex Nevus, they had learned the trick. How to make a fairy die."

"Ignore her," I said.

"Yes. And the children of Adam closed their eyes to the fey, and the mists roared across our world, devouring everything. Our extinction was upon us, and into this terror my mother and my father brought forth three daughters—Lizbeta, May, and Katye. Each of us was gifted a special—peace, power, and love. And then my father took my mother's hand, and leaving their children, they walked into the mist."

"They abandoned you," Jerod said.

"Yes… and set us to rule over what remained of Fey. The mess and the mayhem, a world riddled with holes and the deadly mist. At first we three were one, trying to stabilize a world that because of its magical nature would not hold. But we weren't one. We were three. Had our purpose truly been united, things might have gone differently. But it's not the fey way; it's yours."

"You lost me," I said.

Changeling Mom spoke. "Humans like routines built on logic, Alex… that's what Katye's saying. Stability, normalcy, doing the same thing over and over till it becomes solid. Magic isn't solid, it isn't logical. It's intuitive and in constant motion."

"Twisty," Katye said. "Like the mist. A village of elves here… and then gone. A fairy castle that's stood for millennia, now a grassy hill. The mist is its own magic, that's what Lizbeta would say. May tricked her first. Like me, she used her special as a trap." The flames in Katye's eyes burned bright. "Lizbeta… dark of hair, like you, Alex, and my Lancelot. But skin so clear… like she was made of glass. Just to sit with her… calm… peace. Time, which is different for us, around her lost all meaning. Just be… sit… no matters, no worries." Katye swirled her whiskey in front of the candle, her gaze on the gold in the liquor.

"How did May trick her?" I asked.

"With the mist itself. May encouraged Lizbeta to study it, to know it. It was drawn to her and she to it. I watched it happen. I knew that May was not to be trusted. The mist courted Lizbeta. She'd touch and shape it, making it swirl in giant waves. She'd throw rainbows into its milky waters. She controlled it… or so it seemed. Everything else the mist touched it consumed, but not her. Call me a romantic, but I believe it fell in love with her. It was her constant companion, swirling at her back, around her feet, a cloak of color shooting miles above and behind her.

"May feared what that meant. She saw Lizbeta's control of the mist as a threat. If anyone were to control this terrible thing, it would be May. She demanded to know the mist's intent, and Lizbeta would say, 'It is'."

Katye laughed, "She was magnificent. Lizbeta and the mist. You can't imagine… she was a goddess, and we were in awe and marveled at its meaning. The mist had always been feared, but now…. Lizbeta was its friend, its lover, its queen. Perhaps it wasn't to be feared, but to be studied and understood… which is how May tricked her. She flattered and cajoled Lizbeta into telling her how she controlled the mist… which had no effect. Lizbeta needed no reassurance, she lived in harmony. I think that's what drew the mist, two rare and kindred souls finding one another. May grew furious. She'd watch the fey gather round Lizbeta. They worshiped her and the mist. And for a time, no more lands and creatures vanished. Lizbeta had brought peace between the mist and the fey. May schemed, if she couldn't control the mist, then no one would. She came to Lizbeta, sobbing and tearing the flesh from her face. 'What is wrong my sister?' Lizbeta asked.

"May, who knew our sister's heart, bared her treacherous grief. 'I would know our mother and our father gone into your lovely mist. I would know the children of fey and the marvelous creatures gobbled by your wispy companion. But mostly—' and she ripped the gown from her breast, '—I want my mother!'

"Lizbeta tried to comfort May. But the more she spread her peace, the more May wept, her wails painful to the ears. At last, Lizbeta said the fateful words and sprang May's baited trap—'Tell me, sister, for your sorrow I cannot bear. Tell me what must be done to calm your heart.'

"With tears on bloody cheeks, May stared Lizbeta in the eye. 'Promise me you will do all in your power to ease my paining heart.'

"'Of course, and without delay,' Lizbeta replied.

"The trap snapped shut. 'Then go into the mist and bring back our mother and our father.'"

Katye sighed. "And Lizbeta did…. She turned on the spot, and parting the mist before her, vanished into its depths. Never to return."

"You didn't stop her," I said.

"No." And Katye took the tumbler of whiskey, downed it, and signaled for the waitress to bring more.

"And the mist?" Jerod asked.

"Returned to its old ways, gobbling everything in its path. What remains of Fey—the Unsee—grows ever smaller. As it shrinks, so does May's power. She is desperate."

My cell buzzed. I pushed back and fished it out. It was hard to see the readout in the darkened restaurant. I took the call.

"Alex Nevus?" A woman's angry voice in my ear.

"Yes."

"Where's your sister?"

"Who is this?"

"It's Lydia Greene, your sister's OCFS caseworker." She sounded furious.

"What do you mean, where is my sister?" My anxiety spiked. "She's in your safe house."

"Right. You want to play it like that?" The caseworker wasn't making a lot of sense.

"What are you saying? Alice isn't there?"

"Like you don't know. The cops have already been to your apartment. Clearly you're not there.... Where's your sister, Alex? This isn't a game."

I stared at my phone and then toward the front of the restaurant. I saw the flashing lights of a police cruiser. "You bitch! I don't have her. And if you incompetent morons have let anything happen to her...." I disconnected. "We have to get out of here, now!" Pushing Jerod out of the booth, I turned and spotted a pair of uniformed officers pushing through the front door.

"Come on." I dropped my phone under the table.

"What's happening?" he said.

"I don't know." I headed toward the back of the restaurant. We ducked into the kitchen, and with changeling Mom and Katye following, we fled out the back door and into an alley. At one end there was a cinder block wall that ended in four feet of chain-link fence capped with coiled razor wire. Down the only feasible exit was a parked patrol car. A second pulled up, and two more officers got out. They headed toward us as the door to the restaurant opened, and two policemen came into the alley.

"Alex Nevus," one of them said.

I saw no way out… and where was Alice? They were supposed to keep her safe. Had she run away… or… been taken?

"Let me," Katye said. "Hello, officer." Her voice, like the purr of a kitten, calmed the panic in my head. Apparently, I wasn't the only one affected by it.

"Hi." The officer who spoke seemed dazed as he stared at the beautiful redhead.

"Such a handsome man." She turned to his partner and then to the two coming down the alley. Her hands, like white lilies, floated in front of her. She placed a playful finger on the first officer's nose as the four uniformed men surrounded her, vying for her attention.

I bolted for the street with Jerod, and changeling Mom behind me. I don't think the officers noticed, but I wasn't going to risk it. We ran for blocks, getting off the avenue and zigzagging north. Winded, I stopped in the middle of West Fifty-Second. "What the hell is going on?"

Changeling Mom stated the thing I most feared. "May has stolen Alice."

"How is that possible?" I asked.

Changeling Mom paused. "I can think of a way. And because, like you, your sister is a haffling. She would be able to pass between worlds, perhaps like the Alice in the book—through a looking glass."

"Yes, possible," Nimby agreed. "And if possible, then probable, which is just how it happened."

"We have to go back to Fort Tyron," I said, trying to figure out where the closest subway station was.

"May will be waiting," changeling Mom said.

"I know."

"It will be a trap."

I looked at Mom and then at Jerod. His eyes were wide, clearly frightened… but something more. "You don't have to come with me. You shouldn't," I said.

He shook his head and came toward me.

I didn't move, wondering what he was thinking. My thoughts were a muddled mess of anger and fear. Nothing was working out. I had to find Alice. But I couldn't take my eyes off him.

"I'm coming with you, Alex." His hand was on my cheek and the other on the back of my head. He pulled me close. His lips on mine. My head was suddenly clear and light. I held onto him, our lips locked, our tongues entwined. All of my fears, my panic, vanished. This, this moment was real magic.

Slowly, we pulled apart. Our hands on each other's faces. The scratch of his stubble against my palm.

"We're going to find Alice," he said. His hands fell from my face. "Come on."

# Twenty-Three

IT WAS after ten, and the iron gates to Fort Tyron Park were locked. We helped changeling Mom up first. Jerod and I each hoisted a foot while she grabbed onto the top of the spiked iron fence. She had good upper-body strength, found her footing, and swung her legs over. Then she dropped to the other side. We scrambled up and over, and darted into the park and away from the streetlights. Overhead, the trees formed a thick canopy, through which we glimpsed a full moon. Silver light spilled through the branches and illuminated the paths. We ran up the paved bike lane, found the first hiking trail, and then the dirt deer run.

The towering mulberry was bathed in moonlight, and far in the distance, the Hudson River sparkled.

Of course May knew I would come. This was a trap. We stood at the edge of the mulberry's branches. My actions were rash and ill-conceived. I had no plan. I turned to Jerod. I looked at Nimby perched on his shoulder. She stared at the Mulberry in terror, her red eyes aglow, her lips trembling.

I pressed my hands together and pushed them into the tangle of branches. I waited for that first tingle of magic to thrum up my fingers and my arms. It didn't come. I pushed in further and spread my hands apart, feeling the tug and pull of the twisted limbs as I made an opening.

Inside, there was only blackness. The muscles of my upper arms strained as I pulled the branches apart. I remembered the other two times, like I had fallen through worlds. This felt like… like it was late at night in a park.

The opening was big enough for my head, and I pushed my hip into the branches and let the weight of my body do the rest. Jerod followed with Nimby still on his shoulder. And behind him, changeling Mom.

"Hello?" I whispered, well aware there were rangers and we were trespassing. "Hello?" My voice sounded hollow, swallowed by the cocoon of branches and leaves.

"Shouldn't raise your voice at the end," Jerod cautioned.

"Good point."

"He's not just a pretty face," Nimby tittered. She didn't sound scared. Her pink-jeweled wings sparked with a rosy glow.

"I know that," I said. "He's brilliant."

"I'm blushing," he replied from a couple feet away. His nearness was the only magic.

"She's not here." I felt paralyzed with doubt. What if this had been a dream, or a drug-induced hallucination, or worse still, a sign of the madness I was inheriting from Mom?

"She knew we were coming," Jerod said.

"Yes," changeling Mom agreed. "It's not good, Alex. She fears you—or what you can do—for she has run… and stolen Alice. She has made a choice and will steal your sister's body and use it for her bridge."

"No!" I had to do something… figure this out. "Jerod, tell me that you still have your cell."

"That's better," Nimby replied.

"I've got it…." He paused. "… tell me your mother's number."

I gave it to him, and he tapped it in.

I strained to hear its ring. I heard crickets and frogs and our feet crunching on twigs. No phone.

"I have a GPS app," he offered.

Hope surged and then crashed. Mom's phone had gone days without a charge. The battery was probably dead....

Nimby flitted on his shoulder. Jerod's cell and her sparkly wings the only light under the mulberry. I stood next to him and stared at the screen. It showed our location but nothing for Mom's cell. Either it was dead or May had figured out how I'd found her that first time and disposed of the phone. "Where is she?" I shouted, wanting May to pounce on my question and demand a price for the answer. There was no response, just croaking frogs. My fingers touched Lance's shirt that dangled out of my back pocket. I pictured Alice. "She would call if she could," I said.

"You don't have your phone," Jerod reminded me. "And she doesn't have hers."

I turned in place. "There's got to be a way."

"Maybe Katye knows," he offered.

Something hopped across my foot. I jumped back. "What...." It was a frog. It batted its thick head against my ankle, like a cat that wants its ears scratched. I held still, and it did it again. I knelt down and cupped my hands in front of me. My eyes discerned a dark shape from the blackness as I felt webbed fingers scratch my palms. A surprisingly strong and heavy body waddled into my hands.

Jerod had turned his phone. Using it as a flashlight, he shone it on a plump, green-and-blue bullfrog.

"You have got to be kidding," Jerod said. He placed a hand on my back as he played the light over the frog. "He croaked."

"Not possible," I said. "Has to be a different frog. How could he get all the way here from there?"

Jerod snorted. "Really? A man gets turned into a frog... oh, after first aging a few hundred years in a couple minutes, and you're stuck on the logistics of him hopping a few miles?"

"Good point." Cradling the frog, I eased back on my heels and raised him to my face. I had a moment's guilt, remembering biology dissections, frogs splayed open and hacked apart, with little red and green flags stuck in their various organs. "It's Lance."

It croaked.

"Lance," I repeated.

It stared at me and croaked. "You've got to be joking. Croak once for yes and two for no."

It croaked.

"Your name is Lance."

It croaked.

"Your name is Charlotte."

It croaked twice.

"Tell him to take us to Alice," changeling Mom said.

"Right…." I gazed into the frog's shiny black eyes. I pictured the handsome man and how devoted he'd been to Katye. He was tied to her, and she somehow to us. I felt connections, but couldn't pull them together into anything rational, and maybe that was the problem—*Ditch rational, and talk to the damn frog.* "Lance, take us to Alice. Help me find my sister."

The frog lay heavy in my hands; he blinked. Seconds stretched, and then I felt his hind legs push against my palms as he turned and leapt. He croaked from a couple feet in front of us, hopped several times, and then croaked again.

I followed. He hopped away. He croaked; we followed; he hopped. He croaked; we followed; he hopped. He came to the edge of the tree's canopy. I heard his legs scrape at the branches, and then he was on the other side.

We emerged from the tree. The moonlight was almost blinding after being in total dark. Lance was one gorgeous frog, plump and green, with swirls of blue down his back and haunches. He headed west, at first going a hop or two, croaking and waiting for us to follow. Once it was clear we were on board, he moved in earnest.

"See," Jerod said as we broke into a jog to keep up. "This makes total sense. Frogs can travel great distances if they set their minds to it."

We headed into the woods, not on any particular path. The moon helped us stay clear of twisted roots and saplings. Lance was moving fast and in a straight line. The terrain sloped down, and here and there I glimpsed the Hudson twinkling in the distance.

We came to a paved bike path. Lance hopped straight across and dove back into the woods. Bushes and saplings snapped beneath our feet and tugged at our clothes. Our descent grew steeper as we headed down the wall of a ravine. Traffic whizzed in the distance, and I saw streetlights a hundred feet below us.

Still running, I barely missed smashing my face into the park's outer iron fence.

Lance hopped through and then stopped. He croaked as Jerod and changeling Mom joined me at the impassible fence. It was much higher than the one we'd climbed to get in—probably ten feet. Its iron rods were spiked at the top, a deterrent from people accessing the park. Or in our case… leaving it.

Lance croaked as I stared down the fence to our right and to our left. There were no breaks and no gates.

"There," Jerod said. He jogged to the right, toward a thick-trunked oak that had grown into the fence and bent it out. Not enough for us to get through, but between the bend in the bars and the tree's gnarled branches, a possible way out. He climbed up. "It's not that hard," he said. "Although…." He perched on a branch that rested on the top of the spiky fence. It was a sheer drop to the other side, not just the ten feet of the fence, but the ground fell away over a cement retaining wall. Far below that was the Henry Hudson Parkway. "Give me your belt," he said.

I scrambled behind him, finding the same footholds and branches he'd used. I unbuckled and handed over my belt. He looped it with his. Straddling his branch, he fastened the belts around it.

"It's not enough…."

"Here." I pulled Lance's shirt from my back pocket.

"You'd look good in this," Jerod said.

"Thanks… but use it."

He tied a sleeve to the end of the belts. "Don't worry," he said. "I know my knots."

"Good to hear." I looked from the makeshift rope to the death drop below.

"God, I hope this holds." And over he went.

He moved too fast. I wanted to scream, to tell him we'd find another way over, a safer way. It was too late. I couldn't breathe as I watched him hang tight. His feet scrambled for purchase against the iron gate slats. I reached through and grabbed for his legs. I caught hold of his jeans and guided his foot to the space between the slats.

"Thanks." He was trying to sound brave.

I heard the terror in his voice as his feet moved bar by bar. One hand let go of the blue shirt and gripped the fence, and then he let go with the other, and with a couple more sideways creeps along the iron fence, he was over safe ground, and dropped to where Lance was waiting.

Changeling Mom was at my side. "Help me across," she said. She didn't wait for me to tell her what a horrible idea I thought this was, but she was up and over. I did the same for her, and as she neared the safety of the knoll, Jerod grabbed her by the legs and eased her to the ground.

Then it was my turn. The trick seemed to be in pressing your body as tight to the fence as possible, once over. I shinnied down the branch, gripped the belt-and-shirt rope, and dropped. It was terrifying, hanging there, nothing below but a hundred-foot drop. I felt Lance's shirt strain under my weight. Stitches popped; it started to tear. I kicked at the fence and swung back… and then forward. The toe of my sneaker gripped an iron bar. The backward momentum nearly made me lose it, but I hung fast and kicked my other foot into the slat next to it. I bent my knees and pulled my body in tight. I stared at the fence, and with the subtle back-and-forward swing of my hands on the rope, I waited for the forward surge and grabbed with my right hand. My fingers scrambled over rust and chipped paint. I gripped tight, feeling it rip my skin. I pulled in with my knees, and in a single movement, let go of the rope and shot my left hand to the bars. I caught my breath and clung tight. Now it was just a matter of going slat by slat.

"You got it," Jerod encouraged. "Go slow."

Lance croaked, and Nimby chattered, "Don't fall, Alex."

I moved right foot, left foot, right hand, and then left hand. Slat by slat. Jerod's fingers touched my leg. "Two more to go," he urged. And then he was behind me. I hung tight to the fence, now over safe ground. I dropped back against him, on safe ground, in strong arms.

Lance croaked and hopped away down the steep embankment.

"You okay?" Jerod whispered. His breath tickled the back of my neck.

"Yeah." His closeness was distracting.

"I know this is bad timing.... I want you so bad," he said.

"Same," I gasped, just wishing we could stay there, me nestled in his arms.

"Let's get Alice, get her somewhere safe... then I want...."

It felt amazing to be held. I ignored the voice inside—the one that warned me to trust no one. It was my mantra. At best, people let you down; at worst they deliberately hurt you. "Shut up."

"Huh?"

"Not you... me." I turned into him.

There was an insistent ribbit from a ways away.

"Just tell me you feel this too," he said. The moon glowed on his cheeks, his expression serious.

"You're not alone...." I so wanted to say it, just three words... "*I love you.*" I didn't.

Lance let out a sustained croak, like a foghorn. Then a string of them, loud and insistent.

"We have to go," changeling Mom said.

Reluctantly, we disentangled. My skin tingled where our arms had touched. As we climbed down the embankment, the highway getting louder, Mom called back, "She never told us how *she* got tricked."

"No." Remembering Katye's promise, I held back, waiting for Jerod to get around a dangerous patch of loose dirt and rocks. My thoughts pulled in different directions. Find Alice, stay safe, kiss Jerod.... I guess that was the order I needed to keep. "It might have been important.... May used her older sister's trust to trick her into the mist. It was something similar with Katye. Something to do with love… with Lance. In the poem, the Lady of Shallot looked into her mirror, saw Lancelot, and fell in love. Only there, when she crosses from one world to another to be with him, she dies, and he never knows how much she loved him."

"She still has some magic," Jerod said. "If that girl's boyfriend really gets shingles and like what she did with those cops."

"It wasn't enough to keep her Lancelot from croaking."

He punched me gently in the shoulder. "Joke is losing its steam."

"Yeah." We bumped shoulders, me not wanting to think how wrecked I'd be if anything bad happened to him. We looked across at the Henry Hudson Highway, and beyond that at the river.

"Come on," he said. We zigged and zagged through underbrush and loose rock. "So what's May's weakness?"

"Her hunger," I said. "It's like a poker player's tell." We were stopped by a chain-link fence that cut us off from the highway.

Between the roar of outbound traffic, I heard Lance's croak to our left. The ground sparkled with moonlight and lamplight in thousands of broken bottles.

"So much for don't drink and drive," Jerod said.

"People are idiots," I said, realizing that most of this glass was from beer and liquor bottles tossed from the highway. Lance's croaking was nonstop. I saw something move about thirty yards away.

"He's on the ramp," Jerod said, and we jogged toward a break in the fence.

The frog waited at the curb. He flicked his tongue like a red, flashing arrow. He hopped into the road.

"No! Wait!" I shouted. "Let me." And he stilled as I bent down and cradled him in my hands.

Dodging three lanes of northbound traffic, we made it to the divider. To our left was the George Washington Bridge and Manhattan, to our right the Parkway and the Bronx. I held my hands out, palms open, and watched the frog. His thick legs repositioned, and he faced the river. His tongue flicked.

"He's like a compass," Jerod said.

"Amphibious GPS...."

We darted across the inbound lanes and hopped the guardrail on the other side. We ran across the biking and jogging path of Riverside Park, which even at this hour had people pushing babies in strollers and a trio of skateboarders practicing tricks. Lance wriggled in my cupped hands. His head poked between my fingers. His tongue shot out. I looked around, opened my hands, and he hopped off. He headed for the river.

"You've got to be kidding." My heart sank. What the hell was I thinking? That this was some magic frog… that it was in fact Lance? What a moron; it was a frog that wanted to get to the water, nothing more.

Jerod was at my right, changeling Mom on my left. "He's just a frog," I said. A wave of despair rose inside of me. "Alice...."

"Ssh!" Mom touched my arm. Her gaze was intent on the frog's progress as it disappeared over the concrete breakwater. There was a splash and a loud croak.

"Come on," Jerod said.

I didn't want to infect him with this feeling of hopelessness. *Alice....* Whoever had taken Alice.... My gut twisted as I pictured her. I knew too well what could happen to little blonde girls. I'd been inside that monster, and I'd killed it.

"Something's coming," changeling Mom said.

We stood on the breakwater, the river stretching before us, Jersey on the other shore. A swath of moonlight was like a glittering road on the water.

"Yes." Nimby darted out over the river. Her pink wings sparkled. "Something's coming."

# Twenty-Four

MY EYES strained to pull shapes from the dark water. I heard the night sounds—traffic behind us, lapping waves, a frog croaked… another answered, and a third and a fourth.

Nimby flitted between Jerod and me, her jeweled wings blurred like a hummingbird's. Changeling Mom gazed on the river. "It's coming," she said.

Before I could ask for clarification, there was movement on the river. Something dark pushed up through the surface. It headed toward us. It came fast.

Jerod stared as the weird and impossible thing leapt from the depths of the river. "It's a horse!"

"It's a nightmare… a pooka," Nimby said. Her tiny teeth chattered, and she moaned, "Nooooooo! Bad, bad, bad. You ride its back, and it drags you down. Down, down, down. You drown, drown, drown."

There was no denying its shape, but unlike any horse I'd seen or imagined. Its coat was an oily black, its mane pure silver, and its eyes blood red. It galloped across the river's surface and stopped not two yards from us. It reared back on its hind legs and came crashing down. I expected a wave of water to rush over us—there was no splash. It skittered at the water's edge, snorted, and tossed its massive head. Its red eyes stared at me. The message was clear… at least to me. I was supposed to get on.

It pawed at the river.

I inched toward the edge of the breakwater. No idea how deep the water was.… I was a decent enough swimmer, but as any New Yorker would tell you, a dip in the Hudson is a bad idea.

"No!" Nimby cried. "Alex, no! It's death."

I stared at the horse. It grew still. Images flickered in its fiery eyes. Like I was seeing things the horse had seen, places it had been under the water. I saw schools of dull brown and silver fish, dense seaweed, a rusting can, the hull of a small boat.

"What's happening?" Jerod asked next to me.

"It's like watching TV." I didn't know if he could see this or not. The images in the horse's eyes shifted. I saw a bog with cattails and water lilies. There was an island, like a volcano rising from the mucky water. On the highest point, a fire burned and figures danced.… With the image came music, but not from instruments… frogs.

The horse snorted, and its eyes turned back to red.

"In Katye's book," I said. "Queen May fails when she tries to take over Alice's body. What stops her?"

"She's human," Jerod says. "It doesn't work. Queen May loses all her magic and is captured and thrown back into Fey. So Alice is saved."

"But because my sister, Alice, is a haffling, May thinks it will work. That's what this is about. It's why Katherine Summer didn't write the second book… because it's happening now."

The horse was still, tiny rivulets streaming at its hooves.

"This is a trap. I know that." And there was something more that I would not voice. May had been pretty clear that I'd be an acceptable choice—just give her my name. I reached my hand over the water, and the horse lowered its head. Its mane was slick like algae. My fingers sought purchase, and a stench washed over me, like something baking in a New York dumpster on a hot summer's day. Nausea choked in my throat as I grabbed hold.

Nimby shrieked.

Jerod shouted, "Alex, no!"

I gripped something solid, like braided rope in the middle of the slime. As I did, the horse flicked her head, and my feet flew out from under me. It's like I weighed nothing as she whipped me onto her back.

Nimby screamed, "*Noooooo*!"

I heard someone jump into the water, but couldn't turn as the horse broke into a gallop… over the surface of the Hudson. My thighs dug into to the beast's flank, and gross as it was, I pressed my head against her slimy neck. The smell was rotting eggs and sewer gas. My eyes teared and I gagged. And then she dove. I took a final gasp of rotted air as the river washed over us. Deeper and deeper she plunged, my body pressed tight, my eyes shut. The pressure as we dove hurt my ears. My lungs ached. My thoughts raced, calculating how deep we'd gone and if we'd passed the point of no safe return. Nimby's voice echoed in my head, *"Down, down, down. Drown, drown, drown."*

A calm overtook me. I was going to die. I was going to drown in the Hudson. All of my fighting, my constant struggle to keep things under control… none of it mattered. Memories flashed to mind as the ache in my lungs turned to numbness. I saw Mom before she got sick, and then again at her disability hearing. I pictured the neighborhood thugs trying to shake us down, and Alice in the Chinese bakery as she enchanted the proprietress…. I had to save Alice. I could die another day, but today I had to save my sister. And something else… a pair of brown eyes and the smile that came with them. *I am not going to die*, I thought. *Because I love Jerod, and I need to do something about that.* Fear battered at my thoughts…. *I've been down too long. Just hang on.*

Something lurched beneath the horse's hooves. We'd hit the riverbed. She wasn't stopping. I felt sand and debris against my cheek, and then a thick mud around my legs and closing over my body. She was running into the riverbed, burying us. Bubbles of gas brushed against my face, and then… I felt… air.

I cracked my eyes open. They hurt. I blinked against the sting. We weren't under water, and we weren't buried in the ground. This had to be a hallucination. I gasped, expecting to take in a lungful of water. It was air, and it reeked of filth and slime; it was the best breath I'd ever had.

My eyes burned, and my arms and legs were still wrapped tight around the beast's neck. Cautiously, I rose up, swallowing eager breaths of putrid air. It got better the further from the horse's flesh I rose. I cracked my eyes and then shut them fast against the burning sun.

I tried to get my bearings. Warmth from the sun—how was that possible? It was near midnight when I went into the river. I cracked my eyes again; it was blindingly bright… and green.

"Alex." A man's voice from off to my right. "Open your eyes. Get off the horse now."

I knew that voice…. Maybe I'd drowned, and this was the tunnel on the way to whatever came next. In which case, heaven or hell smelled awful. I eased onto my belly and slid down the horse's ooze-covered flank. I tumbled to the ground. Grass and weeds cushioned my fall. Under the shadow of the horse, it was easier to open my eyes. The first thing I saw….

"No… Jerod!"

Panic took hold. He wasn't moving, his body drenched, his hands overhead clutched to the horse's tail.

"Jerod. Please…." I crawled to his side, his arms like lead pipes, the muscles frozen. His face turned to the ground. "Jerod!" I eased my fingers into his, trying to get them to release. Clumps of the nightmare's tail ripped away in his rigid fists. "Jerod!" I got him free, and he fell to the ground.

He wasn't breathing. I turned him onto his back. "Jerod." Nothing. Terror ran through me like a knife. I pried his clenched jaw open and clamped my mouth over his cold lips. I forced my breath into him, once, twice, and a third time. I checked his neck for a pulse. Nothing. Not allowing myself to think, I positioned the palm of my right hand on his sternum, braced with my left, and started chest compressions. I breathed again and again. I pressed my body against his as the nightmare danced off a ways to chew at a mound of pink clover. "Jerod, please…." I pushed my breath over and over into his mouth. I counted off the compressions. "I love you," I cried. Knowing it was true and that it was too late.

"Alex."

My head turned at the sound of the man's voice. Backlit by the burning sun stood Cedric, and behind him, Liam. "Help him. Please…."

Liam shook his head, his violet eyes and downturned mouth telling me things I did not want to hear.

"Jerod, breathe!" My lips over his. My fingers at the crook in his neck where I should have felt a pulse. "Please…. I need you. Clay needs you. Don't leave." I willed my breath into his lungs. Feeling it travel down his throat, feeling his chest expand as I pressed tight. "Please." Fighting back despair. "Please." Tears streaming. "Please." It was hard to catch my breath. "Please."

Jerod twitched. For a moment I thought I'd made him move, and then a gush of brackish water entered his throat and flooded my mouth. I spat it out and rolled him on his side.

Liam sank down next to me. "Tell me what to do," he said.

"Hold him steady." And I thumped Jerod's back. My fingers again at his neck. "He's got a pulse!"

Jerod coughed and spewed water. He retched and vomited. His body convulsed, and I wrapped myself around his back, wanting to warm him, to feel my life flow into his. I was shaking, realizing what he had done… for me. He'd leapt in after me, grabbed the horse's tail, and nearly died. Why? Why would he do that?

I couldn't stop trembling. I pressed my chin over his shoulder. "I'm sorry," I sobbed. "I'm so sorry."

He was breathing on his own, giant gasps that shook his body.

"He's breathing," Liam said. He looked at Cedric. "I thought he was dead."

I wanted to punch him.

Liam reached a hand out and rested it on my cheek. I flinched. I didn't want him anywhere near me or Jerod.

"You said that you loved him," he said.

I pulled Jerod tight. He was awake and obviously hearing all of this.

"Yes." And like jumping off a cliff, I said it again. "I love Jerod."

To which Jerod choked and coughed. "What?" He twisted in my arms, and gasping for breath, he repositioned himself across from me.

His knees bumped against mine. His eyes were open, his face smeared with green muck, his lips parted. He was beautiful, the most beautiful boy I could imagine. I knew without doubt it was true; I loved Jerod, was in love with him, and there wasn't a damn thing I could do about it. And now I'd told him… and he wasn't saying anything.

He smiled. I watched, fascinated, as the dimples popped in his cheeks. His lips twisted as he pulled a strand of algae from his hair. Our eyes locked. And then he spoke. "Jerod loves Alex."

"Thank you." The only thing I could say. I mean, there was more, but really….

Jerod took my hand, and our lips found each other's. I suppose it should have been gross; we reeked and were covered in slime. It was amazing, the sun warm on our backs, the smell of wildflowers, birdsong, the croaking of frogs, but mostly him. His cool lips pressed against mine. His solid body in my arms, alive and saying that he loved me. It wasn't just that he'd said it…. He'd nearly died for me. And in the warped world of Alex Nevus, actions spoke louder than words.

"Boys." Cedric's voice. "We can't stay here. It's not safe."

*Maybe not safe*, I thought, *but wonderful*. Our foreheads touched.

Jerod whispered, "I had a crush on you for the longest time, this is amazing."

"Boys!" Cedric said. "We need to move, now."

Jerod sighed. "So we're back in Narnia."

I didn't want to add what I was thinking, but somehow the normal filter that kept my brain away from my mouth had been derailed—"Or we died getting there."

"No," he said. "Magic onions don't die that easily." He got up. "Wow… head rush." He reached out his hand. "Come on."

I took it, and for a moment thought we were back at Tchotchke's Fair. It might have been the same field, only not a soul around, unless you counted a rather large army of frogs and toads assembled around us. "It could be a dream," I offered.

Jerod pinched me.

"Ow."

"Nope," he said. "No dream. And just to be clear." He was smiling, but his tone let me know he was dead serious. "You're my boyfriend…." He stared at his feet and then at me. "This is corny, but I need to hear it, say that you're mine."

"Yes," I said, wanting to see his smile again. "I am yours."

"Good. And in case you ever wonder, I am yours."

"Boys!" Cedric's brow was creased with worry. Beside him stood Liam, his blond hair braided down his back, his violet eyes fixed on me. "I could have loved you," he said. "You didn't give me the chance."

"No." Jerod stepped between us. "Alex is mine. And I am his."

"I see that." Liam's lips pursed as though tasting something bitter. He turned to Cedric. "She'll find them."

"I know." And then to us, "Come. There are things I need to tell you, and we have little time."

# Twenty-Five

WE RAN behind the blond duo of my father the fairy and Liam. An army of frogs and toads followed, and rising over them was the black-and-silver horse. It trailed a stream of muck, from which the frogs pulled insects and tiny fish. The green field soon gave way to a dense forest. We crossed a cool stream and came to a meadow ablaze with purple and yellow flowers. It ended in a gentle embankment and a rushing river. Liam leapt onto the horse's back. Cedric grabbed a handful of the beast's mane and turned to us. "Come. Hurry!"

I looked at the river's white-capped surface. I could barely see the distant shore that was shrouded in fog.

"Hurry," Cedric urged. "There's no time."

I looked behind at the sea of frogs as they leapt into the chop, leaving their dull green-and-brown toad comrades behind. The water churned, and schools of rainbow fish darted from the hungry frogs.

"It's the Hudson River," Jerod said. "See." He pointed to the left, where in the distance I could see the shadow of a massive bridge. "It's the fairy version of the GW. And that—" His arm swung across the river. "—We're going to Jersey." He grabbed the other side of the horse's mane.

"Right." And stepping behind him, I put my hand next to his and gripped tight. "Gross." I didn't want him to see my fear.... I felt paralyzed. I wanted to keep him safe. He'd nearly died, and here we were about to go back into the water. I thought of Alice and how I still had no clue where she was or how I could save her, or if... if it were already too late. My teeth chattered. I clamped my jaw.

Jerod must have sensed it. "It's going to be okay. Just roll, Alex. You are the magic onion."

His words were like oil on troubled waters.

"Forward!" Liam spoke into the mare's ear as he dug his legs into her flanks.

The pooka reared, lifting Jerod and me off the ground. We held tight as it leapt the bank.

"Holy crap!" Jerod shouted.

We flew high, maybe thirty feet. We arced and plummeted toward the rolling waters. My breath caught as we landed with barely a splash. Frogs and fish skittered across my legs. I shut my eyes and sucked in a breath, prepared for the dive. It didn't come.

Cautiously, I peeked out. We were moving like a barge across the river. Liam hunched forward on the horse's neck, his eyes on the distant shore. The creature's broad chest, black head, and silver mane were like the bow of a boat, her strong legs churning beneath us.

Jerod was looking around, and then back at me. His face was filthy, and he was grinning. "Awesome!"

"It is."

My fear was still there, but also exhilaration. It wasn't just this unexpected ride that was better than anything at Coney Island. But we weren't drowning. Jerod was safe... and he was mine. There were no words for this happiness. I smiled so hard my cheeks ached. *Oh wait*, I thought. *This is joy*. It didn't last. Even though I tried to hold onto it, as the wind and water splashed my face and I felt Jerod's body against mine, my mood plummeted. This was no party. My sister had been kidnapped. Jerod had put himself in harm's way—for me—had nearly died, and was heading into stuff that could kill us both. "Shit," I muttered. This wasn't going to end well. Things didn't for me. I had no business feeling happy.

By the time the horse made land and we'd climbed the far embankment, I was a jangled mess. I plastered a smile on my face to meet Jerod's look of amazement.

It didn't work.

His smile vanished. My breath caught as he walked up to me and put his face inches from mine.

I tried to look away. "We should go with them," I said, indicating Cedric and Liam, who were making toward a misty clearing in what seemed to be a village.

"Stop," Jerod said. He butted his forehead against mine. "I see you, Alex Nevus. Whatever awful things are running through your head, you need to make them stop. I love you, and I intend to get through this… with you. And when this is done…." He blushed. "I want to do things with you, Alex. Things I have done with nobody." He waggled his eyebrows. "I have no intention of letting anything bad happen to you, or Alice… or me."

My mouth hung open. He didn't wait for me to respond. All the horrible things I wanted to mention—kidnappings, murderous fairy queens, horses made of slime—never made it from my head to my mouth as his lips landed on mine and stopped the words. The moment was perfect, the horse's reek replaced with him. My hands ran up his back and into his hair; it was damp and curled in my fingers. Shivers tingled from my ears to my toes. All the terrible thoughts in my head stopped.

"Uch! Make them stop," Liam said.

"You're jealous," Cedric replied. There was sadness in his voice. "As I was a trap for his mother, that was to be your path. Consider yourself lucky."

"But you love Marilyn," Liam said.

"Yes, now… but in the beginning I was the baited trap, love unrequited. I can never undo the wrong that I caused. Be grateful." Cedric called to us, "Boys, come now."

Jerod pulled back, his eyes fixed on mine. The tip of his tongue flicked between his lips. “Alex, if I were to die right now….”

I pressed a finger across his mouth. “Do not say it. Not here. Not ever.”

He nodded, kissed my finger, and then brushed a kiss against my cheek. My toes curled inside my sopping sneakers. “So where are we?” he asked.

“Ssh… no questions.” I looked across the clearing at a cluster of thatched huts on either side of a dirt road. Beyond them, the mist was too dense, obscuring whatever lay behind.

Holding hands, we walked toward the hut where Liam and Cedric stood before an open door.

“Check this out,” Jerod said.

I bit back the question and twisted the words. “Tell me,” I said.

“This.” Still holding my hand, he focused on a tendril of mist. He pointed at it and moved his hand as if to touch it. As he got close, it moved away.

“Huh.” We veered from the path, and like doing a physics lab, investigated the phenomenon. The fog was a solid wall of white behind the huts.

“No smell,” he said.

“No,” I agreed. “And it doesn’t seem to like us.”

“It’s repelled by us,” he said, noting how the fog fled from our approach.

“Like a magnet,” I added.

We walked toward a dense patch between two of the huts. Sure enough, the fog rolled back, leaving a ten-foot clearing. Behind us was the village, and around us the mist. We pushed forward. I glanced back to see if the hole from where we’d come would stay open, or would it shut around us. It was like a giant wormhole, the river and village still visible through a story-high hole carved into the mist.

“There’s stuff moving in there,” Jerod said.

I hung at his side and could barely see something happening deep in the fog. We walked closer, and the mist fled, taking whatever we’d glimpsed with it. But when we just stood and stared…. "There's definitely something in there."

"Make them stop!" Liam shouted from the hut where he stood with my father.

"They're learning," Cedric replied.

"She'll see them!" Liam spat back.

"She already has," Cedric said. "She's on her way."

"No!" Liam shrieked. "She can't find me here. She'll know."

Jerod and I stopped our explorations of the fog and watched them.

Cedric placed a hand on Liam's shoulders. "The thing is done."

Liam's eyes were bugging as he looked toward the river. He spotted the two of us. "It's all your fault." His mouth twisted, one of his pointed canines visible over his lip. "You were supposed to fall in love with *me*."

I could see he was frightened… but more. I looked at Cedric… my dad. "You were going to explain," I shouted back, my words muffled by the fog.

He swept his hair back from his pointed ears. "There's no time now… but Alex, I am your father, and while it's difficult to believe, I do love you and your sister… and your brother."

"I don't have a brother." Wondering what the hell he was talking about, and hearing the unmistakable roar of a subway heading into a station.

"Yes," he said. He shouted over the deafening sound of an approaching train. "You do, his name is Adam."

# Twenty-Six

THE ground shook and the water churned. Fish leapt into the air. Frogs stampeded the shore as the river—defying the laws of physics—arched a hundred feet high.

Jerod gripped my hand as we stared down our misty tunnel at the towering wall of water. Our ears were deafened by the screech of a train's brakes. The river's edge fell away, sending a wave flooding toward us and the little village. It spilled around our feet and splashed against the walls of the huts, and where it met the mist, it sizzled and vanished.

Liam keened as if in pain. "No. No. No."

I tried to make sense of what I saw. Where the water had fallen away from the river was a dark tunnel. Smack in the center was an old-style Pullman car. It was bright blue with gold trim. Several doors were opening and various creatures were spilling out. There was a gaggle of the pastel-colored sprites, and May's secretary Dorothea with her mantis legs and arms. One of her pincers held a door as May, dressed in an elaborate red Victorian gown, made her entrance. Her blonde hair was swept up, and rubies sparkled around her neck and from her ears and wrists. Taking Dorothea's extended limb, she daintily alit. Her head pivoted, and she made eye contact first with Cedric, then with the panicking Liam, and finally, with a broad smile, she found Jerod and me in our misty tunnel.

She clapped her hands. “Fascinating. You boys are most inventive. It’s the snips and snails. But it’s time to come out. Alex Nevus, you’ve played yourself into a corner, and it’s time to….” There was a thunderous drum roll. From outside our misty nook we heard a screeching of birds. May threw her hands up and traced circles on the ground with her dainty feet. She giggled. “I hate to dance, and sometimes it’s essential. But now, Alex Nevus, come out, come out, because it’s time….” And another deafening drum roll. “To pay the piper.”

I looked at Jerod.

“We could run,” he said. “She wants us to come out. I don’t think she wants to follow us in.”

“You’re right.”

“Don’t even think of running,” she said. “Because….” And the stupid drum again.

I watched as three towering ogres pushed my real mom out of the train. Behind her followed a young woman with long blonde hair, and finally, a little red-haired boy, a couple years younger than Clay. Mom was no longer pregnant. Her hands were bound behind her back. I looked from her to the pretty blonde woman in jeans and a T-shirt. Her liquid-blue eyes found mine…. “Oh shit!”

Jerod followed my gaze.

“This can’t be,” I said. But of course it was. “Alice.” I glared at May, my feet moving fast toward our tunnel’s opening.

“Alex, No!” Jerod shouted. “It’s what she wants.” He ran after me.

“*No*! Stop!” I shouted. There was about fifteen feet of fog tunnel between Jerod and me, and another fifteen feet on the other side. We faced each other. “Look, Jerod… I think you’re safe in here. If you go out there she’ll use you. She’s got my mom, and Alice… and there’s a sea of weird shit headed my way. I don’t want her to get you too. Please, stay safe.”

"I can't leave you," he said.

It felt like something was ripping inside of me.

May was singing from the village. "Come out, come out!"

"Jerod, she's crazy, and she's dangerous, and she wants something from me. She thinks nothing of killing, and the more she has to bargain with…."

He stared at me, and then he was right in front of me. "I get it," he said. "So don't go to her."

My hands were on his face and his on mine. I felt his breath against my cheeks. "I don't have a choice. She'll hurt them if I don't. She already has."

"She'll hurt you."

"Maybe. I don't think she'll kill me. She wants something else. I think if I give it to her, she'll let them go."

"Maybe she won't."

"I know."

"Don't, please."

"I have no choice." We kissed. It was sad, and it was beautiful. I knew it was for the very last time. Our lips parted. "Jerod, promise me you won't follow, no matter what."

"I love you." His jaw twitched, and he was crying. "Don't do this, Alex. Stay with me."

"I love you too. You have to promise. I'll be okay if I know you're safe. You have to get home to Clay, he needs you. I have to try and save my mom and Alice, they're going to need you too. Tell me you won't follow. Please. Promise." I was sobbing.

"Okay." He butted his forehead against mine. "I fucking hate this. You better come back to me."

"I'll try."

"*No*!" he shouted. Tears down his face. "Don't say that. Tell me you're going to come back to me." He sounded angry, his hands tight on the sides of my face. His eyes bored into mine.

"I will come back to you," I said.

"Promise!"

"I promise. I will come back to you." I swallowed. "You have to let go," I said.

"No." I felt his hands loosen.

I pulled back and looked at him a final time. "I will come back to you." The words sounded good, but as they left my mouth, I knew they were a lie.

I turned and left the safety of the mist.

May was waiting, her arms extended toward me. "My goodness," she said. She looked behind me at the tunnel, Jerod still visible. It was too painful to look at him, and I was frightened that he'd try to do something impulsive and heroic. "What a long road it's been, Alex Nevus."

"Yes," I said, trying to steady my nerves. I gritted my teeth and smiled, all the while piecing together the information being thrown at me. Behind May stood my mom, with her hands bound, my sister—who was too old to be Alice—and a red-headed boy of around seven, who looked a little like me. "Tell me about Alice," I said.

"She wasn't ripe," May answered. She glanced back. "And now she is."

"You stole years from my sister." Rage bubbled inside, the kind Sifu warned against. Anger needed to be controlled.

"Just a few," May said. "She's beautiful and nearly as clever as you. If it weren't for your little brother, she would have run away. Thank goodness for the ties that bind."

My eyes fell on the boy. He stared back at me with green eyes fringed with long red lashes.

"I'm Adam," he said. He seemed frightened, his gaze darting from me, to Mom, to Cedric.

"Hi," I said, feeling a rush of emotion. "I'm Alex." I didn't know what to expect. Was he even real.... But Mom had been pregnant, and now she wasn't. I felt sick. How could someone... some creature, do these things?

I glared at May. She was smug, so certain she had me over a barrel. I stepped across the opening to my family.

"Alex," Alice whispered. "I'm sorry."

I took her hands, so used to having to tilt my head down, but now… she was tall and beautiful, her hair loose around her shoulders, a great flowing wave of rippling blonde. Her eyes, still the same liquid blue. "Not your fault," I said. "None of this."

Adam stared up at me… this was my brother. I couldn't imagine what his world was like. How do you go from being nonexistent to seven years old in a day or two? I sank to my knees and did the only thing that made sense. I hugged him. Dangerous questions swirled, and while I held his skinny body close to mine, I felt May's eyes on us.

"Free her hands," May instructed one of the ogres. "She'll play no games with all of her eggs in my basket."

Mom's hand was on my back, and we were having that rarest of things… a family hug. Alice gripped one of my hands, and the other was wrapped around Adam. He was solid; he was my brother… and she'd stolen his first seven years.

"So," May said, breaking the moment. "It's time to pay up, Alex Nevus. And I must say, with a sister, brother, mother, and father in my hand… unless your boyfriend wants to join in, I've got a full house." She chuckled.

I batted away tears and stood. Turning from my family, I met her gaze. "I have what you want… or else you've gone to a lot of trouble for nothing."

"Well said." Her ruby earrings sparkled as she bent her head first to the right and then to the left. "But that is why we're here." She turned her gaze from me, to Alice, and then to Adam.

Dorothea was at her side, her notebook clutched in one pincer, a quill in the other.

"A choice must be made…," May said. "Give me what I want, Alex Nevus, and your family will be safe. That's quite a bargain. Quite a steal. Give me your name, Alex Nevus, and they will all go free."

"No," Mom hissed.

I glanced at Cedric. He was mouthing, "No."

May's head swiveled, and she caught him in her gaze.

He flinched, and Liam ran from his side in terror to hide at the edge of the cottage. "Stupid fairy!" she sneered. "Choose your death, the mist, or me…." She looked over her shoulder at me. "Watch," she said.

"Don't," Cedric shouted back. He met May's gaze. "I don't care," he said. "Just leave them alone. Leave Liam alone, he did all that you'd asked. You don't need them."

"But I do… at least one of them, and you *always* knew that. It was *our* deal. What's amusing is that you actually fell in love with her… and out of love with me. Still, the thing you did, Cedric. She won't love you now. It will be impossible. You will be the cause of unbearable sorrow… the death of her babes. The choice that must be made, to kill them all or just take the one I want. Either way, she will go mad in this world as well as that… she will blame you. And she will be right to do so."

I knew May would make good on her threats. Sometimes, in battle, there was no choice but to charge against a much greater adversary. You would fail, but it was honorable. "I'll give you what you want," I shouted.

May's head swiveled, her eyes bright, her smile wide.

"Well done, let's have it."

I ignored the chorus of my parents, my sister, and newborn seven-year-old brother. Jerod shouted from inside the tunnel, "Run!"

I had a moment's panic that he'd leave the safety of the mist and try something stupid… and brave.

"Don't do it, Alex," Cedric warned. "It means your death."

That couldn't have been clearer. Shit! I was out of choices, my life or my family's. No choice at all. "May, Queen of the Fey. I give you my name, it is Alex Nevus."

"Yes!" She clapped her hands three times. Her skirts swished back and forth as she shifted her weight from side to side. An orchestra of frogs and birds started to play. There was a pounding beat with low croaks in the bass. May's body swayed as crickets layered in harmonies. "I hate to dance," she said. Her voice sounded distant. Her eyes were hooded and nearly closed.

For someone who kept saying that, she did a lot of it. The music flooded my head. My body felt weird—like filled with lead. I couldn't move. I watched May twirl, her dainty feet in red satin slippers kicking out from her gown as her arms drew snaky patterns in the air. She was mad as a bedbug but beautiful and graceful.

Over the dense rhythms, I felt a hand on my shoulder. It was Mom. "Alex," she whispered. "Run. Save yourself."

I couldn't even turn my head. I felt my panic and fear slip away. This wasn't going to end well, but at least I'd done everything possible to save my family and Jerod. My eyes fixed on May. I thought how the woman touching my shoulder and pleading with me to run away wasn't my crazy mother Marilyn. She gripped my head in her hands and tried to make me look at her. Our eyes connected. Hers were clear, the lines around her mouth and eyes deeper than I remembered.

"I can't leave you here," I said. "I can't leave them." I felt a tension in my neck, like it was a rubber band.

Mom winced at my words as though I'd struck her. "You are my warrior," she said, holding my head. "But I never prepared you. Please, Alex… just run." She looked toward the misty tunnel, its entrance still open, and Jerod, who hadn't moved, staring back. "Forget us," she said. "Or remember us, and be sad, but save yourself. Please. What she intends to do… she's going to kill you." She was begging.

Behind her, Alice held Adam's hand. "You tried," Alice said. "But Mom's right. We'll be okay here. It's not all bad, and most of the time—" She shrugged. "—you don't remember stuff."

*Right*, I thought, *like losing seven years of your life.* I whispered, "Today on *Sadly*…."

"Yes." She smiled, and there were tears in her eyes. "Today on *Sadly*. Now run!"

Mom's hands let go of my head. As she did, it was like I had no muscle control, and it whipped back to face May. Her dance had escalated to wild circling stag leaps around the village clearing. Her hair had whipped free of its stays, and every time her feet touched ground, puffs of glittery dust lingered.

"Well then!" May screamed over the dense music.

It stopped. There was silence… not a croak, not a chirp. May put her hands on her hips. She seemed bigger, or filled like a balloon about to pop. She grinned at me. The sides of her mouth were too big, like a snake detaching its jaw to swallow a rat or a cat or… a person. Her mouth opened, and opened and opened. She raised a hand in my direction, and I watched the skin of her fingers, her upper arms, her face begin to bubble and split. A horrible sucking noise came from beneath her gown, like gears grinding and fabric tearing. Her tongue, thick and red and way too long dangled from the corner of her gaping jaw.

"I choose you," she slurred.

"Run!" Mom screamed.

"Run, Alex." Alice joined.

"*Run*!" Jerod screamed.

None of them realized I was frozen, not by fear, not by honor, but by magic. The moment I gave her my name was the moment I ceded the battle, possibly the war, and as I now knew… my life.

# Twenty-Seven

I DIED. I am in hell… possibly purgatory, as not much is happening. No devils poking my flesh, no burning cauldrons, no screaming souls. I'm awake for bits and then I'm not. It's dark; no light, smells, no sound… just black, like floating. I have no body. Nothing with which to touch or feel. I have memories. I play them repeatedly when I'm awake. Brown eyes, soft lips, dimples. "I love you, Alex." *Who's Alex*? I wonder. The last bit…. May's jaw unhinging like a python, but not just her jaw… her. Like the mist, she washed over me… over… Alex. She took possession of Alex Nevus… of me. Like a squatter, or maybe I was now the squatter having given up my rights to my apartment… my body… my name. I'm tired. I'm Alex. I sleep.

# Twenty-Eight

THERE is no time here… wherever here is. I'm aware, and that's it. Which, if maybe I'm still in my body… and that's a big if… then the only place I could be is my brain. Unless kidneys have consciousness… although I read somewhere that the Greeks thought the soul resided in the liver, or maybe it was the heart, and I remember something in biology about the stomach having a ton of nerves. No, definitely the liver. I chew on trivia, remembering the myth of Prometheus who stole the fire of Olympus and gave it to man. As a punishment he was chained to a rock, and every day an eagle ate his liver, and every night it grew back. No, not the liver; if I'm still in my body, this has got to be my brain… or a small part of it that May didn't occupy. Going with that hypothesis, and not wanting to build up hope, I picture a brain and try to remember its basic anatomy. The highest we ever got in biology was the fetal pig… kind of like the human brain, minus the add-ons. I think of Jerod and feel a rush of wonderful… and there's a clue. From him, I picture Alice, as she was before… before she'd been robbed of most of her teen years. Then my brother, Adam…. I'd always wanted a brother, in that stupid way kids want lots of things. So much I could teach him… unless of course she'd turned him into a middle-aged man. These are clues. You have emotions… and thoughts, so it's not just a little bit of the brain… if in fact you're still in the body… your body. My thoughts skitter as I trigger feelings and memories. It's hard to focus. Okay, think of Jerod's eyes. Ohhhh. That's nice. See the flecks of gold. So feeling and emotion… that's deep brain, lizard brain… she turned me into a gecko. But I can remember his words and his name and how he looked carrying his brother's skateboard and how scared I'd been when he wasn't breathing. How good it felt when he did breathe, and I'd realized… he was willing to die for me. So not only am I in the deep brain structures but I have access to the outer layers and possibly the forebrain. A flash of light rips through the black. I stop everything. Where did that come from? Direction is meaningless; there's no up and down, left and right, just space. What was I thinking when the lights almost went on? Outer layers of the brain. I picture the anatomy exhibit at the Museum of Natural History—one of my favorite places. Like a biology textbook, only real. I visualize the brain exhibit… light travels in through the eyes, hits the retina, and then all that information speeds down the optic nerve, which is basically an extension of the brain. Weirdly, it goes all the way to the back of the head where the images get pulled apart, inverted, flipped from side to side, and put back together to create perceptions. As I have these thoughts, something changes. Whatever was allowing me to think and to feel was spreading, and that flash of light, like a search beam, returned. I think of Sifu and of riding the moment in Wing Chung practice. Nothing is forced… the light grows. It's brilliant, and I feel little tendrils of consciousness. This is my brain, and somehow I'm traveling down synapses, hopping from neuron to neuron, and seeing light. Then color. Okay, none of this makes sense. All chopped-apart bits. I feel rushes of anxiety and fear. Not helpful… but maybe I'm not dead. Hope whisks back the doubt. Where there's life there's hope, and then I hear something. After however long in this floating free fall, I just heard… am hearing. Like I'd just touched a wire that hooked up a speaker, someone was singing.

I hold still, fearing that I'll disconnect whatever I'd just made happen. It's a male voice… so beautiful, and not just because I'm thrilled to hear anything at all, but incredibly powerful. A soaring, unaccompanied tenor. I try to focus on the lyrics. It's too difficult. The stream and flow of notes make me sad, and if I had eyes and tear ducts, I'd be crying. When the music stops, I feel drained… so tired. All the gains I'd made; the light, the colors, and the sound, all goes black. So tired. I sleep.

# Twenty-Nine

WHEN I woke, I swept past my doubt and fear and reclaimed all that I'd accomplished before. With a surge of enthusiasm, I leapt through my brain, triggering the connections that had given me light and sound. It was fast, and my world filled with color, and I heard a man's voice. Okay, I kind of knew that voice… it was mine. Only, I wasn't speaking. But the words coming in were just sound, not the beautiful music… was I singing? I didn't sing. Never could. But… that was a beautiful voice. The best I'd ever heard. Information flooded in. Too much and too disconnected. I focused on the colors and the lights. Curious thing, as I followed a particular image, letting it take me forward, it took on substance, and suddenly I was looking at a face… a recognizable face. What the? Why was I looking at eighties pop sensation Carly Casswell? She was smiling and saying something I couldn't make out. I held her image and it grew, like pieces of a jigsaw coming together. No mistaking her streaked-blonde mane, over-collagened lips, and Botox brow. Her smile was bright, and whatever she was saying came with tears. A man's hand fell on her shoulder. I focused on that, and then to the attached arm. From there to a shoulder and another face, this one black, with a shaved head. Wait a minute… Barry Soulfeld—music producer and ex-guitarist for the R&B group Envy. I knew this… May must have been watching TV…. I knew this show. I let the image drift back from Barry Soulfeld to Carly Casswell, because if I was right—and what else could this be—on the other side of her, Morgan Flood. I let the features of his head and face coalesce, from his surgically enhanced hairline, to his taut skin and ski-slope nose. But his eyes. He was crying and shaking his head. His mouth was twisted as though it were too painful to speak. I fumbled around, trying to remember how I'd gotten the audio before, and sent little tendrils of awareness shooting down cells to my right and left. Noise flooded in, clapping and cheering. And a man's voice. No, Alex—your voice. Focus!

The clapping was a solid wall… too much. The man's… my voice, trying to be heard over it. "Thank you."

Oh my God. I could make out words. I was speaking, only it wasn't me. It was May.

"Thank you so much," she repeated.

And I got the weirdest sensation as I felt her/my head turn. The images shifted fast. She was making eye contact with each of the judges. Holy shit! Carly Casswell's red-rimmed hazel eyes were staring straight at me. May wasn't watching TV. She was on it. Holy crap, this was *IT*! I, or rather May, was on the number-one primetime talent show. First there'd been *American Idol*, then *America's Got Talent*, *The X-Factor*, *The Voice*, and last season, the newest and biggest—*IT*. Where the prize was a starring role in a big-budget movie produced by Morgan Flood, whose credits included four of the ten all-time highest grossing movies.

*Calm down*, I told myself, searching for Sifu's mindless path to being. *Just take it in, calm like the surface of a pond. Don't react.* I focused on Carly Casswell's over-plumped lips, the sounds not making sense. I shot awareness off to my right and to my left, to where the audio parts of the brain got their feed. The sounds were different than the ones when I—or rather, May—spoke, but if I relaxed, they pulled together.

"Holy mother of God." Carly's first discernible statement. "Alex, you…." I watched her swallow back mascara-dripped tears. "I can't find the words for how moved…. From your first audition, I just knew…." She was sobbing.

"Thank you, Carly."

What the? So now I was on a first name basis with…. *Chill, Alex, just be… calm like a pond.*

A man's voice, with hints of a British accent. "Brilliant," Morgan Flood gushed. "Just brilliant. I'd love to give you a criticism, I can't. That was… perfect. The best performance this season. No, the best ever. Of this year's final three contestants, it's yours to lose, Alex Nevus. You've thrown down the gauntlet and kicked off an amazing show!"

The audience roared their approval and the images shifted again, and I was looking at… myself. Wow! Someone had given me a makeover. A giant screen focused on my face. *How did my hair get that long?* I'd never really thought about my looks, I was okay, too tall, too skinny… but the teenager on the screen, vivid-green eyes with long black lashes, blue-black hair framing my face, was I wearing lipstick? Really? His skin, right… my skin, glowing, not a blemish, the nose straight, gleaming white teeth. He… I was smiling, but not big, more like a movie star in a close-up. *What are you up to, May? Why this? How long have I been… gone?*

The image shifted, and the show's logo was superimposed over the audience, which was giving me… her, a standing ovation. The applause was thunderous.

The screen went blank, and for a moment I thought I'd again lost my ability to see. I fought against the dark. I heard a woman's voice. "Alex, that was amazing! We need to get you backstage."

"Of course." May speaking through my mouth. "Thanks, nice of you to say." Her tone was modest.

"No," the woman replied. "Nice has nothing to do with it. You're fucking amazing!" Her voice lowered to a whisper. "We're not supposed to say shit like this… you're the odds-on favorite."

"Thanks."

I listened and caught snippets of rapidly shifting visuals: the young woman May was talking to, all in black, earphones draped around her neck, a small microphone hooked under her chin. It was a struggle making sense of things, particularly the dark bits. Where there was light or faces, things came into focus more readily.

I heard a door open and then another, and May was being led into a room with couches and a buffet against one wall. It was filled with crew all in black, and a boy and girl close to my age. This was some kind of holding room for the talent. I sifted through my memories of *IT*. Because Alice was addicted to the show, I had a lot of them. I accessed the rules, hearing them in the voice of the announcer: *"Contestants must be between the ages of sixteen and twenty-five, have no criminal history and be willing... to become IT."*

As I sifted the data—dramatic readings, song-and-dance routines, on-camera challenges—I tried to make sense of what I was hearing. One young woman telling May/me, "I just hate you." Her face smiling... she reminded me a lot of Ashley, the girl Jerod was supposed to take to the prom. "I mean, really," she said, "how can any of us compete with that? It was awesome, Alex. I'm so jealous... but you know, like happy for you too."

"Thanks, Jenna, I think you're great too."

That stopped me. If I'd had a jaw to operate, it would have hung open. The fey didn't lie—admittedly, they twisted things all the way around to where you couldn't tell your head from your ass, but an out-and-out lie—that was one of their rules. May had just broken it. Somehow, in my ferreting through my neurons, I knew she thought Jenna was a mediocre talent scraping by on charm, blonde flirtiness, and surgically altered breasts. It was the first I'd actually sensed May's thoughts directly. They hissed like water on hot coals—alien and calculating. She didn't just think Jenna was a talentless bimbo, she wanted to hurt her... even kill her if she could (a) get away with it, and (b) thought the audience would approve. It was a sick feeling as she played with the options, her/my fingers twitching at the thought of what it might feel like to strangle Jenna.

I listened as the other contestant—a good-looking guy with a crazy head of corkscrew tawny hair—congratulated May on whatever amazing performance she'd just eked out of my body.

"Jeremy," she said to him, "your musical number was so much better than mine." *Yeah, you can sing*, her thoughts hissed out, *but you come off way too gay, and they'll never vote for you.* But there was more, her cool plans to crush him. I could see her working it out, a young stagehand who had a crush on Jeremy. She'd maneuver the two of them together and have a compromising video leaked to the web. It would go viral in minutes.

At one point she must have glanced at a monitor, as I saw myself on stage with an Irish harp in my lap, a soft light spilling across my face as I strummed and sang. At the bottom were words: *"Alex Nevus, 17, New York."*

First, I'd never played the Irish harp, and really… my singing voice—not good. Also, I was sixteen, not seventeen. I strained to hear the audio, but there was nothing. It was weird… okay, beyond weird, but seeing myself on-screen, the way the camera fixed on my eyes. It was me… but it wasn't. Even without the sound she… I… was giving a beautiful performance. I was May's puppet… but my expressions, the way my eyebrow raised subtly and I seemed fused to the harp. I watched my lips and I heard the lyrics… bits of an old ballad. A tearjerker about a young man going off to war, about leaving behind a girl and thinking of her as he died in battle.

Information flooded in. It was too much. I'd been overambitious in trying to feel my way around, and the hissing from May's consciousness made it hard to focus. It was like once I started to touch or feel some thought or memory, I couldn't stop. I was being buried in data. *Shut it down*, I thought, feeling as if I were falling. Too much, *shut it down.* And like all those years of blocking out Nimby, who turns out was real after all, I threw down walls. First, blocking out May's murderous thoughts. I knew I'd need to come back to them, but right now… I had to shut them out. Brick by brick, and then the sounds, and the images, and the ridiculous amounts of stored information about *IT*, the *IT* judges, last year's *IT* champion—Tiffany Sweet—who'd catapulted to stardom. It was like shutting off TV sets that were all connected but not on the same station. Or like the hundreds of panes of glass in May's greenhouse. I needed to think. Finally, there was darkness. It was quiet and black, and I could focus.

I reviewed the facts. May controlled my body. I had been unconscious… dead? … for a while. This raised possibilities. First, was

I dead? Which, judging by my ability to tap into my brain and the fact that I was frantically trying to piece things together, seemed unlikely. I was alive, just displaced. Which brought the next big question.... Did May know I was in here?

Cautiously, I felt around the walls I'd erected and eased back the mental bricks. I could hear and feel May's presence. Yes, she controlled my body, and her thoughts were racing through the circuits of my brain, but there was more. As though she was half in and half out of me. I could hear her, and the quieter I stayed, the more sensations came through. And unlike trying to pull the visual and the audio from my brain, I was getting a moving picture. She was gazing at the other two contestants, weighing their strengths and weaknesses. She saw their fears and insecurities, even listened to their thoughts.

"Lovely," she mused as she stood and followed Jenna to the bathroom.

May pulled out a cell phone as she waited for the girl to go into the restroom. She pictured Jenna on the other side, and padding in on silent feet, entered the adjacent toilet stall. She climbed up on the toilet and looked over the partition. Holding the phone steady, she filmed the girl as she put her fingers down her throat and vomited.

Through May, I heard Jenna's thoughts as she puked. Her mind almost chanting, "I didn't eat that. And I didn't eat that," as she again stuck two fingers far down. "And I didn't eat that. And I didn't eat that."

I expected Jenna to hear her, to turn around and confront… me. But something else was going on here. May was me… but more. *What is that?* I felt her hovering outside my body, as though there were two of her, half inside and half invisible. She was using magic.

*That's the whole point.* It was an epiphany. This was why in the book *May, Queen of the Fey*, she'd failed. A human vessel would rob her of her magic in the human realm, but a being—me—who was half-and-half. *Great!* It was one thing to understand this intellectually, but to realize I had become a bridge between two worlds, and that this barking-mad fairy queen intended to march across and conquer the human realm, it was overwhelming… and real.

As silently as she entered, May and I left the restroom and returned to the room with the other contestant. As she entered, I realized I'd been right. I—or at least my body—had never left the room. I was sitting in the corner next to Jeremy. Whatever had gone into the bathroom was not flesh… but pure magic.

"What you doing?" blond Jeremy asked.

May made meaningful eye contact with Jeremy, and most horribly, listened to his thoughts. "Just thinking," my mouth said.

"You're so going to win this," Jeremy replied.

All the while, May smiled and made too much eye contact. Her thoughts hissed as she seduced Jeremy. He was thinking about my eyes and my lips. He wondered if I liked him… in that way. He wanted to look away, embarrassed that he was revealing things about himself. But hopeful, his thoughts were so clear. *"Does he like me? God, I hope he likes me."*

I wanted to warn him. He was a sweet kid, and May intended to destroy him. I saw snippets of other fallen contestants, like watching video clips. They were memories, only they weren't mine. In one, two teenagers were smoking a joint, in another a young man was trying to sing through a painfully swollen throat. His cheeks were blown up like a chipmunk's and the sounds… like a frog on a bad day. In another, a black girl was swearing at the judges. She caught herself in the monitor as though realizing she'd made a horrible mistake. She broke into tears and fled the stage.

Then came the awful truth, if there were only three contestants left…. I'd been unconscious for months. I calculated how long…. Obviously I would have had to audition, then they went through a process of winnowing down thousands of contestants to the top twenty, and then it was a weekly show where a girl and boy went home. That was why I wasn't sixteen. How long had I been out?

I pulled back, frightened by May's thoughts, feeling a crushing guilt that I wasn't able to stop her from wreaking havoc on all of these talented young men and women. She intended to win. That was clear. But why? May wanted to be a star. Yes, and again the big question, "Why?" That's what all those bizarre shows under the mulberry tree had been leading up to. I felt queasy as I realized I'd been the one who'd told her about *IT*. But why? Why this?

The answer seemed close. I thought about Katye and how she'd sucked the life from poor Lance. I replayed her story of the three sisters, and Lizbeta, who was tricked into the mist. I pictured Jerod. I'd begged him not to follow. And then Alice… who May had aged… to be on this program. Right, when Alice was eleven, she'd have been too young to qualify. May needed her older, and then decided to take me instead.

Still… what was the point? Something Barry Soulfeld said during the last critique—*"Alex, you're in IT to win IT."* What did that get her? Tremendous exposure and a starring role in a big movie… which was even more exposure. More people seeing her, even though it was my body they were watching. She wanted power. Katye lived to love, and Lizbeta's special was peace. May wanted power, control…. She was queen of a dying world, and she wanted to jump ship and come to this one.

But I was missing something. Okay, so she wanted to rule the world, a talent show wouldn't do that, not even being a movie star. And all the preparation… me, Alice, my new brother. Hafflings…. I got that, but something bigger was happening.

I thought back to the village and that final awful moment when I'd given her my name. Cedric and my mom had both said she was going to kill me. So either I was dead or wasn't. And while I didn't seem to have much control… I didn't think I was dead. Unless I was a ghost? Which raised an interesting point… did May think I was dead? It seemed her intent was to shuck me like an oyster, or like one of those crabs that couldn't make its own shell, so it stole one after first killing and eating the prior inhabitant. She thought I was dead. I didn't think I was. She didn't know I was in here.

I startled at the sound of someone banging on a door, and a familiar voice.

"Let me in! I need to see Alex!"

*Jerod!* I couldn't see him, but feelings flooded me, like suddenly being hooked into my brain's mainframe.

I could feel my lips… actually feel my body, I was speaking. But it wasn't me. "I don't know that boy!" May was speaking. "I don't know who he is or why he's stalking me."

I saw a cluster of security guards.

A woman with headphones screamed into her mouthpiece. "How did he get in here?"

"Alex!" Jerod was shouting.

And then he wasn't. A swarm of security blocked the door. I felt May's thoughts. She was furious. Her ability to mobilize legions to do her bidding didn't work in this world. But then, there was that weird sensation again. And like being cut in two, I was floating out of the room and through the television studio. I saw Jerod being escorted out the front of the building by half a dozen guards. I could hear them. "Do it again, kid, and we're calling the cops."

And then we were outside the theater in Times Square.

May's magical body hovered over Jerod. Her thoughts were difficult to read, rage and frustration… and malice. She wanted him dead. There was nothing I could do to stop her. She spotted a yellow cab stopped at an intersection across from Jerod.

"Knock, knock," she said, rapping invisible fingers on the driver's head.

He startled and turned. She dove into his open mouth and took possession. Again, there was a rush of rage as she stared at the cab's console. The key in the ignition. She didn't know how to drive.

"Go!" she screamed.

Through the driver's eyes in the rearview mirror, I could tell she was in control of his body, but not his thoughts.

"Drive!" she shrieked. He slammed his foot onto the accelerator. The cab shot forward before the light had changed, and broadsided a bread truck. The cabbie's head hit the steering wheel with a sharp crack.

"Drive!" May insisted, hauling him back into his seat.

The man's foot never left the gas. The tires spun, and the cab rammed the bread truck out of the way. Horns blared as the cab shot free of the mangled truck and leapt across the intersection and crashed into the side of the TV studio.

May's gaze raked around the intersection. "No!" She spotted Jerod, unharmed and staring at the wreckage. On his shoulder was Nimby.

"Moron!" And she flew out of the driver's mouth, with me along for the ride.

She froze as a beautiful redhead joined Jerod—Katye. May stared at her sister and didn't move. I felt and heard her emotions and her thoughts. She studied Katye, from the way she dressed in pink to how she handled her human form. May's thoughts were a jumbled mix of jealousy and regret. I needed to warn Jerod. He didn't realize how close he'd come to disaster. And from the fury bubbling inside of May, she wasn't done.

Katye gazed at the cab. A crowd had gathered, and someone was helping the wounded driver. A police cruiser pulled up, and then a second. Katye turned away from the accident and stared at May. She shook her head and mouthed, "You missed." Jerod was at her side and Nimby was pointing at us. Her wings fluttered, her mouth moving nonstop. I focused on the two of them. My little fairy that I'd treated so badly was telling Jerod something. She glanced back at us, her pink wings a shimmery blur.

"How dare she!" May's anger was boiling. "How dare she!"

Just as I'd been figuring my way through the connections of my brain, May was still trying to get her bearings. The big difference—she'd had months to do this. But something was happening; she was torn. We were moving again, away from the chaos of the street and back into the studio and my body.

The woman with the headset was leading us out of the room with the couches and the buffet. Someone else strapped a microphone to our chin and clipped a small box to the back of my jeans.

Jeremy called out, "Good luck, Alex."

"Thanks."

And we were being led backstage, then onto a darkened set with a gleaming black piano. Behind that was a massive screen running a video montage of me. I wanted to look at it, but May moved us toward the piano. The audience was on their feet. She paused in front of the piano and scanned the crowd. By now I could read the images fast and clear. She took in the two balconies, the main auditorium, and finally her gaze landed on the three judges—Carly, Barry, and Morgan Flood.

I heard her thoughts and finally understood. She intended to have Morgan Flood make a movie about the fey. Her logic was… bizarre, and it made sense. The fey's existence was based on people believing in them, worshiping them. It's how I was able to block out Nimby for all those years and escape from the mulberry tree. If you didn't believe they existed, then they didn't. But if you did.… Her kingdom was shrinking, her subjects getting swallowed by the mist. Which, considering how she treated them, might have been the lesser of two evils. Still, she intended to star in a movie that tens of millions would see, and like all those goths running around wanting to be vampires after reading *Twilight* and Anne Rice, she intended to not only push back the deadly mist, but return the fey to the human realm. And not for peaceful coexistence, but domination. Not to be queen, but to be God.

She sat at the open piano. A spotlight warmed our face. I felt that, and I stared at the keys as she raised my hands. If she hadn't just tried to kill my boyfriend, I would have found this fascinating.… I didn't play piano, I didn't play the Irish harp, I certainly couldn't hold a tune, and… I started to play… really well. My hands flew up and down the keyboard, my left laying down a steady blues beat that marched in assured cords up and down the bassline. My right riffed a tune that seemed familiar, but that I couldn't quite place. I started to sing.

*Where the hell did that come from?* Marveling at the soaring tenor, I focused on the lyrics and the haunting melody. The words were familiar.

*"If we shadows have offended,*
*Think but this—and all is mended—*
*that you have but slumber'd here*
*while these visions did appear.*
*And this weak and idle theme…."*

I knew this…. AP English. It was Puck's closing soliloquy from *A Midsummer Night's Dream.* She hadn't picked this at random. Where most *IT* contestants sang current Top 40 hits, May had deliberately selected a piece about the fey. There was magic in this, and it was directed toward Morgan Flood. She'd already moved beyond winning *IT*; this was the movie she wanted him to make, with her… me… starring as Puck. A contemporary version of the Shakespearian classic.

Tears flowed down my face as May played and sang.

*"No more yielding but a dream,*
*Gentles do not reprehend;*
*If you pardon we will mend.*
*And, as I'm an honest Puck…."*

I had to hand it to her, this was gorgeous. I barely noticed as raised platforms lit up behind me with a trio of violinists, a pair of cellists, and a harpist.

What did snag my attention… and May's… was the frog.

# Thirty

THE frog leapt from the floor to the piano bench. From there it landed on the keys with a crash in the bass. May stared at it, and not losing time with the music, her—my—left hand went to shove it off. The frog hopped over our hand and landed near the middle of the keyboard with a discordant thud. Apparently, the show really must go on, and May ran my right hand down the keyboard. My fingers made a dizzying trill as they shot for the intrusive bullfrog with its distinctive green-and-blue swirls. It was Lance.

She never stopped singing, and I felt her thoughts gather strength, torn between murdering the frog on stage but knowing that would create a backlash among animal lovers. *They must love me*, she thought. *They must call in and vote.* My right hand grabbed for Lance, he leapt away.

She smiled for the camera. Her voice high and pure, *"Give me your hands, if we be friends, And Robin shall restore amends."* The tune had shifted from its bluesy beginning to a gospel finish. The strings were joined by an eight-person choir, their red-and-white robes swaying as they clapped hands in time to the beat.

Lance the frog, however, marched to a different tune, and frenetically hopped back and forth over my fingers.

As May's fury boiled, I felt more and more of myself. The way my jaw ached as she tried to hold my expression serene. Tension around my eyes as she manipulated the muscles to hold a dreamy, lost-in-the music expression.

And what did I do with this? *Use it, Alex. Feel her anger, her frustration, and use it. Use your enemy's momentum.* An easy concept in sparring and even the occasional street fight, but when your opponent resided in your body….

My fingers laid down the song's last cords, but Lance was not finished with his tune. There was no applause, a stunned silence, and then the first nervous chuckle, and another, and the audience roared with laughter. My hands came away from the piano.

May's thoughts were poison. *How dare they?* She pasted an amused half smile on my lips and scanned the crowd. Let them think this was all part of the act. The frog, now alone on the keyboard, marched up and down, thumping the notes as he went.

The audience was in hysterics. The harder they laughed, the more infuriated she became. *I will not be mocked. How dare they!*

I felt that strange separation as the magic part of May swelled and separated from my body. She was still in control, but she was slipping. The word she'd thrown around, the thing I was—haffling—took on meaning. Half magic and half human, and frankly I'd take the human half. I twitched. It was subtle, but I made a muscle in the side of my neck move.

The audience was on their feet, along with the judges. They howled with laughter. Lance the frog was a hit, and Queen May was not amused.

She'd left my body on autopilot. It was supposed to smile and bow and bask in the audience's adoration, while she went off to…. I'd lost contact with her. *And while the cat's away*…. I managed to swallow… on my own. *Good, now move a finger.* And the tip of my right thumb bent. *Do it again*. I did. It was weird. As I willed my thumb to move, there was an opposing force wanting to spring it back. Like she'd posed my body… but more than that. I was moving and smiling, my gaze serene, everything in place. *Say something*, I thought.

It was too much. I swallowed and tasted the inside of my mouth… salty… and a funny acid feeling deep in my belly.

The laughter was dying out.

A shiver ran down my back. *What is she doing?*

Lance was still hopping up and down the keys. Plunk, thud, plink, crash. He had a bit of rhythm going.

It wasn't an accident, his being here… and if he was here…. Mustering everything I could, I focused on the muscles of my head and my neck. Like pushing a boulder, I turned my head, first to the right, and then all the way around to the left. *This is my body*, I thought. *I want it back.*

It was mine… but May still pulled the strings… and not just mine. The musicians and choir seemed frozen behind me. I strained to turn and face the audience and the judges. What was wrong with them? No one moved. It was frightening. How did she get this powerful? To control one body… to do the twisted crap with that cab driver, or Jenna in the bathroom, but there were thousands of people in this theatre. This was power. Big, scary power.

I felt her fury shoot through my head. Like a whip, it shot down my arms, and before I knew it, I'd grabbed Lance from off the piano. He croaked frantically as my hands squeezed around his juicy body.

"No!" A voice screamed from the audience. "Alex, no!"

"Who was that?" The words flew out of my mouth… but not me saying them.

I felt helpless, trapped in my body, staring out at a few thousand members of the *IT* audience, frozen in space. Their faces were still lit with the humor of Lance's performance.

"Alex!" It was Jerod. "You've got to fight!"

Somehow, he'd escaped May's freeze gun… or whatever the hell she was doing. Nimby buzzed around his head and shoulders. She wielded a sword-shaped cocktail stirrer and was batting at the air around him. He pushed his way past frozen audience members. He made it to the aisle and started to run toward me.

"Leave me be!" The words left my mouth. I felt the muscles in my jaw tense.

I wanted to speak, and I couldn't. *It's not me, Jerod.*

"Alex." His brown eyes searched mine out. "You have to fight her. You can do it."

My jaw moved. I tried to clamp my lips together, but she was too strong.

"Alex is dead," she said through my lips.

"You lie," he shouted. "Alex is alive."

"No." Her thoughts hissed in my head. I felt a twinge of her uncertainty. It frightened her. "He is dead."

"Wrong," Jerod said.

I saw more movement in the audience; it was Katye and Mom… or rather changeling Mom. They pushed past frozen audience members and started down the aisle.

"Hello, sister," Katye said. "Long time. Quite the performance. Very moving." Katye swept her hands out. "And just look at your power. So big and strong. They gave it to you… but you never did have a sense of humor about yourself. The laughter hurts."

"Shut *up*!" May spat out my mouth.

"Truth hurts," changeling Mom added.

"Yes," Katye said. "I'll tell you something else that's true." She stared at me, and then at Lance still clutched and squirming in the prison of my two hands. "You can't possess a property when someone has a lien on it."

I felt May's confusion. "I will kill you, sister," she said, her fear causing her to throw more energy into controlling my body. As she did, I saw movement in the audience. The blinking of eyes, people swaying. A child coughed.

"It's truth… dear sister. It's truth that I will always love you… because you are my sister. It's also truth that Alex was not free for the taking. And that is why you did not kill him when you took his body. He is not dead, May. His body and his soul were not his to give."

"*You lie*!" She shrieked. It was as though an animal had been loosed in my brain. Where I'd been mucking about in here, there was now something else, serpentine and slippery as water. It rushed through all of my hard-won connections and battered up against my consciousness. I felt it, whatever it was, halt as we slammed together.

May opened my mouth and screamed, "Noooo!"

"Yes," Katye replied. "Alex is in there. He's listening to your every thought. He sees you, feels you… he is not dead, and you've taken something that did not belong to you."

"He gave it," May gasped.

"No!" It was Jerod.

I fought through the snaky thing that was trying to hold me back. It was furious but weak. I went on the attack and took back my eyes. It worked, no more trying to pull together images from the back of my brain. I was front and center, using the old eyeballs. I was master of my optic nerves. There was a lot to look at, but really… just one thing. Jerod, tall and strong. He was walking toward me. Nimby flying like a manic satellite around his head, beating at the air—at May's magic—with her plastic sword. I wanted to warn him away. May's thoughts were poison. She'd tried to kill him once today; it was all she wanted now. Her thoughts on this one thing clear: *The boy had a prior claim. Impossible… but true. But if he's dead… the claim is void.*

"He was not free to give," Jerod stated, his eyes on… mine.

*I love you*, I thought as May fought for control of my brain and my body. Like a thousand snakes crawling through my synapses, she wanted to flush me out. *I love Jerod.* It was more than a thought or an emotion, it was strength and truth. I remembered that first kiss and how right and how scary it had felt. I remembered something else.… He'd said he loved me, and more importantly, he'd proved it, again and again.

"Liar!" May screamed.

"He is mine," Jerod replied.

My head turned, first to the right and then to the left.… I'd just done that. The creepy mess snaking through my head and belly flared. *I love Jerod, so do what you do, Alex*. Ignore her, shut her out, make her go away. *Yeah... then say something.* It wasn't easy; a thought flew through my lips, and I felt my tongue flick against the roof of my mouth. "I love Jerod." Something squirmed in my throat. I wouldn't stop as it tried to choke my words down. "I am his, and he is mine. I was never free to give." Each syllable, the way my tongue flicked in my mouth, the feel of my breath against the inside of my lips, the hinge of my jaw going up and down; I was doing all of that.

Katye clapped.

I pushed for more, noticing more movement in the audience. People were staring at me. Lance squirmed inside my hands. He croaked. "He croaked," I said aloud, my gaze fixed on Jerod.

"Yes, he did," he answered while climbing the steps to the judges' platform. He was next to Carly Casswell, who was wakening from May's spell.

She reached a hand to Jerod's arm. "What's happening? Who are you?"

I stood riveted and practiced the one trick I knew. Bricks and mortar--*There is no May, Queen of the Fey. She does not exist, certainly not in this world and not in me. This is my body.* I gently separated the prison of my fingers and made a platform of my palms. Lance sat unmoving, his head toward Katye. I started to shake, like the bubbling of a just-opened bottle of soda.

Carly Casswell looked from Jerod to Morgan Flood. The producer was equally dazed; he shrugged. "Not my doing," he said.

Jerod smiled at Carly, and then bounded from the judges' platform across the catwalk that separated them from the stage.

The monitor behind me was alive again, my image front and center and three stories high. I couldn't stop shaking as the audience came alive, throwing off May's paralysis. My thoughts were a jumble. I was in control of my limbs… but something was wrong. Like feeling the hole after a tooth's fallen out—*This is too easy. Something is wrong.*

I heard movement overhead. My neck craned back, and I stared into the recesses of the stage ceiling. Hundreds of lights and miles of cable, metal gangplanks, one of the crewmembers in black adjusting a heavy spotlight. *Oh God, no!*

"Jerod.... *No*!"

Lance leapt from my hands as I raced across the stage. I felt May's snaky tentacles try to hold me back. Her single thought—*Jerod dies, and the body is mine, mine, mine.*

I saw a metal bolt fall. It bounced across the stage. Time stretched as my legs pumped. I saw Nimby stare in horror from Jerod's shoulder. Something gave way overhead, and I launched myself across the stage toward Jerod, who was twenty feet away. Maybe it was May's magic still inside of me or something else, but I cleared the distance. My hands landed on Jerod's chest and I tackled him. We fell back as a four hundred-pound light crashed to the stage where he'd stood.

Falling, I shot my hands around his head and cushioned his landing. We lay on the stage. His breath fast, his heart beating against mine. His eyes… his lips.

The moment was broken by a tingle down my spine. There was more movement overhead. "No." My word out of my mouth. "She isn't going to stop." I saw half a dozen figures in black, loosening lights.

"We have to get out of here," Jerod said.

"She's inside of me. It won't work." I looked out at the audience, the giant chandeliers; she'd think nothing of bringing those down and killing them all if she thought she'd get her way. "I want her out." I felt like a trapped animal. She was moving in my head and through my nerves. I'd made gains. I seemed to have control… at least for the moment.

Nimby hovered in front of me. In the past I would have shut her out. I almost did that now. The little black fairy flinched as she braced for me to wall her out. I didn't.

Her wings held her in the air inches from my nose. A smile crept across her lips. "You know what to do, Alex," she said. "Make her go away."

"Do fairies ever give straight answers?" I asked.

She put one of her tiny thumbs and forefingers together, placed them on the end of my nose, and flicked me hard. "No." She grinned.

"Ouch!" The pain startled me. I pulled back, looked from Jerod to Nimby. Something twinkled in the light. "Come on!" I was on my feet. I grabbed Jerod's hand as a second light fell. It missed by a few yards, but now we were in center stage, and the scaffolds overhead were a hive of activity.

There was a gasp and screams from the audience. People were uncertain if this was a performance, or if something real and horrible was happening. "Stay close," I told him. "She wants me alive. At least my body."

His fingers twined through mine.

My brain was mostly mine, her presence a single malicious thought—*Jerod dies, and the body is mine.* The bulk of May's power was in the magic she was wreaking on the crew and the confused audience. The cameras focused on Jerod and me. The giant screen tight on our faces… even Nimby was visible. At least to me.

Another light fell; its lens shattered and the bulb exploded.

"She tricked her sisters," Jerod said. "Lizbeta into the mist and Katye into this world."

"Right." Wondering where he was going.

"She used their specials…. Lizbeta to keep peace and Katye… her love for Lance."

From a corner of the stage, there was a loud croak.

"He croaked," Jerod said with a straight face.

"Yes," Katye shouted from the edge of the stage.

Morgan Flood pointed to her, and the giant screen split, half on Katye and half on Jerod and me.

A fourth light hurtled to the stage.

"No!" Katye shrieked. Pulling herself onto the stage. "Lance!"

From the wreckage of the last missile came a three-note croak. And he hopped across the stage.

"Lance! My love."

My thoughts zipped. “Here.” Pulling Jerod back to where one of the lights had fallen, and to where there didn’t seem to be any more overhead hazards… at least that I could see. “She’s inside of me… at least part of her is. Most of her is outside.” I was rambling.

“Keep going,” he urged.

“Right, her special is power and she needs my body… because.”

“Because you’re special, Alex. Your father is fey. What is it she called you?”

“A haffling.”

“Right. You’ve got the body she needs… so she can do this shit.”

“She took my body when I gave her my name. I hate their logic.”

“But it is logic, Alex. It’s rules, and you’re good with those.”

“It’s a stalemate.”

I was on the edge of something. I looked at Katye, now holding Lance. Her face to his… the princess and the frog. May’s voice was faint inside of me, but her power was palpable. Lights crashed, bits of glass flew like shrapnel. I knew she wouldn’t risk harming my body. I also knew once she figured the lights weren’t doing the trick, she’d come up with something else… and with several thousand people in that theatre, the possibilities were horrifying. Her goal was to kill Jerod. Mine was to get her out of me. Somehow, my physical body was her anchor in this world. She was squirming inside of me like that stupid plane full of snakes.

“Jerod…. Whose am I?”

His hand left mine.

I gasped at the loss of his touch, and the squirmy feeling inside surged.

His hand found my cheek and then his other. The tips of his fingers gentle on my skin, his brown eyes serious.

“Mine,” he said. “You are mine, Alex Nevus. And I am yours.”

I heard a pop, and at first thought another light had fallen. It was inside my head. My eyes fixed on Jerod’s.

His voice was solid. “You are mine,” he repeated. “And I’m not sharing you.”

The pop in my head exploded. I doubled over as pain ripped through my gut. It felt like I was being torn apart. I retched and tried to hold it back.

"I will not share you!" he shouted, not letting go of me. His hands gripped my face. "You are mine! Alex Nevus is mine."

Nimby shrieked, "Alex is Jerod's, and Jerod is Alex's. Alex is Jerod's, and Jerod is Alex's."

From the side of the stage, where she was holding Lance, Katye joined in. "Alex is Jerod's, and Jerod is Alex's."

I doubled over. I puked. It was awful. Something slithered from my gut and twisted in my throat and mouth. I saw revulsion in Jerod's eyes as a white snake shot from my lips and plopped wetly on the floor between us.

"Alex Nevus is mine. And I am yours." He never let go, his hands firm on the sides of my head.

The pain was unbearable. I retched again, and this was even worse. It slithered up my throat and out my mouth, a snake… but with feet…. "Salamanders," I gasped.

The edge of Jerod's lips twisted. "Alex is mine," he repeated. "And I am Alex's."

From the judge's stand, I heard Carly Caswell's unmistakable rasp as she joined in. "Alex is Jerod's, and Jerod is Alex's." It spread to the other judges and then to the audience. It roared through the theater as I puked up gaping-mouthed salamanders.

"Alex is Jerod's, and Jerod is Alex's. Alex is Jerod's, and Jerod is Alex's."

The pain was unbearable. A knife in my gut. Jerod's fingers on my skin were the only thing I could hang onto.

"Alex is mine." His voice washed over me.

"I am yours," I gasped. "Alex Nevus belongs to Jerod Haynes." As the words left my mouth, the pain blossomed into something so awful I knew I wouldn't survive. Like my stomach and brain and something where my liver should be were all ripping open. I choked as a mass squirmed from my belly to the back of my throat. It twisted inside of me.

"Alex Nevus is mine!" he shouted, hanging on as I jerked and convulsed.

My jaw shot open, and I felt the corners of my mouth start to rip. This was where I died. My eyes found Jerod's. I saw his terror. Whatever was emerging from my lips was beyond awful.

My belly clenched, and with every bit of strength I had, I hurled and I pushed. Whatever it was, I wanted it out of me.

I gasped when Jerod's hands let go. I wanted them back. My eyes shot open, and he was gripping the thing coming out of me. White and slimy, thick as my leg, with tiny pink eyes and a gaping mouth that snapped at his face. He pulled it out of me, foot after foot, yard after yard. Its tiny legs flapped in space as it flopped and twisted. Pain ripped through my chest and my throat. My hands reached for the giant white salamander and pulled. It seemed like it would never end. Finally, I felt its girth lessen as I retched over and over. And then it was down to a long snaky tail, and with a final awful flick where it tried to latch on to my teeth, I ripped it out. I clamped my lips shut and fell back. I knew I needed to stay away from it, that it needed contact with my physical body. I fought the impulse to help Jerod. I watched in horror as Jerod wrestled the disgusting monster. But outside of my body, it had started to shrink. Its gaping mouth was firm between Jerod's straining hands as it snapped and twisted in his grip.

The audience chanted, "*Alex is Jerod's, and Jerod is Alex's.*"

Nimby danced and flitted around the weakening monster, careful of its violent thrashing. "Alex is Jerod's, and Jerod is Alex's."

The monster lunged between Jerod's hands.... It lunged for his face. The muscles in his arms strained, his jaw was clenched, his eyes staring at the horrific beast. But while it fought, its substance was fading. I smelled something bitter, and there was a crackling. A blinding flash of light, and the serpent burst into silver flame, like when metallic magnesium is pulled from oil and contacts oxygen. It shot sparks and roared; it sounded like a woman's scream.

It took everything I had to not run to him. It was what she wanted… what she needed. *Let him fight this battle, Alex. Let him be the hero.* The flame flashed skyward, a blinding ball of light. My eyes followed. My heart pounded.

It was gone.

Jerod was on his back, his hands holding air. His shirt was soaked in sweat, his hair plastered to the sides of his flushed face. He looked at me. "Any more?"

I stared at the floor expecting to see it littered with the smaller progeny… or whatever they were. There was nothing, just smashed theatre lights and a smell like the chemistry lab after burning off something volatile.

The chanting in the audience fell away. Behind us and off to the sides, giant screens showed Jerod and me and Katye holding Lance.

"Holy shit!" My words, my mouth…. I felt inside, everything hurt, but not like before. I tasted blood and vomit. The nausea was gone. I shook my head, my eyes fixed on Jerod's face. I didn't want to say it, not wanting to tempt fate…. "She's gone."

"Yes," Katye answered. "She was squatting, and you evicted her. You can't possess something that you do not own. You are Jerod's, and he is yours."

"Is she dead?" Jerod asked.

"No. Not dead, but gone." Katye, holding Lance on one palm, looked over the audience. Her flowing hair was loose around her shoulders. She kissed Lance. He croaked, his black frog eyes never leaving her face. Then she looked at me.

"They want you to finish the scene, Alex." She winked at the judges.

"I don't know how," I admitted, still on the floor, my knees in front of me, my hands braced behind. "That was her doing all that stuff."

"Don't be silly," Katye replied. "It's a love story. You know what comes next. Don't be a tease. Your audience deserves the payoff. They were well and truly helpful." Her blue eyes twinkled under the lights. Lance made contented croaking noises as he rested on her palm.

"She's right," Jerod said.

"You're covered in salamander goo," I answered, pushing up from the floor. "And you're beautiful."

"Yeah?" His eyes following me, he bit his bottom lip, and the dimples popped in his cheeks.

I reached out my hand. He took it. It should have felt weird… all those people, the cameras, the judges, Katye and her frog, but it was just Jerod and me. "I love you," I said, and then his lips found mine. We crushed together, like beggars at a feast. It was hot and wonderful, and if the cameras weren't selective in their shots, the kind of thing that was inappropriate for primetime.

Lance croaked.

The audience was on their feet with applause, whistles, and hoots.

Someone started to chant, and it spread through the hall. "*Alex is Jerod's, and Jerod is Alex's.*"

# Thirty-One

AFTER the show I wanted to leave… with Jerod. We stank and looked like we'd crawled from a swamp. When the lights dimmed, a pair of security officers escorted him from the theatre. His name was top on a list of people to be excluded… forcibly if necessary. A female crewmember told me they'd considered a restraining order, but had avoided that for fear of the publicity. "You know, the gay thing," she'd said. She was carrying an expensive-looking camcorder and looked familiar.

"He's not going anywhere," I'd insisted. "I want him here."

"It's okay, Alex," Jerod said. "You know where I live. I'm not going anywhere. I'll wait. Finish this thing, make something good come out of it."

"What are you talking about?"

"This… *IT*. Use it, or at least some piece of it. If not for you… think of Alice."

"Where is she?"

"With your mom."

I blinked, remembering the last time I'd seen Alice, she was years older. "Where?" My eyes searched out his.

"In your apartment with your mom."

“And Adam.”

“Who’s Adam,” the camerawoman asked.

“My brother.”

“Kid,” she said. “I’ve been your videographer for the past six months. You don’t have a brother… do you? Oh, shoot me now. Did I miss a brother? Did your mom ever marry? What did I miss?”

“Six months!” Panic surged.

Jerod stopped me. “Alex, chill! I’m going home. It’s winter… and I love you.”

“Right.” That helped. But the last I remembered, it was spring.

“Alice is safe… at home with your mom.”

“We wanted them here,” the woman interjected, thinking I was upset that my family wasn’t in the audience.

“God, no!”

“Okay,” she said. “At least I got that right.”

“I made sure they didn’t come,” Jerod said. He smiled. “They kept sending passes. It’s how I snuck in, and I gave the other one to Katye. Alex, just chill. Things are going to be okay.”

I couldn’t take my eyes off his face. I chuckled. “Have we met? Really, things are going to be okay? Today on *Sadly*.”

“No.” And he freed himself from the guards’ restraining hands.

They went on the offensive.

“Stop!” I shouted. “He’s not going to…. It’s okay. I want him here.”

Between our bizarre stage show and on-screen declarations of love, no one knew what to do. Except for Jerod. He grabbed my hand and planted a solid kiss on my lips. Pulling back, he whispered, “*Sadly* has been cancelled.”

“I don’t know.” I tried to catch my breath. “It was very popular.”

“The star got a better offer.”

“Good for him.”

"Sure is." The guards pulled him away. "Just float, Alex. Make something good come from this.... I'm not going anywhere. I am yours, and you are mine."

Something in his words. "You sound like Sifu."

"I joined your dojo. Been going since... well, since you became the *IT* boy. Thought I could use all the help I could get. Never know when you're going to need to do some infighting."

"Right." I caught other meanings under his words. I'd been MIA for the past... six months? Holy crap! I was in the final three of America's number-one primetime show, he'd told me Alice was safe... and I believed him. But what did that mean? Safe seventeen-year-old Alice, or.... "How old is she?" I blurted.

"It's back to normal," he said, knowing what I meant. "She's twelve."

"And Mom?"

"Longer story." He glanced at the woman in black, who'd identified herself as my videographer. Her camera was at her side, but I could see the red light; she was filming this.

The guards seemed torn. Clearly Jerod was no threat, but they had their orders. "Guys," Jerod offered. "I'll go peacefully."

"Thanks," one of them said.

"It's just your job," Jerod replied. "Alex, we'll talk. I'm blocked, so you've got to call me. And call your mom and Alice, they'll... just call them."

"I will."

And he was escorted out. Nimby was on his shoulder. She looked at me, gave Jerod a peck on the cheek, and then flitted to her old spot on my right shoulder. "I'm back!" She giggled. "Do not ignore me."

Our backstage drama had attracted a circle of onlookers. Producers, grips, my co-competitors, Jenna, and Jeremy. Everyone was staring. Two cameramen had their lenses trained on us, their red lights blinked.

"What?" Could they see Nimby? That would be news… not to mention my puking up a sixteen-foot amphibian. Was it something else… like I stank and was covered with sweat and puke.

Jeremy shook his head, his corkscrew curls bobbed.

"What?"

He came up to me. "Ew. You really stink."

Jenna looked at the two of us. "That was ridiculous," she said. "I didn't know we could do special effects like that." She was biting her lip and staring at me.

"Talk about pulling rabbits out of hats," Jeremy added. "Those things were gnarly. Salamanders, right?"

"Yeah… I guess."

"And that boy?" Jeremy's dark-blue eyes searched mine. "That wasn't just a scene… was it? I mean, that kid's been trying to get to you for the past… since the auditions. You told everyone he was a stalker from your school. I mean…."

"I lied," I said. "He's not a stalker." I thought about Jerod's words:"*Just float." Don't overthink this, Alex.*

"May lied a lot," Nimby chattered in my ear. "She was good at it. Better than you. You should tell the truth."

I felt like telling her to shut up… but no, Mom—my real mom—complained about my lying, even though it was necessary. But right now… I wanted to tell the truth. I was sick of lies. What had May been doing and saying for the past six months?

"Is he really your boyfriend?" Jeremy asked. "You're gay?"

The videographer grabbed for my hand. "Don't," she said.

I looked at her and at the cameras trained on my face. "Yes," I said. "I'm gay. Jerod is my boyfriend."

"Wow!" Jeremy said.

The videographer shook her head, clearly unhappy with my on-camera declaration.

"It's not a big deal," I told her.

Morgan Flood had been hanging on the periphery. “It can be, Alex,” he said, a wistful smile on his broad face. “But that’s up to the voting public.”

Awed by the famous producer, the crew and onlookers parted as he came up to me. He smiled and made eye contact with Jenna, Jeremy, and then me. “All three of you should be proud of your performances tonight. Pirated segments are already viral. And Alex… Alex, Alex, Alex.” He shook his head and turned. “All cameras off. And if I see anyone filming with a cell phone… I’ll fire them on the spot.” He waited as cameras were lowered and the red lights went black. He gave a pointed look to the videographer.

“Fine.” Her finger hit the button, and her red light went black.

He placed a hand on my back. “Walk with me, Alex.”

“Sure.” He led me to where blackout curtains and dense scrims created privacy.

“Now, you and I… and a few members of the crew, know with certainty that your… magical performance was unplanned. I need you to (a), tell me what I saw, and (b), if you’ve got an explanation for our viewing public, I’d love to hear it.”

In the shadows of our curtained booth, I tried to size up this famous man I’d seen on TV my entire life. His persona was tough but fair, and not a little vain. I wanted to tell the truth. I was sick of lies… but a fairy queen, salamander possession, an Arthurian knight turned into a frog… how could I possibly explain these things? And if I did, wasn’t that what May wanted all along, to make the fey real?

“Oh, Alex.” Nimby’s voice in my ear. “You can’t tell him the truth.”

“No shit.”

“Excuse me?” Morgan Flood’s pale-blue eyes were on mine.

I opened my mouth, and instead of salamanders, out poured lies. “It was pyrotechnics.”

“Fireworks?” His expression was skeptical.

"Yes, it's a long story…." And I'd better make it a good one. Here was one of the most powerful men in Hollywood… in the world. He'd know about special effects.

*Just float*, I thought. "Here's what I did, kind of fused everything I've learned in AP Chemistry about volatile metals, with the best the Chinatown fireworks industry has to offer. You see, I've been doing martial arts forever, and my Sifu…." Once I started, it was like vomiting up May…. I could not stop. Nor did he try to make me, occasionally asking for clarification as lies blossomed onto other lies. The weird thing was, as my stories spun out, I realized what I was describing wasn't so farfetched. "How you wrap and ignite the chemicals is what gives them their shape. The rest was sleight of hand, kept popping them into my mouth, biting down on them, the saliva causing the chemical reaction to start."

Nimby whispered, "Not possibility, synchronicity."

Morgan Flood's expression went from interested to glazed over as I headed into a technical discussion of the combustible properties of Class D metals like magnesium, sodium, calcium.

He shook his head. "And the bombshell redhead… the one kissing the frog?"

"My aunt."

"And how did you get the frog to play the piano?"

"Lance? You have to meet him. You can train frogs to do a lot of stuff. It's basic psych stuff, you know like the dog with the bell."

"I see."

There was silence. He wasn't buying it… or at least not all of it.

"Unbelievable." He was studying me. "I think I'll believe fifty percent of what you've just said, Alex. And if that much is true you can have an amazing career as a special effects expert. I could have made you a star."

"What's changed?" I asked, feeling a rush of relief.

"You," he said.

"Because I came out on live TV?"

"I'd like to say no, but there's some truth there. But it's not that."

He stared a bit too hard. After all the lies, I felt the truth want to burst out. But no, that would only buy me a padded room at Bellevue. And something else. May wanted to bring the fey back to the light of day… to make them and herself real in the human realm. A major motion picture was her proposed vehicle. I'd thwarted that, but to come out and say that, *Yes, it was all magic. I was possessed by a fairy queen*—that might do what she'd intended.

I met Malcolm's gaze and glimpsed flashes of his thoughts. He wanted to believe the performance I'd given was magic. His artist's mind fought against my wild, but plausible, explanations. It's like there was a little boy inside of him, and it's probably what made him such a great producer. That little boy clung to the hope of real magic. For the briefest of moments my—May's—performance had fueled that. Now I was just a smart, good-looking kid who wanted to become a movie star. Nothing special there.

"I'm sorry," I said, sensing the depth of his disappointment. "It wasn't magic."

"I can see that." His shoulders sagged.

"Sorry."

"Me too." He turned and walked away. He stopped and shook his head. "I'm thinking your boyfriend and that redhead aren't union."

"What union?"

"Never mind. I'll have legal handle it."

I trailed behind as we rejoined the others. My head felt light, relieved. Someone covered me in a blanket, and one of the handlers sponged off my face. I thought of Jerod—"*Just float*," he'd said. It was good advice.

I was led with Jeremy and Jenna to a limo. It was snowing. Glistening flakes landed on the windows. The car's heater threw soothing blasts across my face as I pulled the blanket close.

Jeremy sat next to me. "My agent told me not to do that," he said.

"Do what?"

He fidgeted and stared ahead. He glanced at Jenna on the plush seat across from us. "Come out. He said it would hurt my chances. I hate this lie. And I want a boyfriend… a real one. Like yours. Jerod is hot."

"Totally," Jenna chimed in. She gave me a strange look. "And all this time…."

"Yeah, sorry about that," I said. "I tell too many lies. I'm trying to cut down."

She nodded. "We all do."

THE ride ended at the Plaza. The hotel was amazing, and both Jeremy and Jenna thought my reaction to our lavish suite was odd, considering we'd lived there for three months. My first order of business was to strip down and take a shower. I peeled off my ruined designer jeans and a once-beautiful Dolce shirt. Even my suede boots were covered in blood and goo.

The hot water on my skin felt amazing. These were my feelings in my body. The shock of not being aware for six months still sinking in. The non-CGI reality of puking up May was washed down the drain and into New York's sewers. A wave of panic raced into my head… school. I was a senior now. My college applications needed to be in… by? Oh God. January. Jerod's words like a balm on my racing thoughts—*Float, just float.*

I wrapped a towel around my waist and wondered if I could save my ruined outfit. I had a moment's paranoia. What if someone did DNA testing on the goo and found… salamander. I wadded it up and threw the clothes in the tub, filled it with water, and squirted in two bottles of hotel shampoo and left them to soak.

On the back of the bathroom door was a plush robe with the hotel's logo. I belted that on and went to the bedroom. I pulled back the curtains on a spectacular view of Central Park. Snow was still falling. It lay thick on the ground and bent the trees. I grabbed the phone and dialed home.

It rang twice, and then Alice. "Hello?"

"Alice."

"Alex." The words rushed out of her. "You're you. Right?"

"Yes. She's gone."

"I watched the show. When you coming home?"

"Soon. I'll try to sneak away. Or… come and visit here. You wouldn't believe this place."

"Okay, you're sure it's safe?"

I stopped, and for the umpteenth time scanned my body and my thoughts. "Yeah, no one in here but me."

"I've missed you." She was crying.

"I'm back, and Alice…."

She sniffed. "What?"

"*Sadly's* been cancelled."

# Thirty-Two

ALICE arrived at the Plaza with changeling Mom around six in the morning. The on-call producer—who knew there were such people?—descended on them both. He focused on Mom and tried to get an interview—apparently they'd been hard to reach. My background was mysterious and murky.

None of that mattered, just seeing Alice in her puffy parka and snow boots. "You've grown." I couldn't stop touching her, hugging her. The familiar smell of her shampoo.

"I'm in sixth," she said, her eyes focused on mine. Her expression was serious as she tried to figure out if May was really gone. "What's wrong, Alex?" she said with a serious expression.

"Nothing is wrong… well, no."

"You sure? Why was *Sadly* cancelled?" She looked from me to Nimby. "Hi." She waved at the fairy.

"I don't want to be on that show anymore," I said, realizing my sister could now see my fairy. Once true belief takes root, the fey become real. I'd been right about that.

"I liked it. What's going to replace it?"

"Good question." I saw make-believe Mom in conversation with the producer and the woman who'd introduced herself last night as my videographer. The latter looked like she'd just rolled out of bed. "What she's saying to them?" I asked.

"Don't worry. She's amazing." Alice's liquid-blue eyes looked up at me. "You're good, Alex… but Mom number two. She runs circles around you. We're getting a new apartment."

"Cool… same neighborhood."

"Yup. A *real* two-bedroom."

"Way cool." Although, I felt a little jealous. I kind of liked being the one that kept things running.

Alice looked at changeling Mom. "It's better this way. For everyone."

It was hard taking it in. Alice an inch taller than I remembered, and something else was different. "You managed," I said.

"We did." She smiled. "But I missed you… a lot. And Jerod helped, and Mom number two… it's just better."

"How did you get away?" I asked in a hushed voice.

"The mist," she said. "After May… after she took you, everything went crazy. I think May was holding the mist back. When she went into you, it exploded. Like a tidal wave. Everyone was screaming and running. Mom and Dad told me to run into it… to go to Jerod. I thought they were behind me."

"They weren't?"

"No. They were trying to get away from it. It was just me and Jerod, and then it closed over us, and we were in Jersey, and I was back to normal. I think Mom and Dad got away. I saw them on a black horse flying into the river. Mom was pregnant again, and there was no Adam. We have a father, Alex. And I guess we have, or are going to have a brother."

"I know."

She giggled. "Our dad's a fairy."

"True."

"We're hafflings," she stated.

"Yup."

“That explains some things.” She gave me a searching look. “Like Nimby….” She stared at the fairy. “I always believed you, Alex, when you said she was there. This is the first I’ve ever seen her, so maybe I didn’t believe enough.” She glanced at Mom and the two producers. “I think it’s why people give me stuff.”

“Naah. That’s because you’re cute.”

“Not that cute. Not cute as…. Oh my God!” Her hands flew to her mouth. Her pupils widened as she looked past changeling Mom to Jenna and Jeremy, who’d emerged from their bedrooms. Jeremy’s trademark curls were mashed into a weird bedhead. “Jeremy!” Alice gasped. “Oh my God… you’ve got to introduce me. Please, please, please.”

I DID not win *IT*. I was disqualified. One of the producers—not Malcolm—sat me down and explained the list of offenses I’d committed during my vomiting up salamanders performance. It was a long list—nonunion actors, unapproved animal talent, potential abuse of said frog. Then came the fire-code violations, tens of thousands of dollars in damage from all the destroyed stage lighting and wiring. “Didn’t you think to get any of that approved? People could have been hurt… or worse.”

I kept my mouth shut.

With my disqualification, it was close. Jeremy won, and I couldn’t have been happier. Jenna lost out on account of the video May shot of her puking in the bathroom. It was all over the Internet. I felt bad for the girl when the producers told her what had happened. She was horrified that something she found shameful and private would turn into a punch line for late-night talk shows. The jokes were cruel. She cried a lot and sang an angst-filled Janis Ian song at the finale. People loved it and gave her a standing ovation.

Before the live show, Morgan Flood, flanked by Carly and Barry, gave us a pep talk. While disqualified, they still wanted me to go on. “You’re all stars,” he said. “You can all have brilliant careers in the industry if you want them.” Then Carly gushed, and Barry rambled in rhyming couplets. It's what they did, although I wouldn't really know, having been out of it since before the auditions. The craziness of my missing half-year just something I needed to accept. At least I'd taken my SATs in the spring, so I wasn't totally screwed.

The finale was a blur. When it was my turn to perform, I stared into the audience. I found Jerod, and I sang. Considering May was the one who brought the talent, the result was better than I'd any right to expect. A clear tenor emerged through my lips. Startled, I realized May hadn't taken all the magic. Or maybe I was finally accepting the magic that was mine by right. I am haffling, hear me roar… or at least sing an Irish ballad real well.

I was backed by a harp, a string quartet, and a trio of singers. The song was a W. B. Yeats poem, "The Stolen Child."

*"Where dips the rocky highland*
*Of Sleuth Wood in the lake,*
*There lies a leafy island*
*Where flapping herons wake*
*The drowsy water rats;*
*There we've hid our faery vats,*
*Full of berrys*
*And of reddest stolen cherries."*

The music coursed through me. My love for Alice, for Jerod. I didn't question the beautiful voice as it gave life to the words and the melody in a minor key.

*"Come away, O human child!*
*To the waters and the wild*
*With a faery, hand in hand.*
*For the world's more full of weeping than you can understand."*

I sang to Jerod and I sang to Alice. I sang for my brother Adam, who might not yet be born. I sang for my real Mom, who was better where she was, and for my father, Cedric, who I didn't really know. I sang for Katye and tragic Lance. When I hit the final refrain, I felt a rush of sorrow give way to something different. I wasn't sad or scared; I was in love. It coursed through my body. My voice swelled and I hammered out the final verse. I stared across the space and found a pair of beautiful brown eyes.

*"Come away, O human child!*
*To the waters and the wild.*
*Come away, come away, come away."*

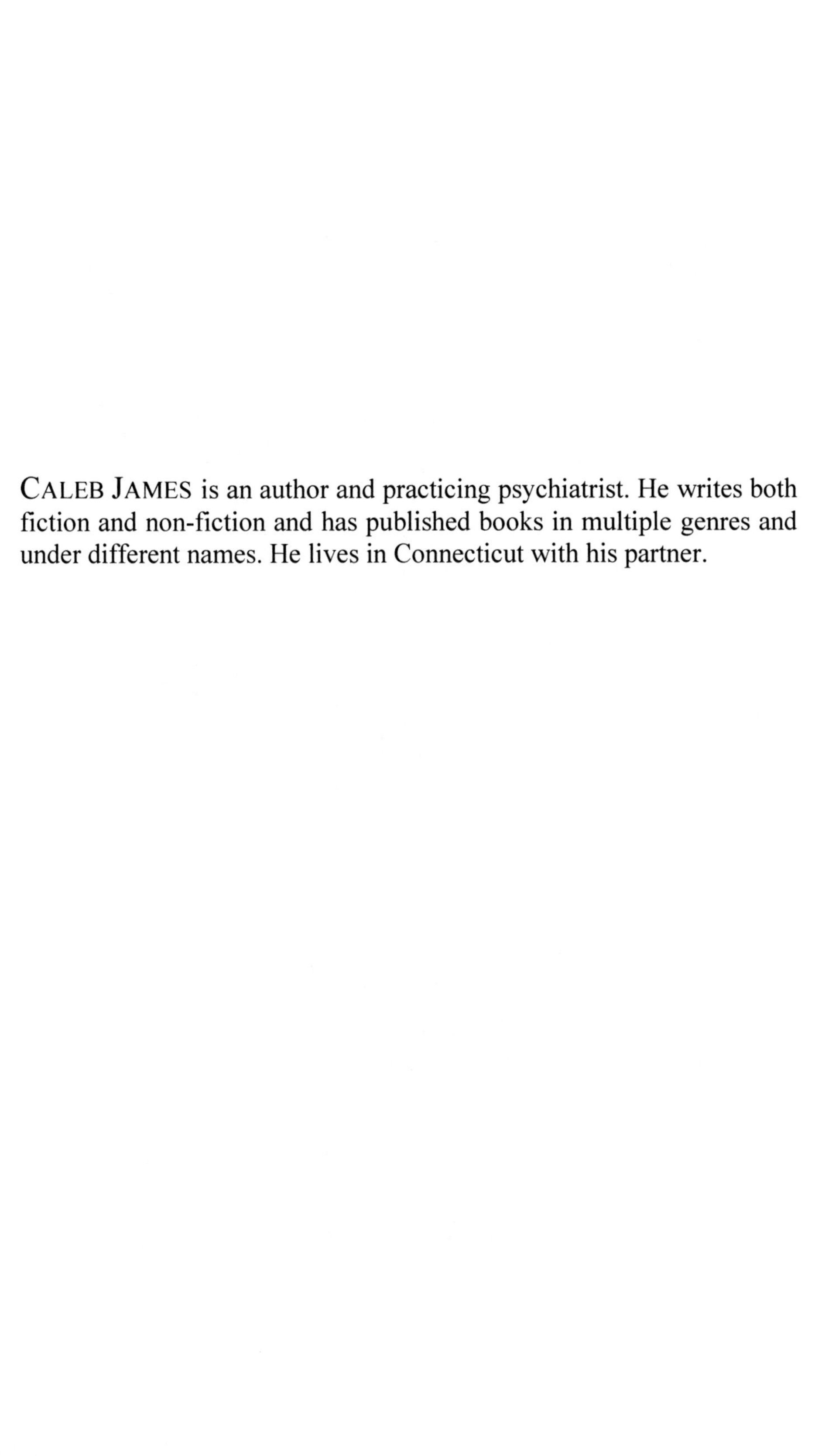

CALEB JAMES is an author and practicing psychiatrist. He writes both fiction and non-fiction and has published books in multiple genres and under different names. He lives in Connecticut with his partner.

Also from HARMONY INK PRESS

http://www.harmonyinkpress.com

Contemporary Fantasy from HARMONY INK PRESS

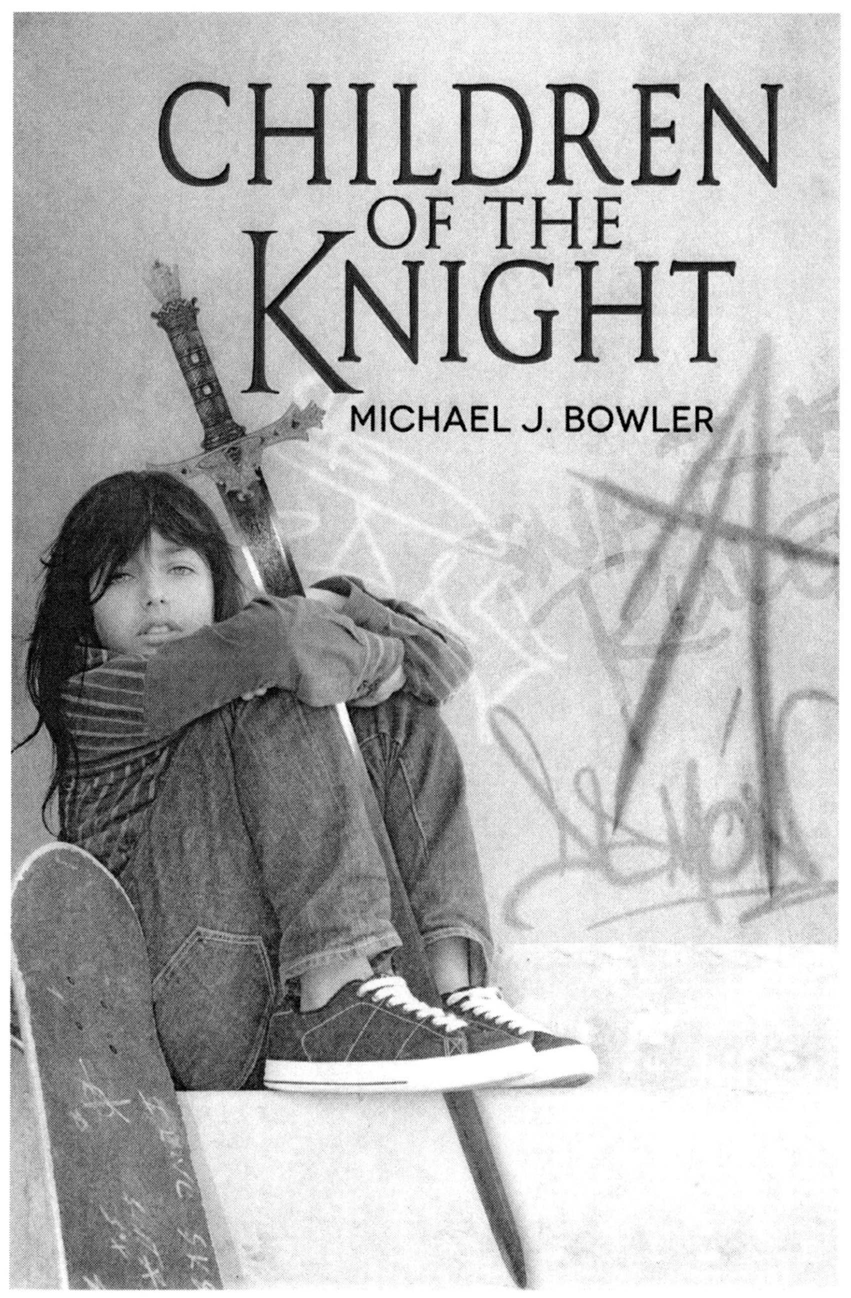


http://www.harmonyinkpress.com

HALLIE BURTON
tapestry

Also from HARMONY INK PRESS

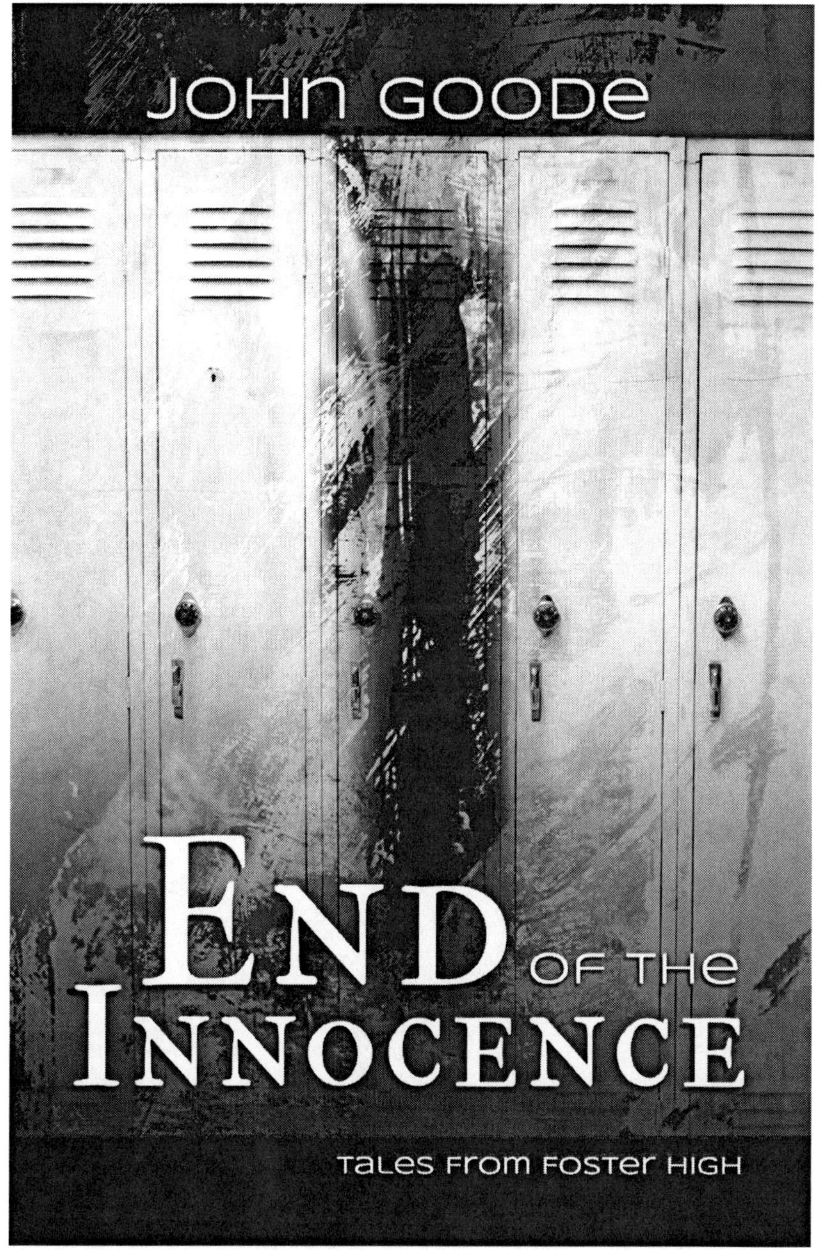


http://www.harmonyinkpress.com

Also from HARMONY INK PRESS

http://www.harmonyinkpress.com

Also from HARMONY INK PRESS

http://www.harmonyinkpress.com

Harmony Ink

CPSIA information can be obtained at www.ICGtesting.com
Printed in the USA
BVOW08s2314190713

326016BV00005B/19/P

9 781623 808945